JAKE

By JOSEPH CASTAGNO

This is a work of fiction. Names, characters, places, and incidents either are the product of the author's imagination or are used fictitiously. Any resemblance to actual persons, living or dead, or to events, or locales is entirely coincidental.

The town of Peakeville does not exist as far as the author knows and was created solely for this book. There are a number of real places in this story, so you can visit them and develop your own opinions if you so choose; any particular descriptions are the opinions and observations of the author and may not represent historical facts or even current conditions.

Chapter 1

Jake had been driving since early that morning, the sweet creaminess of caramel coffee long since erased by the inhalation of acrid smoke from the cigarettes he had been chain smoking. The miles whispered by as his beat up Ford truck picked its way across Florida's I75 toward the gulf. Affectionately called Alligator Alley, Jake hadn't seen one since leaving Miami. *Just as well*, he mused, the son of a bitch would probably have crawled out in front of him; wrecking the remains of what was already a perfectly shitty day.

With the windows down and the day's heat already starting to pile up, deciding not to fix the truck's AC was threatening to add to the long list of poor decisions he'd been making lately. It wasn't just leaving Molly without saying anything either. He had quietly packed up early this morning as the sun shone through the windows haloing her in a golden glow. He had gently kissed her on the forehead and made his way down the back stairs, his cowardly silence echoing loudly in his ears.

He knew heading back to South Carolina wouldn't

solve any problems, he was just running from a month of maybes. Still, like most things for Jake, there was a feeling of déjà vu to his actions; He had come to believe Lady Luck and Fate were conspiring against him once again.

As the morning's coffee kicked his gut up, he wondered how he'd explain this to the boys back home? What had it been? Six… no, seven months since he'd headed south hoping to pick up work helping rebuild South Florida after a long season of storms. Jake was an accomplished carpenter, when he was sober. His buddies had all laughed at his tales of hot Miami women and smuggled Cuban cigars. It hadn't really worked out though had it? Too many missed mornings and too many drunken nights; word got around and no one needed a fifty-something washed up carpenter from Dixie who more times than not didn't bother to show up. So with his tools in the back, a few dollars and change shy of two hundred bucks in his pocket, it was time to head home. If sneaking out in shame without saying a word to the woman that shared your bed was considered heading home and not just running.

Molly, Molly, Molly. He hadn't been able to figure out what the attraction had been, well for her anyway. He had felt something that he thought had died and hadn't been able to take his eyes off her since that first afternoon at Pete's. He had rolled into town looking for some easy work; she had been wiping the bar down and making time till the afternoon crowd wandered in. Now he was running north without having said a word, not goodbye, fuck you, thanks a lot, nothing. Just another commitment he wouldn't be keeping.

At least he'd picked up a decent classic rock station out of Tampa. The damn thing faded in and out but came in strong if he fiddled with it. He fancied himself a crooner more than anything and on a rip roaring Saturday night might let loose with the juke if the feeling took him. Mostly country but good old rock n' roll took him back to his youth. Those hot, dusty nights in the Carolina upstate, racing the back roads to Skynyrd and Marshall Tucker. Him, Jimmy, and the Jordan boys, they had all thought it would never end.

The low rumble of thunder brought him back to the present and Jake could already see black clouds building off the coast. It was going to rain and rain hard. Jake hadn't been able to get used to the afternoon storms down here: rain warm as bath water and heavy as a fire hose. And never mind the thunder. Sweet Jesus, it was like God himself was boxing your ears. He had better start looking for a spot to hole

3

up for the afternoon; he wasn't driving in this shit
that was for sure.

Chapter 2

Jake stirred as a carelessly discarded candy wrapper brushed against his face and swirled into the brush behind him. The cloying sweet oily smell of petroleum distillates carried on the soft breeze, the fine dust eddied like ripples on a pond and lightning teased him of the coming rain while glinting off the crisscross of tracks mixed with the last splashes of brilliant reds and purples of a gulf coast sunset. In the distance a heron mourned the fading twilight and the steady chug of a tanker heading into the gulf drifted in and out. A quiet heaviness tinged with a coiled tension waiting to burst forth had settled over the water.

There was no way to cast this as anything but a setback he thinks. What should have been a quick stop for lunch had turned into an afternoon bar tab and a thirty-dollar card game at a rundown bar and grill called the Crazy Gator. Jake couldn't really afford the setback and winning hadn't been in the cards from the start.

Things had started out simply enough: $1.50 long necks and those greasy burgers you can only find at a joint where the grill has a thousand Saturday nights under its belt. Four cold ones and two burgers later, Jake was feeling comfortable. He was in his element… a bar has an ecosystem all its own and Jake felt like an integral part of it. Just dark enough to hide the signs of too many accepted disappointments and loud enough to silence unwanted conversations. A man could do some real thinking in a good bar if he had something to brood about. Jake didn't, and "thinkin" wasn't really his thing anyway.

Jake drained the last of his beer and motioned for another as he made his way to the head. Passing the card game on the way, Jake sized up the old salts seated around the table. He figured it wouldn't hurt to play a few hands and add to his dwindling reserves. Jake fancied himself a pretty good card player and being well on his way to a six-pack, confidence was running high. Things were seldom as they seemed though, especially down $32 and the cost of another four beers. And as usual he had progressed past the point where things could end well.

Fuckin' Texas hold em. Didn't anybody play real poker any more? Another pot gone and a busted straight was the best he could do. Jake was sure he'd been had and it was time to call these old boys on it. Blowing up and making a scene was a well-refined skill. A lifetime of losing hones the edge of your despair and frustration. Jake let it pour out; the not finding work; not being able to give Molly the things she wanted or needed; the AC in the truck; once again returning home like a lost dog; the missed opportunities; the wasted chances; and now this fucking card game... it all welled up inside him. Jake knew where it was going, he had been here before, but this script had been written with the first bottle and there was no changing the inevitability of it.

Jake slowly rocked to his feet, taking in the brooding storm over the gulf as the last vestiges of color receded into the growing darkness. It had never rained after all. Brushing himself off he tested his legs and rubbed his fingers across his broken lips. *Not going to be pretty tomorrow,* he thought. *Well, nothing broke anyway, the fuckin' pansies had needed three of them to whip his ass.* It didn't occur to Jake this wasn't necessarily a badge of honor he needed right now. With a slow shuffle he headed toward the neon glow and the gentle serenade of the jukebox in the distance.

Maybe Lady Luck had been watching out for him after all, he'd had the good sense to fill the truck up after getting off the interstate. Good sense

7

wasn't something generally associated with Jake these days. Dumb luck was a more probable explanation. Nevertheless a full tank should get him most of the way back to what passed for home. With a last look around the parking lot and shake of his head, Jake headed for the highway as an angry rain finally started kicking up the dust behind him.

As the mile markers flicked by and the city lights faded in the background and the rain let up Jake tuned in the radio and took another long drag on his cigarette. The smoke rushed out the open window and mingled with the scent of hot wet pavement and sweet smell of blooming citrus that seemed to spring up with even the slightest breeze in this part of Florida. Another drag and the soft touch of the filter was an angry reminder of his busted lip. *Son of a bitch!* Why hadn't he just paid his tab and headed out? Jake's introspection rarely led to any clear answers and on this night things didn't appear to be any different.

Chapter 3

Jake had found himself on the far side of opportunity enough times to believe things greater than himself had conspired against him. But it's hard to know what makes a man tread the path he does. Is it circumstance, fate, or is he simply a product of his environment? Maybe it is chance that separates the out of work hardscrabble Carolina burnout from the mahogany row corporate executive with his country club life and health spa wife. Whatever the case, it didn't occur to him that "they" probably couldn't be bothered with him, or maybe he was right and this was all some cosmic joke at his expense.

Reverend Dan Richards had preached it loud and clear from the South Beulah Baptist Church pulpit... "Ye shall be judged in this world and the next..." Jake hadn't really known what that meant sitting next to his mother while trying not to tug at his too-tight starched collar. Jake's father rarely made it home on a Saturday night never mind into a pew the next morning and Randall "Randy" Delhomme wasn't interested in being judged either. Nope, he did the judging and made sure Jake and everyone else knew it.

But for Jake these sermons convinced the young man he
didn't want to be caught now or ever doing anything
needing the Almighty's judging. He believed as
fervently as any of the prim and proper choir ladies
who always seemed to be looking down at him and his
mother. There were mornings he'd swear he could feel
the fire and smell the brimstone. Unfortunately this
healthy fear of the Lord wasn't going to last much
longer. The innocence of a child was destined to burn
away on the lips of a father's smile in the
flickering of a twilight bonfire just months before
his seventh year.

Jake had grown up in Peakeville, a small town
like most any other in the Carolina piedmont. Friday
night high school football games, Saturday Little
League and Sunday Church seemed to fill the social
agenda of most folks. Prosperity had long since
passed by and the town had settled into the
comfortable routine of making do and getting by.

The Delhommes lived at 2114 Orchard Street on
the West side just across the proverbial railroad
tracks and up the street from the dusty ball field
that served as a distraction for the neighborhood
boys and their fathers. It was a mill house like all
the others in this section; two stories of fading
white paint with a porch and front door leading to

the family room followed by the kitchen and laundry room. Bedrooms were on the second floor and functional was probably the best description. There was no front yard, and the driveway on the right side of the house ended at the chain link fence enclosing the small back yard. The Delhommes didn't have a garage, but Jake's dad had built a shed at the end of the drive just inside the fence for his tools, beer fridge, and most importantly a place to avoid the judgmental gaze of his wife.

Three blocks in the opposite direction was Melvin's corner store, a favorite place of Jake's and a sanctuary from the outside world. Melvin's was stuck in time the same now as when Jake had been a boy. Wooden floors polished by the years of traffic, comic books, baseball cards, an old ice cream chest that rattled and hummed, bright red plastic encased bologna, wheels of yellow orange cheese and the biggest collection of nickel candy a kid could imagine. It was one of the few places in town that sold beer. The giant stand up coolers along the back wall had all manner of odds and ends stacked on top, Styrofoam coolers, lawn chairs, pool toys, not that anyone around here had a pool, but if you couldn't find it at Melvin's you didn't need it. On the counter perched a grand old brass register. The story was that Melvin had brought it back from a trip to Atlanta when he first built the place in the mid '30s. Harold, his son, was always telling the tale of how his father had ridden his horse to Atlanta intending to buy a new 1936 Studebaker and had come back with the car and the cash register, but not the horse.

Melvin's survived even as the big textile mills closed up one by one, moving overseas or succumbing to an economy no longer supportive of American made goods. A few small operations persisted, but not enough to lift the small town out of its downward slide. Most folks traveled two or three towns over finding work in the large auto plants the Germans and Japanese companies had built or Michelin's new tire plant. Good paying jobs were difficult to come by and many had turned to the Welfare system just to sustain themselves. It was rapidly becoming a way of life in these small towns. The whites had always pointed a finger at the black community, but simple fact is poverty had wiped out any real distinction between the races.

The vibrant collection of local family owned stores lining Main Street were slowly dying off, while the Dollar General and Wal-Mart on the new bypass seemed to thrive. Sprinkle in a few fast food dives, a couple of Mexican restaurants and Peakeville resembled a dozen other small towns in the upstate. People trying to hang on to identity that no longer really existed, hardly anyone came there on purpose and even fewer made it out.

It wasn't a "bad" little town just one without any prospects or aspirations. The working folk that lived there went about their business day in and day out with little interruption beyond the occasional wedding or funeral. With the monotony of life's metronome reverberating in him Jake seemed destined to embrace the mediocrity of his roots; oh he had left more than once, but never seemed to be able to escape always ending up right back where he had started. "Ye shall be judged in this world and the next…" all these years later Jake still didn't know what that meant. However, the way things were going seemed to point to the possibility that old preacher Richards might have been onto something.

Chapter 4

The rolling hills of the Ocala horse country were a refreshing change from the flatlands of southern Florida. Having left the storms moving off the gulf behind, the sky blossomed above, dotted with the spring constellations and a crescent moon. A peace began to settle deep in Jake's subconscious, a belief that if he could somehow make it home life would take up its natural circadian rhythm and return to what passed for normal. The low thrum of the tires gently removes the regrets, pain, and failures of the past months from him.

It is the ability to "hope" that ultimately differentiates us from the rest of God's creatures. That ability to believe, even when there's no reason to, because logic plays no part in this experience. Man draws on some reservoir of resolve that can't be quenched or reached and even when all seems lost it once again springs eternal. Hope, the unexplainable energy that keeps a hiker alive days after he should have died, that brings a town like New Orleans back to life, allows a soldier's mother to get out of bed and go to work every day, and on I75 North tonight it keeps Jake heading home.

In Florida the highway medians are lined with rumble strips. It seems a jarring vibration and horrendous racket will coerce the everyday driver to take corrective action. Tonight they provided a syncopated serenade to the steady hum of the Ford's engine. It was the roar of an air horn that finally broke through jolting Jake back into this world. He had been driving under the influence of any number of things long enough for instinct take over. *Gently guide that baby back on the highway, no need to rush now, don't want to turn it over or end up in a ditch.* A motel was not in the cards but sleeping in his truck had never bothered Jake. All he needed now was a rest area with a dark corner and no cops. *Nice, there it is.* The sign announced, Rest Area one mile, just outside of Ocala. Jake guided the truck slowly down the exit ramp and coasted to the far corner of the "CARS" section gently bumping up to the curb. With a deep breath and a reflective sigh he cut the engine and listens to the ticks and pings as it cools. Even on his worst days it seems to comfort him. *Damn!* Day one of his journey complete and he hadn't even managed to make it out of Florida.

Chapter 5

Molly woke to the sun streaming through the curtains warming the room around her, but the bed was cold and she had lived enough to know without looking that Jake had made his escape. It had been a silent countdown for weeks but you were never really prepared for that first morning alone. Having to face the reality of another failed relationship, another poor choice. Knowing the sweet whisper of the days passing only picks up speed with every passing year doesn't help either.

Molly wouldn't shed any tears over this one; she wasn't a child. Though it wasn't so long ago there would have been three days of crying and swearing never again, but she already knows the impossibility of keeping that promise. Today she wanders out to the kitchen and brews a cup of coffee contemplating the day while sitting at the small table in the nook. A melancholy smile creases her lips as she remembers the day Jake brought it home with a leg to be fixed and in desperate need of paint. It had been early on in the relationship and he had been as good as his word. She had salvaged a couple of chairs from the bar and had enjoyed sitting there on the weekends drinking coffee and listening to Jake's stories of the road. The stories were a preview of coming attractions if she had bothered to pay attention.

She really did love him or had in the past she admitted. Oh she knew in the end no amount of loving was going to fix him, but it didn't mean she didn't care for him. Now with a deep shadow of sadness lying over her she washes out the cup and sets it in the white plastic rack on the sideboard. With a low sigh she heads into the laundry room to fold the load she had started last night. Life wasn't going to wait for her to heal and no sense brooding over it, reaching down again she pulls out the first couple of shirts. Jake's, and the first tears fall anyway.

Molly's shift ran late that night and it was almost one in the morning before she trudged up the steps to her second floor entrance. She loved this apartment, well really the second story of an older home that had been converted to a full apartment. Most days she could convince herself she had a home of her own. Part of her had hoped to find the lights on and Jake asleep in front of the small TV, but the place was quiet, silent even, all the more obvious in the context of the Jakes departure.

Pete had been sweet, but Molly hadn't wanted to talk about, it even though it was obvious she wasn't herself. She just didn't need another man's sympathy not even Pete, who had become a big brother of sorts to her. She already knew the routine pain, sadness, and eventually anger before she would be able to put things in their place and move on. It was, unfortunately, a process she had become more than familiar with. She bit her lip as she dried off from the hot shower and combed out her honey blond hair. Slipping into the soft cotton nightgown she wore every night, *I'm not crying again*, she tells herself.

The bedside lamp throws a shadow over the far side of the bedroom as she clicks it out. Stretching, trying to fill up the bed, she turns over. It's then she sees the soft silhouette on the dresser of Jake's three shirts and two pairs of socks from the morning laundry. The flood of hot tears is unquenchable she can't help but snuffle into her pillow clenched fist in her chest trying to massage away a pain that can't be fixed. While just short of four hundred miles North Jake cuts the engine and listens to the ticks and pings that normally sooth him. Sucking on his cut lip he tries not to think about Molly.

Chapter 6

There's a special kind of stiffness that comes from sleeping a bar fight off in the front seat of your pickup. It's not an experience easily explained, better to just accept it as fact and move on from there. Jake yawned and worked the kinks out of his back and neck as he shuffled towards the bathrooms. He noticed the blue hairs in the million dollar motor homes were giving him a wide berth. *Hell he must look like death warmed over*, enough to scare the old ladies from up north anyway. He leaned his head against the coolness of the block wall as he drains the indiscretions of yesterday. A quick splash of water on his face and he heads back to the truck. He combs his hair back with his fingers, but it doesn't help. Jake hadn't needed a mirror to confirm what he already knew. His head throbbed and he could still taste the salty residue of his broken lip as he lit up the first cigarette of the day.

Okay now to find a Waffle House, time for two bacon, egg, and cheese on white toast, "wrap em and bag em..." add a large black coffee; Jake had developed a set menu for post ass whipping hangovers and at around eight bucks it fit his budget too. The salty bacon irritated his lip but the hot coffee was bringing him back to life as he headed onto the interstate. As the miles pile up the memories of that first day come flooding back.

Molly, her honey colored hair muted in the dim light, aimlessly wipes the bar down again, losing herself in the midafternoon quiet while the ice machine hums and clinks in the background. Pete is out back wrestling a new keg in from the coolers cursing the whole way. Lost in her thoughts, Molly didn't consider herself a pretty girl, well woman at thirty-six it was getting tough to picture herself as a girl any more. Life leaves its little marks that no amount of Saturday morning infomercial miracles will fix. She had kept herself in pretty good shape though and still tried to watch what she ate most days. The bright light from the street penetrates her reverie tugging her back to the present. *Little early for a regular*, she muses as an unconscious sigh escapes her lips. Putting the rag down and moving up the bar she asks, "What ya have?" taking a closer look.

"Bud Light... in a bottle" Jake murmurs almost to himself. Looking around his eyes adjust to the lack of light that seems to inhabit most bars, *just another jerkwater bar...* he thinks.

"Two fifty on Thursdays," she says. Jake pulls a crumpled ten from his jeans and slaps it on the bar.

"Keep 'em coming till that runs out honey."

"You from the Carolinas?" *What the hell am I doing?* Molly thinks.

"Sure nuff, I guess we all sound 'bout the same huh?"

"Well I knew a fella from up Charlotte way a few years back, I guess hearin' ya just reminded me of him".

"Well there ya go… name's Jake by the way."

"Molly… let me know if you need anything," turning she walks back down the bar, she didn't need to look to know he was watching. *Damn I never do that! "Charlotte way?" Where the hell had that come from?* She had lost her southern twang years ago, South Florida had a homogenized sound all its own. Yet here she was talking like a small town Carolina girl. Lately she had sworn off men again, well bad relationships anyway, which of course they all seemed to evolve to at some point. Then came the inevitable recriminations, the feelings of inadequacy, the heartache and tears. It was a routine she was all too familiar with, yet she still seemed unable to break the habit.

Molly didn't take Jake home that night or the next either, but he became a regular and a friendly face that somehow reminded her of happier and simpler times. Sometimes he would be gone a few days at a time picking up work here or there helping out a local builder or homeowner, but most nights he wandered back to Molly. The warning signs were all there if she had bothered to look. The last calls and early afternoon visits should have been a tip off. It didn't seem to matter though she found herself falling for Jake nonetheless and it was only a matter of weeks before she asked him to move into her apartment around the corner. Loneliness has its own demands and more times than not they trump good sense and knowing better.

Jake wasn't a great lover; too many hard edges and a complete lack of patience, but he had a simple sweetness about him that appealed to Molly. Somewhere inside was a little boy that just needed attention. She believed, like so many before her, that she could somehow love him enough to heal him. Jake's troubled soul needed more love than Molly or anyone else for that matter could muster. They quickly fell into a routine, Jake drinking too much, missing work, and promising it wouldn't happen again… and of course Molly wanting to believe things would be different this time.

Jake wanted more than anything to be a man Molly could count on. It was something he had been striving for since breaking the heart of his first love Annie so many years ago. She had not been able to count on him and her condemnation had become a self-fulfilling prophecy for him over the years. Even before things would begin to slide he would know deep inside that it was only a matter of time before the commitments, time tables, recriminations, and unfulfilled promises would drive him back onto the road. He wished it wasn't so, but he had been here before, the cut and run had become Jake's trademark move.

Chapter 7

Jake left the interstate around Gainesville heading northeast towards Georgia and hadn't passed a car in more than an hour. Finally losing the last traces of a country & western station he turns the radio off and adjusts the vent window on the old Ford. He has become one with the truck and together they lumber on straining to make some headway against the heat, the distance and a shadowy foreboding dancing just out of reach.

The deep purple and grays of a gathering storm fill his rearview mirror as the old ford trundles forward. The silver white leaves foreshadowing the impending storm. Bursting static interrupts the low hiss of white noise, lightning flares ever closer as the percussion of thunder penetrates the cab. Jake senses a feeling of malevolence as if some ancient evil pursues him with a persistence and tenacity born of a long and brooding wait.

Jake has long since stopped believing in the supernatural yet on this two-lane ribbon a slight chill passes through him, unnerved he finds himself pushing the needle past seventy in a subconscious urge to outrun what pursues him.

But just as quickly the feeling passes, the sun once again glares down with a merciless stare with the heat rippling in waves across the dusty ground baking the macadam ribbon stretching to the horizon. The gullies and cricks have long since given up leaving a patchwork of cracked and parched mud. This area of northern Florida and neighboring southern Georgia had been at drought status for more than a decade. The giant oaks lining the road stand as silent sentinels to the destruction, their roots searching deep and far straining to extract the last vestiges of life's elixir. A pointless exercise as life has long since left and death roams amongst them biding its time. On the Western horizon, the thunder gods carry on their battle, more sensed than heard in the distance. Their minions, whipped to a frenzy, chase one another to the northwest and once again, the quiet solitude of an unblinking sun overwhelms the landscape.

As sometimes happens in the universe a man may find himself on a collision course with destiny. He may not be looking for it, and in most cases would undeniably prefer to avoid it at all costs. However destiny is a force all its own and the whims and weaknesses of mortal man have no bearing on it. Jake was headed for such a meeting and he was wholly unprepared for it. For at this moment events were conspiring, and the true mettle of the man was to be tested, tried and scrutinized by forces beyond his comprehension. It was a day fraught with equal measures of peril and opportunity for there is a filament that lies within the human experience that ties all things and all beings together. It allows the soul to absorb all that is beautiful, horrific, agonizing and uplifting. It transcends time, space, geography, prejudice, and understanding. It creates coincidence and allows for missed opportunity. It is a sharp intake of breath, an ache deep in ones chest, an uncontrolled smile, and an unrestrained single tear. It is all that we are, all that we wish to be, and all we wish we weren't... and today on a deserted road it bids Jake "pull over".

Chapter 8

Maria soldiered on wishing there was a bit of shade or even a ripple of a breeze to cool the stagnant air of what passed for late spring in Florida. She had kissed her little brother and sister as they slept three days ago and silently made her way out of the two-room shack that passed for home these days. She had carefully packed her backpack the night before, removing the normal accumulations of a high school senior and replacing them with as many clothes as she could cram in, an extra pair of shoes dangled from the strap. With her eighteenth birthday a few weeks behind her it was time to go. Life in a migrant family can be unkind at best. The constant moving, the barely veiled hostility of the locals, the gangs, the drugs, the forced sex, but the worst was being unable to turn to anyone. It wasn't fair didn't she have dreams? Was it her fault her parents had paid the "coyotes" to bring the family across the border when she was just a babe in her mother's arms? She didn't really remember any of it, but had heard the stories enough times that it seemed like she should. She had played the game, learned the

language, tried to fit in and unlike so many of her
friends had managed not to fall into the trap of
getting pregnant and dropping out of school becoming
just another statistic people with no understanding
of things could complain about. She felt like there
had to be more. Something deep inside seemed to call
to her, but she hadn't been listening until now
anyway. But now after two relatively stable years her
parents wanted to return home, back to a country she
didn't know and didn't want. So she had left with
tears in her eyes, a fervent hope they would just let
her go and a secret she couldn't share with anyone.

Truly on her own for the first time she was a
complicated mess of feelings, excitement, fear,
loneliness, and deep down, maybe the first tiny
sparks of hope. Hope that maybe this was the right
thing, the way it should be, and the opportunity she
had always dreamed about. But she had a growing
feeling that things were not all they seemed. She
knew there was strength in her yet untapped; was she
not the child of Hector and Graciella Lopez? Had they
not braved the desert of the American Southwest
wading across the Rio Grande holding their daughter
and small bundle of possessions above the swirling
waters in the dark of a moonless night? Surviving for
hours in the sweltering heat of a box truck. Forging

an existence in a strange new world that was intent on destroying their dreams and shipping them back. What was a hot deserted road in Florida compared with that? "Self doubt is a killer", "fear is the greatest obstacle", cliché phrases she had heard somewhere from a teacher or coach probably, but this morning she was beginning to understand the reality underlying those oft parroted phrases. Although she was pretty sure none of her coaches or teachers could possibly relate to what she was experiencing. In fact with the arrogance of youth she was sure nobody could relate. Well, maybe her parents, but that was different wasn't it?

The soft thrum of a truck approaching intruded into her internal conversation. She hadn't been paying attention and turning Maria saw it was closer than she expected. Too close to miss her, she was going to have to take her chances. Lowering her head she prayed softly they would pass by, but she could already sense the diminishing speed as the truck rolled to a stop waiting for her to catch up. Maria had every intention of walking by without looking up, but like so many things in this life our will appears powerless when we think we need it the most. Unable to help herself she looks over. Maria isn't sure what she notices first the dangling cigarette, the trash strewn across the dashboard or maybe the hopeless

anguish in the man's eyes. A strange sadness

overwhelms her in that brief instant and she

whispers, "Jake?"

Chapter 9

Jake searches her face trying to pierce through the haze his memory has become. Does he know this girl, he doesn't think so, but the soft measure of her voice seems to touch him deep inside. Deeper than he is willing to acknowledge, deeper than he really understands and slowly tears well up in him. Not just tears, but that aching in the chest, an inconsolable sadness, that clenching we feel at our very core. Jake shakes it loose, letting the moment escape unwilling to acknowledge the authenticity of this experience. Coming back to the present he growls, "need a ride?"

She is already sitting next to him when he glances back over. Lighting up another he pushes the truck into gear and guides them off the shoulder. Neither says anything, what's the point? There aren't any answers to the questions that lurk in the cab between them as the silence takes over and acrid wisps of smoke envelope him. The tires have once again taken up their steady cadence. But it is there just out of reach - a whisper - the soft breath of something new.

A few moments pass but for Jake it seems an eternity. "Do you know me?" he croaks. The space between them seems to stretch and he can barely hear her whisper.

"Yes, but it's not like that…"

Jake can feel the icy hand of fate twisting inside him as destiny softly laughs and the filament of his life begins to softly glow. For a moment Jake is so filled with equal parts terror, apprehension and excitement everything seems to fade around him. He struggles to control the wave of emotions he is drowning in. The road seems to fade in front of him as sudden calm steals over him. Her soft hand gently touches his arm and as if in another room he barely catches her voice reassuring him, "it's okay Jake."

Jake steadies himself, willing himself to breathe, his eyes to focus, white knuckles betray him as he barely holds on to himself. It doesn't make sense, why here, why now, why me? There are no answers to his questions. But Jake knows that here on this road, today, he has a decision to make. A decision of the greatest import, a far reaching decision, a decision that will ultimately change his life. For deep inside, deeper than he cares to acknowledge Jake knows this is a choice between finally living or continue this diminishing illusion

he has created for himself. Unfortunately for Jake
there is a big difference between knowing something
and turning it into action, and this has always been
Jake's biggest problem.

Chapter 10

As the truck picks up speed she gazes out the window lost in memories of another time. The dough magically forms under her small palms as she gently mixes the simple ingredients in the ancient wooden bowl. She wonders if it is the same one her mother learned with. Dumping the soft doughy mass on to the table she gently forms the balls her mother will press into tortillas for the family dinner.

It's late summer in the northern reaches of Maine. They had arrived earlier in the week having spent the summer harvesting tobacco in Virginia and vegetables farther north in New Jersey. The summer fades as August leans toward an early fall and only a few weeks remain in the blueberry season before they caravan south to Florida. There they will begin the cycle of harvest again. A small fire crackles in the old iron stove they cook on. Later it will heat the small shack as the damp chill seeps up through the aging boards that pass for a floor. They are luckier than most though having a roof over their heads and a raised floor to sleep on. Of course they share with two other families, but no one minds; it's better than living in their cars or the tents lined up like so many lost kites along the tree line. While Maria watches, her mother stirs the cast iron pot of beans and checks the simmering chunks of pork while adding some spices: ground chilies, cumin, garlic, and salt.

Maria knows it won't be long till her father and the other men come in still smelling of the wet earth, sweat, and the sweet berries they have been picking all day. Sometimes her dad will bring a small cardboard carton of berries with him. For the kids it's a special treat and they eat them as slowly as possible hoping to make them last.

He kisses the top of her head as he greets her mother, his rough hands still wet from washing up tousle her hair. Not old enough to understand the frustrations and despair that can creep into a man's soul Maria knows that at least tonight there won't be any yelling and her mother won't be left crying in the dark. No, whenever she gets the dad kisses, as she likes to call them, it will be a good night. A quiet night filled with the warm murmurs and her mother's soft laughter. The other times frighten her. Those nights she lays quietly nestled up to her mother hoping her father doesn't come back in a drunken rage. But tonight is a good night though and she sits on his lap listening to the tales of the day and looking forward to blueberries after dinner.

Chapter 11

Maria sits quietly watching him in the
periphery of her vision. He seems calmer now but she
senses the anguish, the struggle in him. What haunts
this man she wonders. She's seen this pain in men's
eyes before, the torture of unfulfilled dreams, the
hopelessness of failure. Their pride destroyed by an
uncaring society, it is hard to hide the mix of shame
and anger brought on by prejudice and hate. She has
seen it at her own table, in her father's friends.
She sees it in her people as they struggle to scrape
out a living here in the land of opportunity. They
are forced to compromise their values, heritage, and
culture. She knows she has been lying to herself for
a long time, dreaming of just being an American girl.
Thinking she can live the life she sees on
television, it's the real reason she is running isn't
it? Fleeing from the culture of her forefathers into
a society hell bent on homogenizing individuality
until all are indistinguishable from each other. She
is finally beginning to understand there is no
escaping the struggle and there is no perfect life
around the next corner. She knows she must create her

own dreams, her own opportunity. Assimilation provides no comfort, no safety net, and no answers. The realization that the very things she was trying to escape were really her strength suddenly overwhelms her.

And just that simply, two strangers share opposing yet identical sides of the broken dream that is America. Traveling in silence together toward a destination neither understands nor recognizes. Neither believing any longer the plasticene imagery doled out to the still hopeful masses. Life has a way of opening one's eyes to the reality of their own existence. It isn't all cherry vanilla coke and Victoria's Secrets models. No, this existence has more than its fair share of heartache, disappointment, hate and failure. But isn't that what living is really all about? Finding the beauty, the moments of happiness tucked among the struggles, the insignificant successes that provide just enough hope to continue. Or is there more to be had? Are we destined for greater things, for true happiness, for that elusive peace we all seek? Sure, there are exceptions, they dot the digital landscape like lamps in the darkness, but like so many mirages they are unattainable. Our journey in darkness is inevitably interspersed with brief flickers of happiness, like so many fireflies, just enough to keep us chasing the dream, but never enough to light our way. There are no answers for these questions in an old Ford truck lumbering down a back road toward a destination neither of its passengers is sure of any longer.

Jake wasn't clear where this was going. He wasn't even sure exactly how this had happened. But here he was with a young woman he didn't know, obviously not a white girl, and it scared the shit out of him. He was old school, didn't need or want these people invading the States. Didn't need them taking American jobs, speaking a different language; it just wasn't right. They were even showing up in little southern towns like Peakeville. He knew of at least three or four families that had moved in down on the east side of town. They had even opened up a restaurant down there. Everybody said the food was great but he would be damned if he was going to go support them. Now that he thought about it most of the guys working down in Florida had been "wetbacks". Probably why he hadn't been able to stay on anywhere, undercutting him at every turn.

Jake could feel the slow burn beginning, the anger, the resentment. And the unfairness of it all crept over him taking on a life of its own. He couldn't control it, didn't want to control it. Jake needed someone to blame, needed a target for his disappointment. Inadequacy and ignorance had been the bedfellows of prejudice since the beginning of time. The fear and anxiety bled out of him following the steady stream of cigarette smoke out the window. It was slowly being replaced with his long ingrained attitude of intolerance and prejudice. Glancing over at Maria, Jake only sees what his warped perception allows. He misses the pain, the fear, the basic human need for compassion and missing this he misses another opportunity. He misses the chance to finally make a real decision about his life.

Chapter 12

In the distance heat lightning crackles through the clouds, the muggy air stands still without a breeze to move it on. Jake can see the dancing shadows cast by the bonfire as they ripple and caress the surrounding trees. He knows he is supposed to stay in his dad's truck but he can't really see and he needs to, wants to, as curious as any six year old would be. He also knows the sting of his father's belt well enough to be torn... stay or go? His dad and his buddies had been drinking beer and telling stories till the dark had settled in. Now they were all up by the fire and sometimes a boy just needs to know - to see - to understand.

The "nigger" had been beaten, his eyes swollen shut, blood drying and becoming crusty on his head and chest. He was stripped down to his pants, no shoes on his feet. With his hands tied behind his back he stumbles unable to right himself and falls to the ground. The men seem to enjoy this and laugh and jeer. Desperately trying to understand, Jake sees his dad kick the man and yank him to his feet. His dad's voice carries over the clearing drowning out the other men, "nigger, stand up when we talkin' to ya."

In Randy Delhomme's world every black man was a "nigger". Jake could already recite by heart his dad's ranting, "they's different from us, they ain't equal, they ain't got the brain God gave white folk, and now they want what we got..." " Ya know son we ain't got no need for niggers and ya don't have nuthin' to do with em."

Jake had never really thought about it. There were no black kids in his elementary school and definitely none in his neighborhood. But standing here in the shadows with the still air, the smoky smell of burning Carolina pine, the mix of engine oil and spilt beer in the background it was all very real. And at six years old Jake was about to come face to face with the legacy of his heritage.

The mind of a young child isn't ready to process brutal violence, the degradation of one human being by another, or the unfiltered hatred of ignorance. Add to the mix a young boy's natural idolization of his father and you begin to understand the paralysis Jake felt. He didn't want to watch, couldn't tear himself away, feeling emotions he couldn't begin to understand. His dad had looped a rope around the man's neck. Now his dad and Jimmy Sewell's dad were taking turns yanking him up just high enough to get him off the ground before letting him down again. Looking up Jake locks eyes with his dad across the clearing. He wanted to move, needed to move, a small smile plays across his dad's face as he looks away and pulls the rope tight tying it off to the tree. Jake ran for the truck, he could taste the salt of his tears, his breath ragged, numb.

Jake was no different than many of the young boys his age, stuck between the hatred, fear, and prejudice of their parents and the dawning of a new age in the American psyche. It was the early sixties and the oppressed had found their voice - a new version of America was being forged in the crucible of the Civil Rights movement. Only weeks away from Martin Luther King Jr.'s "I have a Dream" speech, Randy Delhomme and men like him fought on. Not knowing or caring that the battle was already lost. They insured their legacy of hate and ignorance would live on for at least another generation or two.

"Is he dead daddy?" Jake head down timidly asks.

"Nah son, we just teachin' em a lesson, niggers need to remember their place..." turning to glance his way "... and next time stay in the truck."

Jake prayed there wouldn't be a next time. It was one thing to listen to his dad go on and on at the dinner table, but he didn't ever want to see anybody hanging like that again. He swore to himself as young kids often do that he would never do anything like that. Unfortunately Jake was destined to be a product of his environment and even with that horrific night burned into his memory the indoctrination of small town prejudice was inescapable. He would grow up parroting the poison of his father. There is an insidiousness to ingrained prejudice: it permeates a person's soul, it's in a look, a word, the offhand comment, a lack of compassion. There are a million little ways to wield the sharp edge of intolerance. It was as much a part of Jake as his arm was. How do you begin to change a man's very essence, extract a part of him he doesn't even understand? Where and how does a man gather the courage for self-introspection, for confronting the very core of who he is?

Chapter 13

Jake had nearly forgotten that night in the clearing, or more to the point had chosen to pretend it had never happened. He had never spoken to his father about it, not even at the end sitting in the silence watching his father slowly waste away in the county nursing home. Long since betrayed by his years of abusing tobacco and alcohol his father offered no explanations, no apologies, or wisdom. No, there was just the tired wheezing of an empty husk struggling to resist the burgeoning darkness. There was no hope in his passing, no light, no redemption. Jake wasn't even sure why he had spent the seeming endless days and hours in a silent vigil. He and his father had a mutual antipathy for each other and in the end nothing had been resolved.

They had spent a few days trying to reconnect when his mother had passed, but neither had the words or the heart for it. The one thing that had provided some small connection had lain in a red satin lined box at Hemley's Funeral Home having finally found the peace she so fervently prayed for. Now his father was making the same pointless journey in much the same way. Only this time it would be blue satin enveloping the final remnants of Jake's past, leaving him finally and hopelessly alone.

Jake had left town the next morning, packing his meager belongings into his Father's Ford truck. He had closed up the house, dropping the keys at Attorney White's office and set out searching for something but without any real idea what.

Lost in the memories the miles piled up and the sun continued its journey west chased by the lengthening shadows. He had been gone, what, three maybe four years that time? He had headed West looking for a new start, something different. It would take more than a change in scenery though. Lasting only a few months in any one place Jake had traipsed across the Southwest steering clear of the bigger cities picking up odd jobs in a dozen towns before heading out to the Northwest landing in a small town just outside Olympia.

He had run about as far as possible and the grey days and nights suited his mood. He had talked his way into operating a forklift for one of the smaller lumber mills that dot the Pacific Northwest. Seemingly the perfect job it offered routine, and solitude with few distractions. Jake had been flopping at the Hilltop Travel Lodge. Really just a

roadside motel offering individual rooms for sixty
dollars a week framed by the faded sign on top and
the flickering vacancy neon below. One of the
seemingly forgotten places that dot the landscape of
America paint peeling from the baby blue ramshackle
exterior, the window AC units laboring away creating
a steady trickle and film of algae along the broken
sidewalk. The odd collection of older sedans and
pickups that always seem to inhabit the gravel
parking lots the only indication anyone was there. It
was well within his budget though and just up the
road from the mill. Most days he would walk to work
stopping at the service station across the street,
well, the gas Metroplex with its mini grocery store,
yogurt bar, hot food, and bank after bank of soda
fountains. Jake had seen these monster one-stops
supplanting the traditional service stations as he
had trekked cross country. Still nobody ever seemed
to get the simple things right. Usually he settled
for the inky black liquid that they passed off as
coffee and a Honeybun spun for a couple turns in the
microwave.

Jake had been off the juice for almost seven
months, well, except for the occasional six-pack of
Coors on the weekends. It was a beer he hadn't drunk
a lot of before heading out West. Spring had

progressed to August and the remains of summer were quickly running away. The lengthening nights had already begun to carry a chill. Jake had been suppressing the itch for more than a few weeks at this point. He didn't really want to move on as there was a freshness imbedded in the anonymity of the Northwest and he had settled into a comfortable, even if a bit lonely, routine. He knew it wouldn't last and wondered some nights how you could be somewhere this long and still feel like no one knew you existed? He was just another smudge the coming rainy season would wash away.

Chapter 14

It had been early September; maybe right after Labor Day, he didn't have a clear recollection of the date. But it had been a Tuesday morning when he had left, no notice, didn't even ask for a refund on the balance of his weekly room rent. Tommy his foreman had handed checks out that Friday and let the fellas know there was only about three more weeks of work before they would start cutting people for the season. Jake hadn't needed to wait around to see who was on that list, he had long since convinced himself that lady luck wasn't fond of him. Packing up didn't take very long either. Never one to accumulate very much, he was on the road early munching a Honeybun and trying not to spill the blazing hot coffee he had collected when filling the truck up.

That had been a long fucking drive home. Took him more than two weeks and he had managed to rekindle his drinking habit on the way. And why not? There was nothing to look forward to where he was going, three and a half years gone and he was sure nothing had changed. Aside from almost getting himself killed in a 7-11 parking lot just outside of

Gallup, New Mexico by the biggest damn Indian he had ever seen it had been pretty uneventful. Apparently Native Americans appreciate "wagon burner" about as much as African Americans appreciate "nigger". He had nursed those bruises and a busted nose for three states before the Goody Powders finally started making some headway against the constant mind-numbing ache. Just one more scar on what was already a broken soul that couldn't seem to understand why he continually generated these episodes.

Fortunately his father's attorney Harry White had taken care of settling the estate, paying the taxes on the house and pretty much everything else Jake hadn't shown any interest in. The house was still standing when he rolled into town, needing a fair bit of work, but at least it was work he was skilled at. He had spent pretty much the entire winter getting it back in shape... well livable by his standards anyway.

"Jake I'm hungry and we need to stop..."

Jesus Christ, he had almost forgotten she was there he had been so caught up in his memories. They had been on the road for nearly three hours and the afternoon was winding down - *damn if it didn't look like rain again.* "I'll pull off the next place I see," he grumbled mostly to himself. *Just what I need a woman, hell girl, telling me what to do,* he thinks.

Pulling off the highway and making a left at the bottom of the ramp Jake spots the sign for Jimmy's, looks like one of those middle of nowhere truck stop / diner type joints. *Well the coffee usually ain't bad,* he thinks and *hell its damn near impossible to screw up a burger and fries... and I bet they even have a "blue plate special"* known the world over as... meatloaf and mashed.

Easing the truck into a spot right up front the parking lot is empty except the hot little BMW parked off to the side, *weird place to find one of those babies,* Jake thinks as he shuts the truck off and listens to the ticks and pings that always seem to soothe him.

Chapter 15

Josh Pickering had been staring out the grimy
side window for what seemed like hours, the gnawed
blue cap of a standard issue Bic pen a visual
testament to his boredom. Upstairs he can faintly
hear the back and forth of his older sister Rachel,
well half-sister, and their father no doubt working
on some dramatically important case he would never be
privy to. It was technically spring but a few left
over fall leaves and what seems to be a never ending
supply of trash blows in circles through the alley
outside his office and the deepening grey seems to
foretell another rain later in the afternoon. He
guesses he should be happy he has a window at all. He
is stuck on the first floor of his father's law
practice, no upstairs suite for him, that was
reserved for partners, partners like his sister that
is. Not for the last time he wonders how he ended up
back here the very place he swore never to return to.
But when no big city firms came calling after
graduation what choice had he really had. His father
ever magnanimous in his condescension had regulated
him to title searches, typing briefs, and whatever

other low-level legal scut work made its way through the office.

Josh was eight years old the last time he had seen his mother, he of course hadn't known it would be the last time, but nonetheless his final memory would be her tear streaked cheek still blotchy and flushing scarlet where his father's heavy hand had recently left its mark... again.

"I'm sorry Joshy", she murmured, leaning down to kiss his forehead before fleeing out the front door to the waiting red Porsche at the curb.

He still remembers her hand pressed against the window, watching long after the car has disappeared, not feeling the cold seeping through his socks or the icy wind drying the salty streaks on his cheeks.

He hadn't noticed his father standing there, one a small imitation of the other, the hand on his shoulder heavy through the thin fabric of his plaid pajama shirt. It didn't cross his boy's mind, lost in the fog of his breath, standing there struggling to understand his crumbling world, but many times since he had wondered at the comfort his father's touch had lent. The very touch that had moments ago executed a parting blow to his mother's porcelain cheek.

He had suffered quietly through those first

early years, the drunken lectures recounting his mother's infidelity, never quite sure if it was somehow his fault, a byproduct of his very existence. Or was it just a flaw in her nature as his father so often said. Every rant ending the same way, "you can't make a silk purse out of a sow's ear", as if this somehow explained everything thereby absolving his father of any responsibility in the matter.

It had always seemed like he was more tolerated than anything else, not that his father didn't love him, but he would never have the bond his sister shared. There was no explaining why he continued to torture himself with unresolved memories of his mother and there would never be a way to rationalize the obsessive need to please his father. He was pretty sure a therapist would chalk it up to compensating for his mother's sins. Not that any of it mattered today or any other day either. His existence was cast in stone and there was no sense pretending escape lay just around the corner.

Grabbing up his battered briefcase, a hand me down from some long forgotten shlub that had finally withered and fled under his father's endless invectives, he makes a break for the back door muttering about the Whiting title. Sure that Evelyn and the other para's are shaking their heads and no doubt clucking in unison. Heading out route 117 to one of his favorite hideouts, Jimmy's, a diner / truck stop / coffee shop out by I85. The humiliation of interviewing with his sister and father plays through his mind in a torturous loop. Pulling in he can see Shirley wiping down the counter and the place is empty, same as most afternoons. Most traffic opting for the bypass that no one seemed to understand the need for but somehow was built anyway.

His coffee is waiting as he slides into his favorite stool, second one from the end with a good view of the empty parking lot and the soon to arrive storm. Josh doesn't know it, but his life has already left its intended path and his father's Bic pens have no need to fear him again. The old blue Ford pulls up in a cloud of dust pulling Josh out of his self-loathing just long enough to take a look.

Shutting the truck off Jake looks over, "will this do your highness?" Maria just nods, she knows better than to indulge his acidity...

Chapter 16

"Hmmm, not from 'round here for sure", Josh mutters to himself watching the two slowly approach the diner entrance. The man looks like any number of local rednecks that occasionally make their way through his father's office trying to fight their latest DUI, domestic violence charge, or delinquent child support. Not that his father bothers to handle any of that personally. Nonetheless there is steady stream of work and most of it falls on his desk. He doesn't give Jake a second look; he has seen enough of his kind to know the man's "woe is me" story without having to hear it again... but the girl, *ahhh the girl, now what is that about* he wonders. *Obviously she's not the old fella's daughter and way to young and attractive to be "with" him... What was it about her though?* Something tugged at him a curiosity, the feeling she didn't belong here, not that she didn't belong in this diner, but that she somehow belonged to a different existence altogether. *God he had been in a strange mood today, what the hell was wrong with him?*

"Good Lord boy, you never seen a Mexican?"

Shirley whispers breaking the spell and pulling him
back to the present.

"Sweet Jesus"... he murmurs, "of course I have,
it's not that..."

"Well I thought we had lost you there for a
moment..." She chuckles wandering over to the booth
to take their order, condensation already forming on
the water glasses she had carried over with their
menus several minutes earlier. *Christ, how long had
he been staring* he wonders?

Josh drops a couple of bills on the counter and
makes his way to the door desperately trying not to
glance over, *almost there*, he thinks. His palms
sweaty, he grasps the cool polished handle of the
door, and everything seems to slow down. He can smell
the faint odor of ammonia from the Windex Shirley
must have used on the glass that morning. The hum of
the neon open sign in the window to the left, the
faded and peeling visa sticker on the glass just
above the handle, the muggy air seeping through the
worn weather stripping between the doors, the
slightly out of kilter whir and clack of the old
cook's fan in the back. Each little piece separate
but yet together playing a discordant symphony in the
background. In that moment an involuntary turn, just
the slightest glance back, but he already knows it's

too late. She looks almost through him with a gaze both sad and playful. It's only a moment, but he is pierced through, breath escaping him in a mad rush. He is through the door gulping the dusty air wondering what the hell that was. Leaning against the door of the beemer attempting to put things in order to clear his head, the sharp crack of lightning brings him back. He can hear the first few drops ping off his roof as he backs out of the parking lot and with no warning the storm opens up before him.

Maria watches the dark grey BMW turn slowly in the parking lot, it seems to hesitate suspended in time. The rain starts kicking up the dust and beating against the window like some mindless force trying to reach through the glass to where she sits. Jake never takes his eyes off her as she watches, his coffee cup carefully balanced in his calloused hands halfway between here and there. Shirley hums as she mindlessly wipes down the counter pocketing the bills as she deposits Josh's cup in the washtub unaware of the events playing out around her. Time is moving slowly, like a spinning top that has reached the end and begins that inevitable wobble. Every motion, sound, thought elongated, exaggerated and stretched. Jake watches intently as Maria slowly turns back to the table a lone tear sliding down her cheek, "I don't think he is going to make it Jake..."

"Jesus Christ, what does that mean? What do you mean he isn't going to make it? Make it where...?" Jake shakes his head, sipping on the hot coffee thinking *what a weird fucking day this has been*.

Chapter 17

The rain turns to steam as it hits the hot
engine and through the silence Josh can hear bits and
pieces of a familiar refrain... *what was the name of
that song...?*

*Where have I heard that before? Damn, none of
this makes sense*, he thinks as the light fades, the
rain falls and the music slips away.

What a mess, this was not what Sergeant Wilson
was in the mood for, especially at the end of what
had been another uneventful shift. Jerry liked being
a County Sheriff. Loved it! In fact, the freedom from
an office, knowing most folks in the area, driving
around taking care of his peeps, as he liked to say.
Sure, there was the occasional DUI, or kids acting
up, but this was a quiet town and he liked it just
fine that way. Setting the flares out he keeps an eye
on the EMTs working to extricate the Pickering boy.
What had once been a marvel of German engineering was
now just a tangled mass of steaming metal. The annual
training programs he attended in Columbia always
emphasized not making a personal connection in
situations like this, but everyone in town knew the

Pickering story. You couldn't help but feel bad for the boy, what with his mother running off. Jerry was pretty sure growing up with old man Pickering hadn't been any picnic after that.

The rain had finally slowed to a misty drizzle, the flashing red and blues careening off the wet pavement like some macabre light show-casting shadows across the wet grass. The newly carved furrows leading toward the trees as if some wayward farmer had decided to plow up the side of Route 117. The flares had mostly burned out leaving cones of white ash in their wake as the old Ford idled to a stop behind the backed up traffic. Half a dozen cars were waiting for the cop to wave them on. Maria can see his dark green uniform, the yellow rain jacket and the plastic covering his wide brimmed hat. He seems to be carved of stone standing perfectly still watching the blue shirts scrambling across the grass towing the stretcher behind them. The siren screams its echoes grow dimmer in the fading twilight, the cop is waving them through now. Jake doesn't even glance over, tightening his grip on the wheel he drops the truck into drive and lumbers past the sputtering flares. He doesn't need to look, doesn't want to look knowing already and scared, more scared than he can remember. *How did she know?* But maybe the better question is did she know or did she decide?

Maria doesn't need to look either but she does, pressing her hand to the window a silent farewell a parting prayer for a young man no longer here.

The hills take over and the thick pine forest seems to close in as the light fades away. There is a chill to the spring air here, the unwavering heat of Florida now left behind. The sweet smell of pine mingles with the tarrying smoke of what seems to be Jake's endless supply of cigarettes. Somewhere in the distance reminiscent of the forlorn call of yesterday's heron a lone whip-poor-will wavers. Jake trundles down the beltway intent on nothing more than making it home. He hangs the right on Mill Street, six blocks up and left on Orchard almost there. He can see the glow of the ball field up ahead, *must be finishing up a Pony League game*, he muses pulling into the drive at 2114. Home, finally... it was time to get some things clear, make some changes, figure some things out. The ritual was the same as it had always been for him: the wash of relief and the fervent belief that somehow things would be different this time. And like all those times before Jake believed it was true. He shoved the brief thought of Molly aside; he couldn't deal with it, not yet anyway.

Chapter 18

The laughter of children echoed across the
fields while the breeze carried the tantalizing smell
of grilling meat and fresh mowed grass. Maria could
feel the warm sun on her cheeks as she watched the
white patches high above playing tag as they
disappeared beyond the end of her cleats way down
past her knees and dirty shin guards. The older boys
would be playing now. She heard the dads shouting,
"ándale! ándale!" and smiled. It didn't matter how
fast she ran, her father always urged her on in the
same way. Saturday afternoons at the fields were a
family tradition. The children played the early
games, their brightly colored jerseys and
unquenchable smiles chasing the ball back and forth.
On the sidelines the fathers urged them on and the
mothers caught up on each other's news. The older
ones would play in the late afternoons as the food
carts were setting up. The older ladies would be
making tortillas and grilling the pork, beef and
chicken. The thought of the fresh fruit sprinkled
with tajin, frozen juice bars, tacos, duros with lots
of hot sauce and of course the freshly made donuts

with cinnamon and sugar were making her hungry again. She knew she would have to wait though, the family always watched her father and his team play first. A patchwork blanket would be set up on the sidelines, her mom rocking the baby while they cheered and ate and ate and ate.

Tempted to just leave her in the truck Jake starts to get out barely hearing the murmurs of her dreams behind him. "Jesus, what a pain in the ass this is", he mumbles to no one in particular. Crossing round in front of the truck there is a quiet only found in small towns, none of the constant noise of bigger cities. Jake can smell the honeysuckle in the night air and hear the gentle hiss of the streetlight at the end of the drive, for all its imperfections this is home. Hand on the door handle he hesitates, Jake can see her clearly even in the shadows of the cab as there is enough light filtering through to illuminate the profile of her cheek and her dark hair cascading to her shoulders. She is beautiful in an innocent, pure, childlike way, the earlier sadness smoothed away by the blissfulness of a dream world Jake can't relate to. Standing with tears clouding his eyes Jake feels the terrible weight of his emptiness, a deep sadness that wells up in his chest, unwelcome, unbidden, and unstoppable.

She is standing beside him now, why does time
seem to slip away around her like pages missing from
a book. Taking his hand she pulls him back into this
world. Heading for the porch door while fishing his
keys out of his jeans he unlocks the door and
reaching with the familiarity that comes from years
of repetition, he flips the lights on. The
fluorescents flicker for a moment before settling
into a soft hum brightening the kitchen. It is what
you would expect, white clapboard cabinets, porcelain
sink with the requisite iron stains, white fridge in
the corner, faded linoleum floor and a gas range. The
curtains were once a soft blue with bright yellow
flowers but have faded to grey. It's obvious that
what was once a warm room filled with smells of
Sunday dinner and a mother's love is now barely
holding on to the last vestiges of her memory. Like
all older homes it was quiet and still in that
peculiar way only an old and experienced home can be.
Its years of stories, joys, heartbreaks, loves, and
arguments intertwined with each other like a tapestry
of the lives that had lived there. Now slowly
diminishing with each passing year replaced with the
emptiness of the lonely soul that still remained.

Striding now with a feigned purpose Jake flips
the lights on in each room, more tour guide than

resident. Pointing to the stairs, "you can stay in the room on the right, beds already made up and it has its own bathroom." It had been or actually still was his parent's room. Nothing had been moved or changed since they passed on.

"Good night Jake, thank you..." barely a whisper she slowly ascends the stairs, no look back, no hesitation, a purposefulness beyond her years. At the top of the hall the door closes with a soft click. Retreating to the kitchen he lights a cigarette, drawing in a deep lungful of the acrid smoke. He leans against the sink, staring past the faded curtains into a simpler time, brighter days, and a time when the future was still something to look forward to.

Chapter 19

The sun-dappled counter seems to shift in an ever-changing pattern as a soft breeze plays through the branches of the old maple outside the kitchen window. The gently fluttering curtains, their small blue flowers dancing gracefully in a sea of bright yellow, ripple in the breeze. The rich aroma of fresh brewed coffee mixes with the piney odor of floor cleaner. The mop bucket sits by the old fridge waiting tackle the old linoleum floor for a second time that morning. Small delicate hands wash the coffee cups, placing them in the old wire rack on the counter, all the while humming a nameless anthem reminiscent of some happier time and place. There is a soft glow, a warmness, a feeling of life's energy emanating from her diminutive frame that seems to chase the shadows from the corners and filling the kitchen with a sense of peace.

"Coffee Jake?" she asks without turning already moving to pour a cup for him.

"Sure, why not?"..., not exactly surly and of course he no longer lets the surprise show when she speaks. How the hell she knew he was there he hadn't quite figured out yet. It didn't seem to matter how quiet he was, he never got past the doorframe without her saying something. She must have some weird sixth sense or something he figured. In fact there were a lot of things he didn't understand about this girl and he wasn't getting any closer to the answers as spring began to fade to early summer. It had been three weeks; well, eighteen days nine hours and thirty-seven minutes, since they had arrived back in Peakeville. They hadn't really discussed anything but both seemed to be waiting for something.

Jake was sure the town was having a heyday with this and no doubt it started that first morning. She had left his carcass sleeping on the couch and had walked the three blocks down to Melvin's pretty as you please. She had picked up coffee, milk, eggs, and plenty of five cent candy, and he was sure she had answered plenty of questions. He had been pissed at her for that, but couldn't find the words to say why. He had been standing in the kitchen smoking the first cigarette of the day when she had walked in. Not usually one for reflection Jake couldn't help a small smile. She hadn't even put the bag down, just pinched the cig from his mouth, dropped it into the sink and announced there wouldn't be any more smoking in the house. She had rocked him, that was for sure, without a pause she had started babbling about the unbelievable selection of candy and did Jake know about that cash register? *Well of course everyone knows about that damn cash register* he had brusquely replied. That had earned him a hard look and Jake had decided then and there he probably didn't want to cross this one. She looked and sounded like an angel, but there was something else there as well. Something he didn't think he wanted to turn his back on.

"Jake? Your coffee", she murmurs softly touching his arm.

Blinking his hands wrapping around the old cup feeling the warmth soak into him seeming to travel up his arms. *Shit!* He had been gone again hadn't he? *Damn what the hell*, he couldn't get his head around it. It was happening a lot lately, he would come to feel like he had been waiting on standby till she was ready for him. It was damn strange, he had never been one to daydream or get lost in his thoughts. Hell not even as a kid when his mother had dragged him off to church on Sundays. But now he had a hard time staying focused around this girl. Funny thing is he knew that it wasn't a man-woman type deal, she was beautiful in her own way, but he didn't feel that familiar tug. No, he felt like she was somehow above those things. When he looked at her he felt a longing for better times, for something beyond this simple existence. A forlorn feeling that he had wasted too much time, time he might not now have a chance to make up for. Jake felt stuck, unable to untangle himself from himself. All around him he could see things changing. The house was coming back to life. Maria was infusing her spirit and will into everything around him but he couldn't move, didn't know where to turn, what to do or even what to think.

It had been earlier that week she had cleaned out his parent's room, reverently packing their things into boxes and moving them to the basement. Her only explanation: "it's time to let them rest", she had gently said. And she was right of course, but even knowing that he hadn't been able to say anything. No, he had just stood there nodding like some mute creature destined to watch the world turn around him.

Gazing into his coffee he knew there were no answers to be had, and maybe that's what he was waiting for, the realization that it didn't matter what Maria did or anyone else for that matter. He had been asleep at the wheel missing all the signs, the opportunities. The second, third, infinite chances to change things. Now this stranger was in his house breathing new life into everything around him, but he could only watch and wonder at it. Whatever was happening had decided he was not included, wasn't worth the energy, the effort, the whatever it was, that he was missing. The coffee was long gone by now so he slides the cup into the sink and heads out to the Ford finding comfort in the one piece of his life that seems to still fit him.

Chapter 20

Molly ran the soft cloth over the bar one last time, generating the glass like shine from the deeply lacquered wood, she hollers for Pete letting him know she is getting ready to leave. He had insisted she take the weekend off doing something fun for herself, hell he had even given her an extra two hundred dollars in her tip share. He pretended to be all gruff and tough but underneath it he really was a nice guy. He really did care for Molly like a little sister.

She had decided a trip to the Keys was just what she needed to wipe the last vestiges of Jake out of her life. The healing had been slow, but like every wound time healed, where even the best medicine failed. Sure, she still had her moments, a song here or that stack of shirts in the closet she should have gotten rid of already. But she was better and a weekend on the water was just the final piece in moving on. She planned to leave first thing in the morning. Pete was lending her the old Toyota pickup he used for hauling stuff at the bar. It was a straight shot down Route 1 and she figured to be there by lunch. Pete didn't believe her, but she was a museum junkie and hitting the Hemmingway Home and the Harry Truman House was at the top of her list. Most folks went for the parties and the bars, but when you worked in one the last place you wanted to vacation was in another bar. She would spend her time walking the town and refilling her emotional tanks.

Saturday broke bright and warm as she packs her backpack into the seat beside her and heads out. The quick stop at Starbucks for a caramel macchiato and butter croissant doesn't even trigger a "Jake moment" this morning. Pulling out into traffic she tunes in a nineties station, singing along she heads south towards Homestead and the Overseas Highway. The highway is a series of bridges between the islands of the Florida Keys stretching for over a hundred miles. She had spent a bit too much, but had booked a room at the Blue Marlin right in the heart of Key West and within walking distance to both the Hemingway Home and Duval street.

As the miles rolled by the wind blew the salty smell of the sea through the truck windows and she could feel the stress and blues of the past weeks starting to recede. Pete had been right, she had needed this. She planned to hit the two museums today followed by a special dinner at Louie's

Backyard. She wouldn't normally have spent this much at a restaurant but Pete had insisted it was his favorite place and he had called ahead and was picking up the tab. Apparently Pete was "known" at Louie's.

The day was perfect, the two museums had taken her back in time and dinner on the back deck watching the sunset had been breathtaking, never mind the best shrimp and grits she had ever even imagined and a sangria to die for. Top it all off with the tart coolness of key lime pie and she was one happy girl.

Sunday was a carbon copy of Saturday bright blue skies, warm but not sticky. Molly hit the breakfast buffet for a plate of fruit and a bowl of yogurt with crunchy granola and headed out to spend some time by the pool. Laying there basking in the sun she promised herself she would take better care of herself going forward. Seriously, why shouldn't she indulge in little treats like this? Why else work as hard as she did? The sun had crossed the midpoint and it was time to get back on the road. She packed up heading for the truck and the long ride home. Deciding to grab a couple of fish tacos from one of the nearby food trucks she heads North feeling better about herself than she has in a long time.

Chapter 21

"Listen Jake I'm tellin' ya son you got to do sumtin' about it... you can't have some Mexican girl livin' in your daddy and mamma's house like that, hell boy are you even sure she is legal? She don't look hardly old enough to be out on her own, never mind living with you"!

Harry White had been his dad's lawyer for near about everything he could remember and had known Jake since he was just a small boy. Having turned eighty-two that spring he was officially retired and had been for many years. Harry still made his way into the office most days, probably for the routine and no doubt for a nip of the bottle and a smoke. Although his beloved Martha had been gone for a number of years he still didn't have the courage to smoke or drink at the house. He had grown old though, the black mop of hair was white and patchy now, the roadmap of capillaries on his nose and cheeks a testament to his struggle with the bottle. He still wore his suspenders but they flared out around the old man's belly now. His looks and manner might seem otherwise but Harry was still sharp as ever and saw more than he let on. His country ways belied an Ivy League education and an insatiable curiosity. Why he chose to stay in this little town was anybody's guess, but his family had been here for as many generations as anyone could remember and all of them had been lawyers. Harry would be the last one though as mother nature had never seen fit to provide him an heir.

"I know sir, but..." Jake's words trailed off, Harry would always be "sir" to him and he trusted him as much as his dad had maybe even more. But how was he going to explain this he didn't even understand it himself? "It's just that..." running his hands through his hair there were no words for this, how was he supposed to describe how he was feeling? There was no logical explanation for strange things that had happened. Or what about the fact that everything around him seemed to be coming back to life except him.

Harry rested a hand on his shoulder, "it's okay son, sometimes a woman will do this to you, there's no explainin' it, never understood them myself."

"It's really not like that sir, she is different, I don't even understand it, but there is something about this girl that scares me and gives me hope all at the same time..." biting his lip Jake hears himself talking but it's like watching someone else. *Gives me hope?* He thinks... *is that really what it is? How can that be and hope for what? I must be goin' nuts this is crazy.*

"Well son I can't say I understand what you're trying to say, but listen to what I've been tellin' ya, you know how our little town can be."

Chapter 22

Jake headed down Beecher road. It twisted back and forth on itself in a slight but steady decline as it followed the Broad River basin heading for one of his dad's favorite fishing spots. It was really no more than a small clearing fifty yards off the road along the gentle banks of the slow moving water. No one lived out in this part of the county anymore. With no one to slow its march the kudzu vines were taking over the landscape obscuring the few old crumbling buildings that still dotted the landscape and advancing on the gravel shoulder here and there. His dad had showed him the remnants of an old Cherokee fish damn many years ago. It was one of just a few fond memories, a treasure to be polished and kept close to his chest, used sparingly so as not to wear out the specialness of it. The waters had receded over the years. Some of the old stones poked their heads above the surface in a jagged line wandering out towards the middle of the river before dropping back under the gently drifting brown water.

Propped up against a fallen tree with boots pointed toward the water Jake let his mind wander, fishing had never really been about the fish for him. More a chance to clear his head and take a break from whatever chaotic reality he happened to be immersed in at the moment. The red and white bobber drifting gently occasionally dipping and confirming the interest of one of the river residents. Jake let it go, there was no appointment with a fry pan tonight.

He could almost taste the smoky tang of pimento cheese on soft squishy white bread, a staple in the Delhomme household. His mom would cut them in diagonals for him served up with a heaping handful of greasy Lays chips. Smiling as she watched him from the sink, the soft blue apron tied neatly around her. Nobody made sweet tea like his momma, the glass glistening on the table always on a carefully folded napkin so as not to leave a ring, the Oatmeal Pie lying just out of reach beyond his glass.

The whip cream mustache made her laugh and he smiled in spite of himself, Molly loved her Starbucks, that's for sure. He would never admit it but the sweet caramel coffee laced with whip cream was better than any desert. He had stopped more than once on the way to work in the morning to have one. Of course he couldn't own up to that, teasing her that it was a girl's drink no self-respecting Southern man would ever drink such a thing.

"I thought that was your truck Jake." Startled out of his reverie Jake looks up shifting slightly on the stump, his back telling the tale that he has been drifting for some time now.

"What the fuck Jimmy, you don't go sneaking up on people like that..." he had known Jimmy Sewell since they were in grade school. The big man was as mean hearted as his dad had been and they had definitely had their moments when they had both been drunk. Jimmy usually whipped his ass pretty good when it came right down to it. He just didn't care and that made him dangerous or at least unpredictable in a predictable way.

"Hey, I heard ya was keepin' a spic down at yer place, ya know yer Daddy wouldn't had known of that" a nasty smile playing over his face. "She any good? Maybe I'll drop by and have a taste."

"Fuck you Jimmy it's not like that" *shit here we go again,* "and my dad is dead just like yours so who gives a shit what that asshole would think." Jake hadn't meant to go there but he was tired of it all and the simple fact was Jimmy had been a bully for a long time and enough was enough.

"Whoa buddy-ro I'm just messin' with ya, don't go gettin' all fired up." Shaking his head and giving Jake a puzzled look, "some of the boys are gettin' together over at DJ's later. Just saw yer truck and figured I'd see if ya wanted a stop by..."

"Yeah maybe, sorry just tired and you caught me off balance there... it's good to see ya, been awhile."

Over his shoulder, "yep, see ya later" a quick wave and Jimmy's lifted truck was fishtailing back onto the road, the roar of the throaty diesel engine chasing away the silence.

Son of bitch, Jake muses, he knows that is just going to make things worse and never mind being lucky Jimmy didn't beat his ass and leave him lying out here. If Jimmy knows about Maria then it's got to be common knowledge around town. Oddly though, he no longer really cares what anybody thinks... *That was interesting,* he thinks and a small smile, but just a small one.

Chapter 23

He watches intently through the window as the young girl, her green smock perfect, a few wisps of blond hair escaping her visor, just a hint of freckles caressing her nose, carefully applies the drizzle of caramel to the perfectly formed swirls of whip cream. She reminds him of someone from long ago.

He hadn't been able to stop thinking about Molly or the damn coffee since the run in with Jimmy that afternoon. He had driven two towns over just to make sure no one saw him. Hell, he had even called it a "grande" like she had taught him... laughing every time he insisted it was a "medium"!

Sitting in the parking lot listening to the familiar soft tick and ping of the old Ford alternately chewing the green stir stick and sipping the sweet hot mix of coffee and cream Jake rewinds the past few weeks. No questions just simple reflection, Jake wasn't one to indulge in second thoughts, recriminations, or normally even simple introspection for that matter. But he couldn't shake the feeling that he was missing something, something just out of reach.

The tears caught him by surprise, that familiar tightness in the chest the burning cheeks the soft huff of gently caught breath, he hadn't felt this way since he was a young man a teenager. But you never forget what a broken heart feels like and Jake had been broken for a very long time. Sitting watching through the filmy lens of his tears a slow parade of young people circulate by coming and going with an exaggerated sense of purpose. It hadn't been like this for him and his buddies. No, there had been a palpable sense of tension between the young bucks and any young lady created measurable angst. No, these kids had a casual comfort with themselves and each other that was foreign to Jake and his generation. Oh, he had been around his fair share of girls growing up, but if he was honest, even on the best of days it was awkward and nerve wracking. The free love of the sixties was fading in the early seventies as the disco age approached. Not something you talked to your buddies about but he was pretty sure now that they had all dealt with pretty much the same thing growing up.

He had that first heartbreak at fifteen, Annie Tildon. He could remember it like it was yesterday, her long brown hair and the handful of freckles. He had been amazed she even spoke to him. This delicate

83

beautiful young woman with an impish grin and the brightest blue eyes he had ever seen, her small soft hands lost in his calloused mitts. Time had stood still that summer and fall and Jake had been happy, truly happy like he had never dreamed possible. If he was honest with himself happier than he had been since. But even with just fifteen short summers under his belt he was more than capable of self-destructing in spectacular fashion.

He hadn't meant a word of it and the hurt in her eyes had pierced him through. She had called him out then and there with the tears magnifying her freckles. "Jake" she had said, "I thought you were a man, someone I could count on, someone I could love, but you're just a little boy like the rest of these idiots you call friends." Books tight to her chest, head held high, she had marched out of his life and all the slaps on the back and guffaws of his buddies hadn't made a bit of difference.

Oh, he had tried to apologize, to explain but Annie wouldn't even look at him, much less speak. He had spent more nights than he cared to count crying himself to sleep, head buried in his pillow the hot silent tears flowing, the hole in his teenage chest empty and hollow. He had swallowed it, unable to talk to his father and too embarrassed to tell his mother.

There had been other girls, but he knew he was just going through the motions and it didn't take them long to figure it out either. Crazy as it seemed he hadn't loved anyone like that since and that was a long damn time ago... well, maybe Molly, but shit he had managed to screw that up as well.

What was the point in dredging up these old memories anyway? The whole thing just seemed ridiculous to him. Yet he felt powerless to move to drive away. Unable to don his usual casual attitude of disdain and indifference he remains in the parking lot softly sipping. Rain begins to spot the windshield when he finally turns toward home. The now empty sweet caramel reminder of happier moments rolls around the floorboard matching the syncopation of the old Ford's tires and Jakes melancholy heart.

Chapter 24

Harry dipped the sugar cube in the steaming hot coffee, watching intently as the black liquid absorbed into the crystalline square before popping it in his mouth and crunching down. He always anticipated the explosion of sweetness but never tired of the surprise when it flooded his senses. He hadn't meant to stop, just ride by and take a gander, see if Jake was home, but the girl had been standing on front porch almost like she was waiting for him. No choice at that point but turn in and introduce himself, besides he really was just trying to help.

It had started almost the moment he had put the car in park, that feeling that more was happening here than met the eye, a sixth sense he used to call it. Happened sometimes in the courtroom, those times when you knew what a witness was going to say before the question had even been asked. It didn't happen often but enough for Harry to know it wasn't pure coincidence. No he didn't indulge in the arrogance of the intellectuals, Harry was well aware that there were forces at work in the universe well beyond his ability to understand. The question was why here why now? And maybe the biggest question of all... Why Jake, he seemed a most unlikely candidate to be experiencing anything larger than the next happy hour. He loved Jake like son, most wouldn't have believed that, but he had watched the tortured young man grow up and felt a sense of responsibility for him. It went well beyond that but most folks weren't ready for that story and Harry wasn't really in any hurry to tell it. But the truth of the matter was that Jake had seemed to attract heartache, trouble and bad luck like some human vortex for the ills of humanity. Now here he was with this strange young woman, a shining gem, a light in the darkness an ethereal beauty and presence about her that just didn't seem to fit with Jake, this town, hell she didn't seem to fit at all.

A soft tap on the window had brought him back to the present, damn how long had he been just sitting here in the drive? He was not prone to daydreaming and distraction, but he had definitely been off somewhere. "Come in for some coffee Mr. Harry," she had said softly, and here he was sucking on the last remnants of his second sugar cube. *Mr. Harry... hmmm* he hadn't remembered introducing himself *yet she had known him hadn't she?*

She hadn't had much to say actually, just sat

87

there across the table small delicate hands wrapped around the coffee mug. It seemed as if she was waiting, on what he couldn't fathom, but there was a peacefulness about her that just seemed to envelope you. Jake had been right, there was something different about this girl, something unexplainable. Jake had said something about being scared and hopeful all at the same time. He could see that, but more than anything he was intrigued, curious, and well he felt a bit of excitement, yes that was it, excitement. Like some great adventure or discovery lay ahead.

Chapter 25

The first dreams had scared her, waking up
shivering not understanding what she had seen
everything seeming so real. Maria had never dreamed
or at least she never seemed to remember them the
next morning. These were different though, there was
a vibrancy to them, even an urgency she didn't really
comprehend. And with these dreams she remembered
everything clearly. It was not every night the first
ones had started shortly before she had left home
that early morning that seemed so long ago. In fact
she had dreamed Jake that very morning she had known
he was coming. Knew he would be on that highway, she
hadn't realized it until the moment the truck had
stopped but deep in her heart she had known along.
She had dreamed about that boy in the grey BMW too,
she had known he was going to die in that car. She
had almost told Jake in the diner, but how do you
explain something like that?

Strangely she didn't feel scared anymore. The
dreams had frightened her at first, but not in a "bad
dream" way but the clarity and precision of what she
saw and felt was so real it had been unnerving at

first. She certainly didn't understand why this was happening or even what was happening, but she wasn't scared anymore. No there was a purpose to this, she might not see it yet, but she knew there was a reason she had been given these dreams. She had not had a "Jake" dream since that first time, but she couldn't help feeling that he was tangled up in this somehow. Why else had she dreamed about him that morning and why else would she be here?

There were no answers to these questions, but she didn't dwell on it, they would come when she needed them. The only question right now, today was how to explain to Mr. Harry any of this. She had known he was coming and she also knew he could be trusted but that didn't make things any easier. That was the difficulty only having part of a story made it hard to piece things together. You couldn't tell if you were at the beginning, the end or somewhere in the middle. There were often people she didn't know, pictures of the past or future; it was impossible to tell and of course each person had their own story making it even more complicated. The end of one could be the middle of another or anywhere in between. You could chase this string forever if you let yourself.

It was like trying to write a book report in Mrs. Timmon's class without having read the book. She knew some of the characters but it wasn't clear what their roles were or how things turned out. Maybe that was the point, this was a story that hadn't been written yet. It was a lot for a young girl to absorb and make sense of. Then again she didn't want to over think this, just trust herself and see where things went from here. One thing was for sure, she had not imagined being here when she had kissed the little ones on her way out of what had been her home, humble shack that it was. She missed them all desperately but had resisted the urge to call them, what was there to say? She knew she could never go home. Leaving her cell sitting on the dresser that morning might have been the single most courageous thing she had ever done.

Chapter 26

The tires softly crunched over the gravel as
the truck comes to a stop, the light from the kitchen
spilling out through the pulled curtains cast a
patchwork of shadows on the back steps. Jake pushes
through the door hearing the murmur of voices and
soft clink of dishes in the sink, Maria must be
washing them he thinks. Hesitating, trying to catch a
word or two standing in the dark of the rear foyer he
can see the light seeping under the swinging door to
the kitchen. He knows its Harry she is speaking to,
his car had been parked at the curb. In a strange way
he feels like an intruder in his own home and he
stops with his hand on the door.

Harry watches the young woman as she pours a
fresh cup of coffee and sets it on the table. She has
a fluid gracefulness that only the youthful seem to
possess. He can sense as much as see the small smile
playing across her face. The creak of the kitchen
door interrupts his thought as Jake lumbers in the
very antithesis of grace and youth. "Hello sir,
didn't expect you here this evening" as he sits at
the table and picks up the coffee. It's not the sweet

caramel mix, but it's warm and milky the way he likes it.

"I was in the neighborhood Jake, just wanted to stop by and check on you after our talk earlier..." Jake's smile was uncontrolled and followed by a bit of a chuckle.

"Couldn't stay away could you sir, I told you didn't I, didn't I? Now do you see what I am talking about, do you get it sir, it's not me is it?" He is almost pleading, his voice rising leaning into the table searching the old man's eyes for the right answer, some explanation, desperately needing someone else to see it too.

"It's okay Jake, Mr. Harry isn't here by accident," she softly whispers sitting down between the two of them. "We all need answers, maybe me most of all, but a lot of this doesn't make sense yet."

"Hmmph, tell me something I don't know, you've got me pretty convinced I'm crazy cause I don't know what's going on with me and I ain't never been like this before."

"Let me tell you about my dreams..."

There were questions and more questions and those led to more unanswerable questions, and of course not nearly enough answers to please any of them. Jake was stuck on the Pickering boy and how could Maria know and not try to stop him. It was an unusual sentiment since Jake rarely bothered to be concerned with anyone beyond himself. Turned out Mr. Harry had known the boy's father and had even sat across the courtroom from him a few times many years ago.

Maria spent most of the evening trying to describe how each dream felt, the detail, the "realness" of it all, but her words swirled around each other and without a way to explain the very real but very strange experience she was left repeating herself.

Harry was enthralled with the mystery of it all, how it happened, the why, what could it mean and the world of possibilities it opened up. He had not had his curiosity piqued like this in a long time, well maybe never actually. This was so far beyond his experience it was thrilling and overwhelming all at once. Sitting back watching the two dramatically different individuals in front of him he began to understand the danger this posed and the delicacy with which this had to be handled. These two would need protection, mostly from themselves, but Harry had a feeling that there was probably more to it than that. He was going to have to help them manage through this, whatever this turned out to be. He had been around long enough to know that something as outside the ordinary as this was had the power to inflame this little town without a great deal of provocation. No this wasn't a bad town, but it definitely had a limited perspective on things, and it hadn't been that long ago when ignorance had ruled the day, *what had it been, the summer of 1981?*

Thirty or so years later people still whispered about the old plantation just outside of town and the strange happenings of that summer. It was still there but the property had become overgrown and the house had fallen into disrepair over the years. All in all still an eerie place and although the town didn't openly talk about it no one had really forgotten.

Chapter 27

The plantation house set alone on the hilltop,
the long gravel drive winding down to the two-lane
country road. The grass had grown up around the
pillars flanking the entrance to the drive and the
kudzu was slowing taking over the fences that lined
the sides of the road leading back down toward fields
that played out behind the old homestead. The place
had been built back in the 1820s and had supplied
indigo to the early textile industry in the area.
Surprisingly it had been bypassed during the burning
and pillaging of the North's advance forty years
later. Since then it had passed from family to family
until finally laying empty for a number of years. The
old slave's quarters still stood upright behind the
house and small garden and arbor off to the left was
mostly weeds and vines at this point. The summer
kitchen directly behind the home had become a resting
place for birds, the front door leaning to the side
partially unhinged. Little remained of the stately
glory she had once known.

The long sleek profile of the gleaming white
BMW 740 was an incongruous interruption to the quiet

forlornness of the old place as it slowly pulled around the drive encircling the property. It wouldn't be more than a few weeks later that the string of moving vans would show up, the fifteen or so young people and one very out-of-place family. That's when the real trouble would start.

It would begin simply enough, the calls for local electricians, plumbers, carpenters as there was enough work to keep more than a few local companies busy. The transformation was happening rapidly, the young people worked in teams clearing the land, putting up fences, and planting. Within weeks the plantation was coming back to life, horses, cows, chickens, and sheep had been delivered from somewhere. All the while the town watched and whispered.

It really was impossible to know what the trigger was, the cash only payments, the massive shopping trips to local grocery stores, the expensive foreign cars, the young folks working around the clock, or maybe it was all of it in combination. But it was just a matter of time before the town would demand to know what was going on up there. The town needed to know exactly what these outsiders were up to. How else were they going to protect themselves? As is usually the case when ignorance is faced with circumstances it doesn't understand it manufactures hysteria, hatred, prejudice, self-justification and unfortunately this time would be no different.

Chapter 28

The candles lit the sunroom with a warm glow as the brick oven grill combination in the attached garden came to life. The twilight settled in punctuated with the soft strumming of a guitar and the careless laughter of friends relaxing after a long day working the fields. In the kitchen succulent lamb chops and chicken were marinating in preparation for the now hot grill. Nearby fresh vegetables from the garden lay waiting to be cut and added to a large wooden salad bowl. The plantation was beginning to bear fruit and this evening would be a celebration of many weeks of hard work, the culmination of many efforts and the recognition of new beginnings.

Her name was Sally and she had created this place through sheer force of will. The long trip from the Southwest followed by bringing this plantation back to life and infusing it with a life force a spirit of love and peace. It was the realization of many years of preparation and planning. She came from a long line of teachers and healers. Her people were from the northern Native American tribes and the early English settlers of the Hudson Valley. She was wise in the lore of Native American medicine, botany, biology, and the philosophies of the Middle Eastern mystics. Although a wise and virtuous woman she had no illusions about man's capacity for evil and his special talent for hurting those around him. No, she knew better than most what man was capable of. But she also knew the power in the earth itself, the mysteries that eluded modern man and the energies that co-existed in this universe hovering just beyond the ability of most to grasp. It was this wisdom that guided her life and allowed her to bring this patch of earth back to life. To sense the souls and spirits that had inhabited this place before her. She had a virtual communion with the hardy folks that had carved something out of nothing, as well as the frightened oppressed spirits of those whose life energy and blood had seeped into this earth thousands of miles from their homeland. It was the confluence of all these things and the final maturation of her plans that had led to this place and point in time. This was the school that she had prayed would finally come to be.

Teaching these young people the value of introspection, heightened self-awareness, hard work, and self-reliance was the living proof that her dream was finally within reach. They were the first ones, the groundbreakers. The school would make a difference, have an impact, and bring a generation of lost narcissists back from the brink. She believed firmly that the self-discovery and enlightenment, as well as, the energy of the sixties had been lost on the current generation. They needed to be saved from the complacency, rampant materialism and image consciousness that pervaded current society. Coming back to the moment she picks up the tray of lamb and chicken and heads toward the grill. She senses the dream is already under attack and the forces of ignorance and hate are being arrayed against her. There are powers in the universe that work in a continuous struggle against each other. There truly is an equal and opposite reaction for every action. Well versed in the powers that lay beyond the comprehension of the unconscious man Sally was well aware of the constant struggle. She had planned well though and only needed a foothold, enough time to establish a base from which to combat the inertia of a decaying humanity.

The first Molotov cocktail struck the left pillar of the front gate shattering instantly. Flames spread across the freshly painted wood and the nearby shrubs. The second landing further down the fence line caught an old scrub pine on fire. It wasn't immediately obvious what had happened, as the main house was a few hundred yards up the hill. However the flames quickly grew fanned by the night breeze demanding attention. Although the fire was brought under control without any significant damage the war had begun and it would not so easily be quenched.

The coals had burned down to embers as the marinating meat, that had hours ago represented a triumphant beginning, remained forgotten and uncooked. The flashing lights were gone, statements taken, noncommittal reassurances given, and a cold determination was born that would eventually have an unforeseen and lasting impact on this little town. It would create its own set of consequences requiring an accounting before all was said and done.

Chapter 29

Standing on the front porch Harry hesitated a moment, turning to Jake he takes his arm gently, "Son, I know I don't have to tell ya this but don't be talking to anyone, and I mean anyone about any of this... you understand?" And then giving him a sideways glance, "you remember what happened with those folks out at the old plantation all those years ago right? This town got all worked up thinking they were devil worshippers or some such nonsense. I know it sounds funny now, but everyone was sure quick to believe it back then. Well you may not believe me, but this could bring some of the same kinda trouble. And before you go protestin' too much, don't for a minute think I don't know your own little part in that mess, never mind what your father and his hooligan friends did."

Jake honestly didn't know his father had been involved. But he and his best friend Jimmy had been right in the middle of things, well maybe right at the beginning of things. It had just been another bored Saturday night drinking beer and riding around. It had been Jimmy's idea to make the Molotov cocktails using the empty beer bottles that were rattling around in the rear floorboard. They had both thrown one, but he had never told anyone that story. Things had escalated pretty quickly after and they had both sworn an oath to never tell. Obviously someone had known, or more likely Jimmy had run his mouth at some point.

"Come by the office Tuesday and we can talk about it," Harry said, sensing the questions rising up in Jake. "Now isn't the time or place, come by then I have a few things to double check and a couple of items to discuss with you anyway."

" Yes sir," and without really knowing why "thank you sir, I appreciate you always watchin' out for me."

"Think nothin' of it son, I owed your old man, but that's a story for another time..."

Inside Jake heads for the kitchen, but Maria has already cleaned up and headed upstairs. The kitchen is dark, only illuminated by the light of the muted street lamp outside. He sits quietly at the table trying to make sense of it all, it really was just too much to absorb and Jake was way out of his depth with this. *What had the old man meant he owed my father?* Jake tried to recall those early years, but it was mostly just a blur. He had been so caught up in himself and his buddies as a teenager he didn't really have any significant memories of his father. And although that may seem strange to many others, for Jake it's just the way it was. His father hadn't been around much and when he was it was generally unpleasant. Truth was neither had been really interested in pursuing a traditional father son relationship. The fact that his father had something to do with the old plantation mess didn't really surprise him. What was surprising was he had never heard anything about it and this was a small town after all. But his father had never mentioned it and neither had anyone else as far as he knew.

He hadn't thought about those days in a very long time. It wasn't just the oath he and Jimmy had sworn, that was also the summer he had tried to see Annie again. It had been almost ten years since he had been an idiot. Things hadn't changed enough for him and too much for her to ever set that clock back. *It kept coming back to that, didn't it? Damn, it had been what forty years since that day in high school, when was it going to be long enough?* By now Jake knew better than to expect an answer to that question, but it didn't stop him from reviewing his seemingly endless catalogue of failures and disappointments. They paraded in front of him like some familiar book, the pages worn from constant turning.

Chapter 30

Jake was sitting in a side booth at McElroy's Family Restaurant drinking coffee and wishing there was something interesting to read in the Tuesday edition of the Peakeville Times. Anywhere else but in the South, McElroy's would be considered a diner: decent coffee, open 24/7, breakfast all day, an extensive dinner menu and the deserts looked like something you would see on TV. The seven layer cakes perfectly frosted, the chocolate and creamed filled pastries, and the pies, oh man, the pies were really special. Peach was the local specialty, but there was always apple and sometimes cherry as well. The menu leaned decidedly toward southern comfort food, but old man McElroy had moved south after World War II looking for a break from the northeast winters and had brought the framework of the quintessential northeast diner with him. His son ran the day to day but the old man was still around most of the time. Jake had been eating here most of his life along with most everyone else in town at some time or another. Nothing fancy but it was simple good food and the girls were quick with a refill and pretty good-natured with the lecherous old men sitting at the counter stools.

Harry had decided breakfast sounded better than meeting at the office so here Jake was, waiting. It wasn't like Harry to be late but he was well past twenty minutes this morning. That didn't necessarily worry Jake. He figured everyone was entitled now again, he had never been the on-time type himself.

Jake looked up as the door chimed just as he figured Harry had finally made it, he looked around, a bit flustered before catching Jakes eye and hustling over. The old battered briefcase banged down next to him papers spilling out of the top as if they had hastily been shoved in without much thought. Damn, the old man was sweating and muttering to himself, he had never seen him like this... Harry White was not prone to panic or even nerves for that matter, he was the coolest, calmest, most reserved man Jake had ever met. Seeing him like this was, well it was disturbing and with the craziness of the past few days, past weeks actually, disturbing was not exactly what Jake was hoping for this morning.

"Are you okay sir?"

"Yes, yes, just as I thought though. Yes, just as I suspected, Jake things are going to get pretty interesting for a bit young man. I'm not ready to tell you everything yet, but well, let's just say things are never quite how they appear."

"Sir, I don't even know what that means, what isn't how it appears, what are you talking about?"

"Jake, son you are just going to have to trust me on this..."

"You know I trust you sir, I just don't understand what is going on... In fact I don't really understand any of this."

Leaning back in the booth Harry lets out a long exaggerated breath, "I know son, but it will be okay I promise you, I just need a little more time got a few more things to check out." Leaning back again signaling the young girl standing at the counter... "Black coffee, two sugar cubes."

"We don't have sugar cubes," is the bored acerbic reply.

"Yes you do young lady, they are on the back counter there in the blue bowl, now be kind to an old man and fetch them for me." Harry glances back at Jake, "now where was I... oh yes, I just need a little more time then I will bring you and the girl up to date on everything." The young waitress brings the coffee and sugar cubes with an acid smile, not noticing, Harry mumbles, "thank you miss."

Jake slumps down in the booth, brow furrowed,

looking like a scolded schoolboy forced to listen to the familiar refrain of an all too well-known lecture. In fact he had already stopped listening, caught up in the dissonance of the mingled conversations going on around him. Harry's remonstrations continued unabated while he simply floated away lost in his own little world.

"Jake!"

"What, what?" suddenly back in this world looking a bit dazed at Harry sitting across from him. The old man was shaking his head at a complete loss for words.

"Son what the hell is wrong with you? You were gone, just not here."

"I don't know sir, I guess I just got a little distracted."

Harry gives him that over the glasses look he usually reserved for smart-ass law clerks. "Now listen son, I have some work to do, but I need you to take your tools up to the office and fix the porch railing, and there are a couple of loose steps in the back. Think you can handle that without getting distracted?"

"Yes sir, I'll have it done this afternoon for you. Are you stopping by tonight? I was thinking I would take Maria over to that Mexican place on

Bridgewater, thought she might like it."

Harry pauses for a moment, "yes, I think she would like that Maybe I'll stop by later this evening but don't wait on me. Make sure that railing is tight, if you need to buy anything just put it on my account down at Sanders and I'll take care of it," and with that he was gone.

Jake watched him leave, waddling down the street in as much of a hurry as he had ever seen him. Well, at least he would have something to keep him busy for the better part of the day.

Chapter 31

It felt good to be working with his hands
again. The simple truth was that Jake loved building
and fixing things. The precision and attention to
detail required by good carpentry appealed to a part
of him that he mostly kept hidden. He wasn't sure
where he had picked it up but he had adopted the old
carpenter's adage as his own: measure twice cut once.
Rules to live by, not that Jake lived by any
particular set of rules when it came right down to
it.

In his usual way Harry had seriously misjudged
the amount of work the old porch had needed. Jake had
started with stripping out the rotting floorboards
only to find that at least two of the joists would
need replacing as well. *No matter though, anything
worth doing was worth doing right... ahhh, there was
another one*. With all the old wood torn out he had
made his list and headed down to Sanders to pick up
the new lumber and a couple of pounds of galvanized
nails. He liked Sanders, an old time lumber yard and
hardware store where you could still buy bulk nails
and hand pick your boards. After having settled up he

signed the slip for Harry's account and headed back to the office. A quick stop at the Bantam Chef for a couple of slaw dogs, crinkle cut fries and chocolate shake seemed like a perfect idea.

Feet up just relaxing on the tailgate of the old Ford Jake was sipping the sweet chocolate of the shake alternating it with the overly salty, but oh so crispy fries, of course the dogs were long gone. Jake could down those in just a couple of bites. He loved the way they got lost in the soft bun, the sweet coleslaw and the occasional tangy bite of the bright yellow mustard was a perfect match. A final slurp and it was time to get back to the porch.

Pulling out his carpenters pencil, now whittled down to not much more than a nub, he takes his father's old square, the wood worn smooth and the measured etchings fading along the metal edge. It was square and true though. Working quickly he marks the lengths he had recorded earlier whistling as he goes. The power saw sings through the treated pine throwing a rooster tail of sawdust behind it and filling the air with the sweet pungent scent of fresh cut wood. It reminds Jake of that long summer in Olympia. He had considered those good times even if it had been a bit lonely. The heat was building as early summer set in and this would normally have been about the time to break for a cold one. He had been trying to cut back and Harry would not have been happy to come back to a half done porch and a half-baked carpenter so, back to it. Replacing the joists went quickly since he was able to reuse the metal brackets. Time now to begin attaching the decking. Jake knew a lot of fellas that slapped it on and then cut along the edge trimming the decking all at once where it extended over the porch edge. He had never liked the rough look of it though, preferring the precision of a perfectly matched board. It took longer but the overall impression was one of quality and care taken.

It didn't occur to Jake that the rest of his life could use a bit of this type of attention. With the last board in place the shiny heads of the new nails reflecting in the afternoon sun he begins reattaching the railing and cleaning up. It's been a full day but he feels good about getting it done and accomplishing something worthwhile. Somewhat sheepishly he thinks, *you know I am pretty good at this.*

As he pulls away from the curb thoughts turn to home and Maria. He had told Harry he was thinking about taking her out to the new Mexican restaurant El something or other. Something spicy might be nice for a change and maybe they had that guacamole dip Molly had introduced him to. Made out of avocados or something, better not to think too much about what was in it. It sure was great on chips with a couple of cold ones, no doubt about that. Pulling into the driveway he lets the old Ford settle into its symphony of pings and ticks as he rewinds the day. If he set aside the insanity of the dreams, the girl, and the flight from Florida, today had been a good day. Not for the last time he asks himself, *why aren't there more days like this? What is it about me that's so damn hell bent after fifty plus years on this earth that's still so intent on fucking it all up? I'm a good carpenter, generally a likeable guy, sure I drank a bit much but I can control that if I want to... so why was it so damn hard to just keep it on the rails?*

This wasn't the first cycle of self-inspection Jake had undertaken, but it was the first sober one in a long time. As usual there were no clear answers forthcoming from the cab of that old Ford but he felt like maybe, just maybe, he was starting to ask the right questions and it scared the shit out of him. With a deep sigh he opens the door, *you know something is different* he mutters... *Hmmm, son of a bitch no cigarettes today! Holy shit how long had it been since he had gone a whole day without lighting up, hell he couldn't even begin to remember. Had to be years though, didn't it?*

Maria is sitting at the kitchen table with the paper open on the table, "nothing good in there," Jake announces from the doorway.

"Jake you startled me, that's not funny."

"Well, there is a first time for everything isn't there? You always seem to know where I am before I even know I'm going to be there, serves ya right," he says laughingly. "How about we do dinner at El El um El whatever, it's a new Mexican place over the other side of town?"

Giving him a look trying to figure out if he was somehow making fun of her, "sounds great, by the way Harry stopped by earlier today and left this for you," she says handing him the plain white envelope.

"So what's in it?"

"That's not funny Jake, you know I can't do stuff like that."

"Hey hey, I am just kidding, I thought he might of told you. I guess we'll just find out together." Jake slices the envelope open and takes out the note and three hundred dollar bills:

Jake, thanks for the quick work on the porch...

Hard work is its own reward... except

today!

…….Harry

Wasn't that just like Harry, the three hundred was more than a fair price for a day's work. He never would have asked for it, probably the reason for the note in the first place. Of course there was always some little phrase or as Harry called them "pearls of wisdom", if he had thought to keep them there would probably be hundreds of them by now. Well the cash would come in handy and apparently dinner was on Harry tonight.

"Okay, I am going to take a quick shower then we can go, I am pretty nasty after working on his porch all day. I'll tell you about it at dinner if you are interested." Nobody had ever really been interested in Jake's carpentry but it had been a good day and he wanted to share it with someone.

Chapter 32

Why on earth they would want to call it Carne Asada instead of just steak was beyond Jake, I mean this was the United States after all. Take Olive Garden for God's sake, you didn't see them calling spaghetti something Italian did you? No, spaghetti is spaghetti, but setting that aside it had tasted wonderful. There were spices he had never heard of. Well, anything beyond salt and pepper was going to strike Jake as exotic, but still it had been excellent. The steak was served with a rice dish and beans, the whole meal had been really good. Maria had ordered something in Spanish he couldn't pronounce, and he was afraid to ask what was in it. She was in her element and had seemed to be practically one of them - the wrongness of that thought didn't occur to him — she was speaking to most of the staff, laughing, and smiling like a fool. He couldn't imagine how anyone could talk as fast as they did and it was impossible to understand anything they were saying. But the girl had seemed at ease, at home, finally among people she could relate to. He finally had a small glimpse how difficult it might be to find oneself as out of place like she was. Jake didn't go so far as to imagine himself in her place but he wasn't completely oblivious of how hard it was to be different, and pointedly unwanted. That's as far as his introspection could take him tonight, but it was a slight bit farther than he had ever bothered to go before.

Walking out to the truck she had thanked him again, telling him how good it felt to be able to speak Spanish without worrying what someone might think. She had spent much of the evening sharing stories and laughing with the waitresses not much older than herself. "It makes you miss your folks doesn't it," he asked her.

"Yes it does, but I have no regrets Jake, this is just something I had to do. My parents were moving the family back to Mexico and I just couldn't see myself surviving there."

"Oh, I am sorry I didn't know..." and he really didn't know, Jake had no experience even remotely related to being an immigrant, his family had been in this general area for generations.

"It's okay, I get sad sometimes and I miss my little brother and sister, but my life is here in this country, I grew up here and I don't want to leave."

"I guess I understand." A lie, he really didn't and more than that Jake had spent a great deal of time honing his prejudice for anybody that wasn't clearly white and what he considered "American".

She gave him a look, one of those you are full of shit and you know it looks, "Jake you don't understand at all, how could you? People don't hate you because your skin is too dark, or treat you like a criminal because you speak Spanish. Or better yet think you are taking their job cause you weren't born in this country." Leaning against the truck bed she sighs and continues, "Jake, you can't imagine what it's like, boys would treat me like a whore because they think all Mexican girls are easy. It doesn't help that many girls get pregnant as teenagers, but it's a cultural thing in Mexico as most fifteen and sixteen year old girls are already getting married and having kids. I am not saying it's okay but its different down there, it's one of the reasons I won't move back. I want more for myself. Then there are the gangs, sure there are lotsa Mexican gangs, but that doesn't mean every Mexican is a gang-banger does it? My parents didn't take anyone's job either Jake!" She was getting worked up now, "Jake they pick the strawberries, squash, okra or whatever for next to nothing while we live in houses no one else will. But you know what? They are happy to have the work cause they get to be here and no matter how bad it is here it is better than living in the slums of Mexico."

"Whoa now, I didn't mean nothin' by it," Jake splutters feeling himself get defensive and angry at the same time. "I'm not stupid you know, I see how it is too, you people come here and live off the system expecting to be taken care of with your hand out all the time while hard workin' Americans..." he stops looking across the truck at her. He can see the hurt in her eyes, the deep sadness there and he has seen it before in a young woman many years ago.

"Do you really believe all that," she asks, her voice starting to quiver. Determined not to cry she shakes her head, squeezing her eyes shut. "Really do you believe that, is that what you think my parents did, what I will do? Did we come here just to live off YOUR system? All my family has ever done is work hard and try to make enough money to get by and make it to the next job. We were luckier than most Jake, we usually had a place to stay, clothes that fit and I got to go to school. I know lots of families that lived out of their cars, didn't have food, couldn't put clothes on their kids, but we are the ones taking advantage?" Her anger was beginning to show through now and this was going to escalate to a full-blown argument right here in the parking lot of El Casa Robles.

"Maria, Maria, please, I am sorry I don't want to fight about this, you're right, I don't know anything about you or your family or most any of the stuff you are saying, sweet Jesus, give me a fuckin' break." Hands in his pockets leaning against the door of the truck he takes a deep breath. "Fact is... well, I don't know what the fact is, but that's just how people around here have always felt about people that's different from them. I ain't saying it's right or wrong; it just is."

"You think I don't know that? Really! But guess what... that doesn't make it okay... listen, can we just go get a coffee? I haven't had a Starbucks since I left home, maybe we can get a Caramel Macchiato, do you like those?" she says with just a hint of a smile obviously trying to diffuse the tension.

Jake sees it coming and still can't get out of the way. *Son of bitch, how could she know about Starbucks and the caramel coffee, sweet baby Jesus, she scared the shit out of him sometimes.* "You can wipe that grin off your face and stop acting like you don't know, probably dreamed that shit too didn't you?"

Chapter 33

Molly carefully folds the apron, setting it down on the back of the bar trying not to let the tears come, but she can't help it. Pete steps over and gives her a big bear hug, kissing the top of her head, he holds her out in front of him and gives her a huge grin. "No tears now pretty lady, this isn't good bye, you'll still be working weekends. I am not letting you go that easily!"

She smiles through the tears, "Oh Pete I know I just can't believe this is happening and you're helping me out so much I feel bad about it."

Pete shakes his head, "now, now, nothing to feel bad about, you have been a blessing here and if I can't help a friend out what's the point anyway?" He grabs the bar rag and mindlessly starts wiping his eyes growing misty, "look you go back to school and make a better future for yourself, I'm happy to help and you know anything you need I'm here for you."

"I know Pete, you are like the big brother I never had..." He smiles ruefully at her as she asks, "you do think I can do it right?" She had been asking that question a dozen different ways and he always answered the same.

"Of course you can do this, you're great with numbers already. I have no doubt you'll make a great bookkeeper, besides your first job is to come back here and straighten my mess out..." he says laughing.

"You know I will, I really can't believe I am actually doing this, I never would have believed I could go back to school after all this time."

He smiles again, "go on get out of here, you have an early morning tomorrow, make sure you stop by and let me know how it was... and Molly... I'm proud of you honey."

She couldn't believe it herself, she had seen Miami Dade College advertising an associate degree in accounting on TV and something had just clicked inside. She knew it was time to take stock of her life and make some changes. Pete had been a little skeptical at first, but once he realized she was serious he was her biggest supporter, well, only supporter for that matter. They worked out a schedule that allowed her to take classes full time in the mornings and early afternoons while still catch enough shifts to pay her rent and make ends meet. Pete had insisted on covering her tuition and upped her hourly enough to help with everything else. It wasn't going to be easy, she was sure of that, but she hadn't been this excited about anything since moving to Miami in the first place. She didn't think there was ever going to be a way to pay Pete back for all his kindness, but she was going to make sure he didn't regret it.

Sleep didn't come easy that night, the excitement, nerves, and a touch of fear surrounding this new journey had her restless. Strangely, she finds herself wondering what Jake is up to, funnily enough, it didn't bother her and with a smile she drifts off knowing that chapter is finally closed.

Chapter 34

Harry didn't make it over that night and neither of them had heard from him the next day either. Jake had circled around to the office to put a coat of water seal on the new decking. It had that closed up feel to it the mail still stuffed in the mounted box by the front door untouched. It didn't appear that anyone had been there since he had finished the deck. The afternoon was drawing on when Jake had finally finished cleaning up and stowing the paint gear he headed back to the house. He could feel that brooding sense of doom he had grown quite familiar with lately. Nothing he could put his finger on, but it was never quite that obvious was it.

The air was heavy and he could see the dark clouds building to the West, looked like an early Carolina summer thunderstorm was on its way. Living in the upstate you learned the signs: that smell of earthiness that seemed to carry on the wind, the silver backs of the leaves dancing in the growing breeze and there it was the low rumble of distant thunder announcing the impending storm. Jake didn't mind these storms they weren't anything like the torrential insanity of Florida thunderstorms that would kick up every afternoon and had a fury all their own. These storms tended to taper off to gentle nourishing rain lasting for hours. The big drops announced themselves on the roof of the truck as he was pulling into the driveway. Making a dash for the back door before the downpour catches up to him he can smell something truly wonderful coming from the kitchen. It's something familiar, reminiscent of a happier time in his life. Jake can't quite place it, but something inside him breaks just a little. He can't help himself, he is standing there in the doorway blubbering like a child, great heaving silent sobs the tears streaming down his cheeks coupled with that all too familiar tightness in his chest.

"Oh my God Jake, what's the matter, what happened?" exclaims Maria turning and seeing him standing there in all his vulnerable glory. His hard shell of indifference beginning to crack and whither.

"I, I, I, don't know," he stammers. "What are you making, it reminds me of something, I don't know what it reminds me..." shaking his head.

"Jake, it's one of your Mom's recipes, I found an old handwritten cookbook today, I figured it was hers and just thought I would try to make you something... I'm, I'm sorry I didn't know."

Coming over to the kitchen table set with plates, utensils and a soft yellow tablecloth that seems familiar but he can't quite place it though, he sits down catching his breath. "No, it's okay, I remember now. It was my Dad's favorite meal and we would have it on Sunday's whenever he was home, which really wasn't that often, but I remember it like it was yesterday."

"Well, just sit down, I'm almost finished, I didn't mean to upset you, it just sounded so good when I read it."

"It's okay, those are good memories and my momma always baked the best biscuits too."

"Well, no biscuits, I don't have any idea how to do that, but I made fresh tortillas the way my mom taught me when I was little, I hope that's good enough." Turning back to the stove she stirs the green beans remembering her own good times with her mom cooking the evening meals for the men. "I'm pretty sure I did this, umm, cube steak thing right, but I've never ever made mashed potatoes. I boiled them but after that... do you know how to do them?"

"Sure do," lumbering over to the stove he checks the boiling potatoes with a fork and moves the big pot over to the sink. Reaching into the old refrigerator he pulls out the milk and butter trying, not very successfully, to keep composed. With the potatoes drained and steaming in the big pot he measures in the milk and adds the chunks of butter. Next a dash of salt and pepper and his mom always added a small pinch of garlic powder. The mashing had always been his favorite part as a kid, no blender for the Delhommes; his mom had always used an old fashioned masher. He can't shake the feeling that somewhere she is watching with a smile as he is trying to work out all the lumps, he never had been able to get it smooth like she did. "Okay, I think these are good now, should I put 'em on the table?"

"Yes, next to the green beans so I have room for the steak things. Why do they call them cube steaks anyway, they don't really look like steaks."

"Well...," with just the hint of a raised eyebrow, "I honestly have no idea," Jake says trying to stifle a laugh. "But my old man loved 'em and mom would make 'em for Sunday dinner when I was a kid; don't really know why she stopped." Jake scoops two onto his plate with a heaping spoonful of potatoes and some green beans. "So tell me about tortillas, how do you make 'em and how am I supposed to eat 'em with this?"

"Well I make them the way my mother taught me, pretty simple really it's just flour, salt, water,

and lard when she could get it. Most times she just
used that vegetable shortening that comes in the blue
and red can, hardest part for me is she never
measured anything. Anyway, you mix it all up and
knead the dough, let it sit a little then form into
small balls before you roll it out real thin. Drop
them into a hot pan and flip them when they start to
puff up. It's really easy once you get the dough part
right, you gring... well most people put everything
in them but we use them like bread, just roll them up
and eat them like you would bread."

"Gringos is that what you were going to say?"
Jake shakes his head pretending to be upset. "Well I
might be a gringo but these are pretty damn good
anyway."

"I'm sorry I didn't mean anything by it."

"Don't worry bout it, doesn't bother me none,
and I am sure you've been called plenty worse by
white people."

Sometimes it's the smallest stones that create
the biggest ripples, Jake had a momentary glimpse
into another world, a world of prejudice and
intolerance. A world he had long been a prominent
resident of.

Chapter 35

The kitchen had that quiet stillness a room acquires after a bustle of activity has dissipated. The dishes neatly stacked in the strainer gleaming in the soft light streaming through the window. The residual warmth and wholesome smells of dinner permeate the room in an almost whimsical reminder of all the dinners ever brought to life here. Further along the counter the soft bubbling and smell of freshly roasted coffee brewing rises above the rest. It seeks out the nooks and crannies traveling stealthily into the rest of the downstairs.

In the living room a somewhat battered plaid cloth covered couch sits along the outside wall below the picture window facing Orchard Street. To the left sit matching bright red, well, somewhat faded now, naugahyde recliners. Jake's father had picked them up for next to nothing at one of the many flea markets dotting the Carolina upstate. As his mother had been fond of pointing out any price would have been too much to pay. But as proud of them as Randy Delhomme was you would have thought they were top of the line Lazy Boys. Maria was ensconced in one, her legs curled up under her reading through the recipes she had found earlier, occasionally asking Jake to explain some of the finer points of southern cooking to her. Surprising himself he remembers a lot more of his mother's cooking than he would have guessed. Lounging on the couch he tries to interest himself in the local paper without much success. Where the hell was Harry and what had he been so worked up about the other morning? And why can't he shake the feeling that the old man is mixed up in something?

The bitter overtones of juniper and coriander mix with the briny saltiness of three green olives floating in the half empty martini glass, the sweet background wisps of vermouth dance in and out. The glass is almost empty, its two brothers already drained, are pushed off to the side patiently waiting for their sibling to catch up. The deep mahogany of the bar is polished to a glass like sheen. It doesn't hide the nicks and scars of a lifetime of long nights but they exist as a marker of the many years and souls that have passed through these doors. Harry knows he should have stopped with the first one or probably even before that, but he needed the time think, *damn how much could he tell them. What was today? It had been let's see... two, no, three days since he had met Jake for breakfast. Christ, this was all moving way too fast.*

Even the brightest and most wise among us sometimes make the mistake of believing they are in control. That if they are smart enough, quick enough, cautious enough that somehow the laws of the universe won't apply to them or at the very least will leave a window of opportunity open for them. It's an illusion of course, but then again the intellect has its very own blind spot no different than the fully unaware man who sleeps through his own existence.

Tonight Harry was augmenting his already dangerous blind spot with the "martini brothers" and this was a family reunion that was becoming more dangerous as the night wore on. The barkeep barks "Hey Harry, I gotta close up, you need to call it a night, you okay to drive?" Slapping a twenty on the bar Harry steadies himself and makes his way to the men's room, his bladder as impaired as his judgment.

"Yeah, yeah, I'm fine he mutters..." waving off the barkeep.

The cool air tinged with a hint of moisture clings to him as he makes his away across the parking lot. The earlier shower had left a fine sheen of moisture on the road and his car, as a late night fog starts to build. Sliding into the pearl white Lexus LS460 he brings the 4.6L V8 engine effortlessly to life. Harry loves this car, it is as luxurious as any vehicle he has ever had and with plenty of power too. It didn't matter to him that it was Japanese, it was an amazing vehicle. Sitting in the stillness smelling the sweet aroma of the leather and letting the defroster clear up the windshield Harry tries to collect his thoughts. He had known a little about the folks out at the school and had spent the last few days trying to track down what had really happened out there all those years ago. The files had been a gold mine, but the visit to PA had split things wide open for him. *Fucking Larry Johnson, no-one would believe it*, even if he hadn't promised to keep the whole meeting confidential. The whole town knew the basic story: the harassment, the supposed devil worshipping, and of course the cross burning. Followed by the need for the state police to get involved, but what hadn't been told was what had happened after. The really strange happenings had taken place during the long summer that had followed. The only reason Harry knew anything at all was because Randy Delhomme had continued to hold him to an agreement he had made in his first foolish days as an attorney. The symmetry had been too much for Harry to ignore. Jake showing up with this girl Maria, her dreams having a strange prophetic quality to them, it was too perfect to be simple coincidence.

Well he would lay out the whole story to them tomorrow and maybe between them they could find some string holding it all together. Or hell, better yet maybe the girl already knew all about it... but Larry Johnson he just couldn't believe it.

Taking a deep breath he drops the car into drive, the rain sensor triggers the wipers to start their intermittent cleansing of the spotted windshield. The headlights seem to move with the turns and twists of the road ahead as Harry peers into the fog. Unconsciously Harry feels the weight of discovery and its partner anxiety bearing down on him and as if with a mind all its own the Lexus is accelerating through sixty miles per hour.

You can call it an accident or nature's way, inconvenient coincidence, or even fate if you will, but then again nothing on this journey has been by chance has it? There are always deer on these Carolina back roads, everyone knows it but nobody slows down. You take your chances and you roll the dice. The trajectory of the Lexus as it leaves the road misses the largest of the pines and crashes through the scrub and into the gully below. The red clay dirt spatters the luminescent white paint like some country fair spin art. Maybe it's the Japanese engineering, the side, front and knee airbags; whatever the case Harry survives the impact with the old oak. He isn't awake to know it, the shock of the dash crushing his lower body rendering him immediately unconscious. The LS is equipped with a state of the art safety system and for the most part it's kept Harry alive tonight. The LS takes things a step further and comes standard with the Lexus' Safety Connect system; an integrated cell phone and GPS system that can locate the vehicle and automatically dials an emergency call center in the event of an airbag deployment. Thirteen months ago the dealer had explained in detail the system and its one-year complimentary subscription, unfortunately the renewal email was thirty-two days old and unopened in Harry's Email box. There would be no help dispatched tonight and Harry's fate lay in the hands of his mangled Japanese marvel of engineering and the fitful dreams of an eighteen year old Hispanic girl.

Chapter 36

When the dreams come it's like being in a movie you can't leave, or watching a TV show you can't turn off. Maria is unable to wake up, the dreams are in control until they decide to release her. Suddenly waking Maria is shivering in the quiet of the living room having fallen asleep in the big recliner, the recipe book still in her lap. Jake is still on the couch staring at her, fear in his eyes mixed with something else, curiosity maybe.

"What, what is it," he demands more forceful than he intends.

"It, It's Harry, Oh my God Jake, I don't know, I don't know if he is okay..." trailing off with a sob.

"Slow down now, just tell me what you saw, everything, don't leave nothin' out..."

"Okay, okay let me see... well first he was at a bar I think but I didn't see the name, but it was a long shiny wood one with a big mirror behind it, he was drinking something, um yeah something with like a green olive on a toothpick..."

"Fuck me, there is only one place Harry drinks

martinis, what else?"

"He's hurt real bad Jake, the car ran off the road and its down in a big ditch with lots of trees around it..."

"Ok, let's go. I know which bar he likes and we'll just go up there and trace his route home. Come, we gotta go. Hey wait a sec can you tell if this already happened??? Or maybe is it going to happen like that kid in the BMW?"

"I don't know Jake, but the boy in the BMW was different, we saw him, besides I had already dreamed about him, I think this just happened... umm, it was like getting a message, like someone was reaching out to me... I don't know, I just don't know..."

"Oh man that's fucking weird as hell... come on we gotta go..." Jake backs the truck out of the drive wheels spinning and spraying gravel before they catch on the roadway. The old Ford trundles out of town heading into the inky black of the Carolina country side racing to catch up with the beams of its headlights. Jake pulls into the empty parking lot, only an old Chevy Nova parked in the back by the dumpster remains. There is no way to confirm whether Harry had actually been here or not. Jake drops the truck back into drive as a sliver of light plays out across the still wet blacktop of the lot. The screen door at the back of the bar slams shut piercing the quiet night as a barely discernable figure hauls two large trash bags towards the dumpster. Jake drops the truck back into park and gets out heading towards what turns out to be the young bar-back taking out the last of the trash before heading home for the night.

"We're closed buddy, come back tomorrow," the young man hurries back toward the bar.

"Hey, wait a sec, I'm looking for someone who might have been here tonight," Jake blurts out hoping to slow him down. "Don't mean ya no harm fella, just need to know if you saw an old man drinking martinis tonight."

"I don't know, we get a lot of people in and out, what he look like?"

"Older fella, white hair, always wears suspenders and drinks martinis with lotsa olives."

"Yeah there was a dude in here like that, last one to leave in fact, old man, and he was hittin it pretty hard, left outa here about midnight probably not more than ten minutes ago... I remember pretty good cause I was just shutting down the gas for the grill," pointing to the two large propane tanks by the door.

"You see which way he went?"

"Lit outa here in a big white car, like I said couldn't have been more than, um, ten minutes ago, headed north back toward..."

"Thanks buddy 'preciate it," Jake is already running for the truck.

"Hey wait, what'd he do?" But the old Ford was already pulling back onto the road headed north.

Even their best efforts and the rapidity of their response to the dream would not have saved Harry's life. No it was the call Russell Martin, the closing bar-back at the Walnut Grove Bar & Grill, made to the local sheriff even as Jake was speeding out of the parking lot. Figuring something was up, and probably something not good for the old man he had walked inside and dialed 911 to report the strange encounter. It was a slow night in the county so dispatch had sent the call out for any car in the area to cruise that stretch of road just in case.

Deputy Ryan O'Neill had only been on the force for about four months so of course he had the graveyard shift and happened to be in the area already. To be honest he was glad to have the monotony broken up for a change, nothing really happened in this part of the county after midnight. Passing the bar on his right he continues North figuring this was leading nowhere. Cresting the hill

by the Fischer farm he immediately hits the brakes. He can see the red glow of emergency flashers filmy in the growing fog, *must be at least a half-mile up* he thinks. *Better call this in*, all he needs is to be out here with some lunatic all by himself. Picking up the mic he immediately thinks better of it. Nothing but ribbing would come of this if it turned out to be nothing. *Ok I'll just drive up on them slowly with the spot on*, he tells himself. The fog swirls in the concentrated beam of light like wraiths attending the dead in a macabre dance ignoring the living. The old Ford is pulled off the road straddling the grassy shoulder. Ryan can see the lights of the sedan probably a hundred feet further down the ravine. Rolling to a stop behind the pickup he is already on the radio to dispatch calling for fire and rescue...
"Yes just past the Fischer farm on 149 North and tell them to hurry the hell up, this car has gotta be close to a hundred feet off the road, y'all better send someone over to get Tommy Jasper and his wrecker, tell em to bring the big one."

Ryan turns on the cruiser's red and blue light bar, pops the trunk grabs two flares rapidly setting them behind the cruiser, takes the first aid kit and starts to scramble down the embankment toward the wrecked Lexus. Slipping and sliding on the slick red clay he balances the kit in one hand while grabbing at the trees trying to maintain his balance. The only light is the blue and red strobes cutting through the fog and the lights of the old Ford.

"Hurry up dammit he needs help..." a deep and trembling voice rings through the trees.

"I'm coming as fast as I can, EMTs are on the way, that your truck up there?"

"Yeah, that's mine, how'd you know to come?"

"Young man at the bar called it in said you sped off in a hurry, didn't seem right to him," Ryan said having made his way down to the Lexus. "We'll talk later, how many people in the car?"

"Just one, his name is Harry White, he's an attorney over in Peakeville, I can't get in there but I think he is breathing," Jake's voice breaking as he tries to cover his emotions.

"Alright, help me out here let's see if we can get one of these doors open, those front ones looked wedged in pretty good," Ryan says reaching for the back door. He finally notices Maria quietly standing off to the side, "where did she come from?"

"She is with me, we are friends of Mr. Whites," Jake says before she can answer.

Ryan gives him a dubious look, not Jake's first from a police officer, "alright, you can explain it

to me later, I think if we can get this open I can
squeeze in there and check on him."

With both men pulling on the frame they are
able to create about a foot and half opening. The
metal on metal screeching even dampened by the fog
still seems to reverberate in the night. Ryan
squeezes in and Jake hands him the first aid kit. The
sirens wail in the distance, far off but getting
closer.

Jake whispers to Maria, "go wait in the truck,
lock the doors, don't answer any questions, they
can't make you talk to them."

"But Jake what about Harry, I don't want to..."

"Look don't argue with me, he hisses. "You
don't know these small town cops, we don't need to be
answering a bunch a fool questions trying to splain
this to anyone, now go get in the truck!"

Maria turns and starts to make her way up the
hill, Jake turns back to the car, "What ya think, is
he gonna be alright?"

Ryan turns shining the light back at Jake,
"look fella, I don't know, he's breathing okay, but
he isn't conscious and I can't really see anything in
here, we got to get him out of here and to a
hospital. I cut the seatbelt off, but we need to wait
for the EMTs and fire and rescue guys before we can

move him. Besides I think that dash has him trapped."

Harry was twelve minutes into his "golden hour". It is the sixty minutes emergency medicine considers the highest priority for treatment in trauma victims, especially those with significant shock, internal injuries, or major trauma. There is no special formula, but survival rates seem to drop dramatically after the hour expires. Jake and Maria could not have known but the timing suggested that the "call" had gone out to her as the accident was taking place. They had pulled up only minutes after the accident itself and Harry was a little more than a mile from the bar. This combined with the phone call from young Russell Martin had placed Deputy O'Neill at the scene only minutes later. Luck? Probably not, equal and opposite forces balancing each other out again.

Chapter 37

Maybe it was the martinis, maybe the three days of not getting enough sleep and pushing his tired old body beyond its limits, whatever the case Harry had no time to react. The car was already airborne the screams of tearing metal bringing him back to the moment, but too late. The sudden jolt and blinding white light as if a bomb had gone off in the car the excruciating pain in his legs and Harry can feel himself drift into the darkness. The incessant ding of some warning sensor the last sound he hears before the nothingness starts to swallow him up. His final conscious thought is: Maria! Her gentle voice whispers something in response, but he just can't make it out and the pinpoint of light fades into total blackness.

Harry hurries into the Monroe building taking the steps two at a time to the third floor. Its 8:28AM, tie askew, trademark suspenders uneven, he looks like he hasn't slept in several days and his shirt is already soaked through with sweat from the muggy July temperatures. He just makes it before the doors are locked sliding into a desk in the back of the room. He is the youngest by two and a half years of the probably thirty young men sitting for the South Carolina Bar Exam this morning. It's the second and final day of the testing and it seems that there are almost half as many of them today as yesterday and half of the remaining ones won't pass.

Harry's tardiness has nothing to do with anxiety over the test, no, his Harvard Law education has more than prepared him for series of essays. However his predilection for dry dirty martinis and southern blondes has definitely impaired his punctuality this morning. One might have wondered why an obviously brilliant if somewhat self destructive young man with his education would be sitting for the South Carolina Bar, but even a casual conversation would quickly reveal his country boy roots. Harry White was home and he was going to pass the bar on the first go round. He would then settle comfortably in at the White Law Group in Peakeville, just as his father and grandfather before him. He didn't long for the grandeur of the big city or the politics of the New England blue bloods he had met and befriended in Boston. No, for Harry becoming a lawyer was a sacred calling; they were the defenders of the weak, advocates of the truth, arbiters of fairness. He knew there was a greater need here in the South than most anywhere else for these ideals. The South was at the very doorstep of the Civil Rights fight and there was going to be plenty of need for objective, fair, and intelligent attorneys. Let his friends up North debate the politics of race. He would be living the realities of hate, prejudice, and basic human rights every day. Well at least that's what he thought anyway, and it had sounded great last night with a couple of martinis behind him and a pretty blond next to him. However, the reality was destined to be quite a bit different than his grandiose visions. Oh, there was plenty of injustice, hatred, prejudice and subversion of human rights, no doubt about that. But he had not been prepared for the unfiltered brutality of it all or the maddening pig headedness of supposedly intelligent people. However, on this hot July morning, this son of the South believed his state, his community and people he had grown up with were ready for change. He believed they would embrace the simple yet elegant truth that "all men are created equal." He was dramatically and emphatically wrong and he would spend the rest of his career carefully balancing the unseen line between "white" and everything else.

Eighteen minutes in and the first EMT and firemen had finally reached the car. Sherry Johnson had already climbed through the rear door and was starting her assessment of Harry immediately finding him unresponsive and suffering crush injuries on his lower extremities. Knowing she can't wait for the rescue team to extricate him she starts with preservation of the airway intubating Harry. Next she quickly starts an IV line stringing up the first bag of lactated Ringers solution and finally placing the heart monitor leads. The first of the rescue team has already called for the "Jaws of Life" and the "Ram" praying silently the hundred feet of hose reaches the car. They will use the jaws to wedge open the front driver's door, the front impact has pushed the frame far enough back that it won't open on its own. With the door removed they can place the ram under the dash, the simple hydraulic tool is a piston type expander that creates space by lifting whatever its placed under, in this case it will be the dash that has Harry trapped.

The team works with the precision that only comes from hours, days, and years of training and experience. They all know that every minute, and in some cases every second actually does count, it's a reality of their profession, not just a cliché on prime time television. The site commander has communicated with Life Flight and they will be waiting in the parking lot of the Western Sizzler four miles ahead on the outskirts of Leesburg. They both agree that the combination of fog, trees, power lines, and lack of level ground make the accident scene out of the question. The flight to Catawba will take less that fifteen minutes cutting off almost forty minutes of transport time.

It had taken sixteen minutes to cut the car door away, place the ram lifting the dash off Harry, place him on the backboard and slide him out the broken out rear window. All the while Jake continues to hover on the periphery unwilling to believe Harry won't be okay, but starting to feel an empty hopelessness at the same time. They had him out of the car now and were heading up through the trees as rapidly as possible desperately trying not to jostle the basket stretcher with each slick step in the red clay. The fog is swirling around them angrily finally engulfing them completely thirty feet from the top. Count the additional four minutes in the basket during trip up the hill to the waiting ambulance and thirty-eight minutes have expired from the Harry's golden hour. The doors slam shut and the sirens begin to wail.

Chapter 38

For just a moment there is a peaceful silence, nature's silence that isn't really silent at all but is devoid of the thrashing around of humanity. It came back slowly, the drip of moisture off the trees, the far off song of a lone whip-poor-will a chill wind passes over Jake. He knows many old Native American legends hold that the cry of the whip-poor-will is a harbinger of death.

"Hey, help me carry these things up to my cruiser," Ryan said returning Jake to the present.

"Sure, no problem, did they say where they were taking him?"

"They are going to meet life flight over at the Sizzler and fly him to Catawba Regional, they've got the only trauma center anywhere near here." Handing Jake a briefcase and folders, "you need to explain to me what you were doing out here anyway, I'm going to need to write this all up."

Jake knew this wasn't going to go the way the deputy wanted, he had no intention of telling him a damn thing. "Yeah, well, there's not much to tell so..."

"I'll be the judge of that," Ryan quips, "now let's go, I'll follow you up."

Jake was more than familiar with the routine by now, cops always assumed you were guilty of something. Didn't much matter what you said or what it looked like. His newly found introspection and self-awareness didn't quite extend to his interaction with the law. As it is with most people it never occurred to Jake that his attitude and composure invited suspicion from deputies like Ryan O'Neill. Accustomed to being on the wrong end of the truth and having a defensive attitude about it radiated from Jake like a heavy dose of bad cologne.

As he crests the hill and looks up Maria is staring at him from the truck, he can sense her reaching out to him telling him to be calm, it will be okay. With an almost perceptible nod of her head she motions back at the police cruiser and he knows that everything rests on him, that this moment is his and their very future hangs in the balance. Jake could not have explained any of this and on a strictly intellectual level he doesn't understand it at all, but on a visceral level in his gut, so to speak, he knows he has to get this right. "So officer what can I help you with?"

Ryan turns and gives him a look, not quite

believing this hard ass' respectful tone. "Let's sit in the car, you can tell me what you know about tonight."

As Jake reaches for the door handle, "hey, sit up front, I just want to talk this through." Sheepishly Jake closes the back door, reaching for the front handle. This should probably have been a moment of clarity for him but the deputy's change in attitude had thrown him. "Alright, start at the beginning... tell me why you were out here and what made you ask about this Mr. White back at the bar... And don't leave anything out. I'm going to have to write a report on all this and honestly you being here doesn't make any sense to me."

Chapter 39

Harry couldn't believe it, he had joined his father's practice six or seven months ago but this was his first truly significant case and probably most controversial. It wasn't everyday a black man got a fair trial in this town. Actually it probably had never happened before, never mind having access to one of the sharpest young lawyers in the state. This was a locked down for sure win, and he couldn't wait to put that fool Hancock in his place. The prosecutor was an ass and Harry had his number, but not without his only witness, Larry Johnson on the stand.

Thomas Jefferson Jeter was on trial for theft and not simple burglary either. No the local police had him pegged as the brazen criminal that had two weeks ago stolen three of the new Kenmore canister vacuums and two Singer sewing machines in broad daylight off the rear loading dock of the local Sears & Roebuck. Now it didn't seem to matter to anyone that not only did Thomas not have a car to transport all these items but neither could anyone definitively place him at the scene that day. It was well known however that Mr. Jordan, the owner of the local store had occasionally hired Thomas to clean up the back lot for him. The presiding logic was that he must have known the items in question would be there and had waited for the perfect opportunity to spirit them away, all without being seen of course.

It was this kind of nonsense that made Harry White mad, not just mad but furious, the stupidity of it was just overwhelming. Thomas' aunt cleaned house for Harry's father and had asked if they would help. Harry had jumped at the chance and insisted on taking the case pro-bono.

But here was the wrinkle, the prosecutor had no case, but this was 1957 rural South Carolina and he didn't necessarily need a case to convict a young black man. No he just needed what sounded like a reasonable suggestion of guilt it didn't even need to be that good a story. It hadn't even been fifteen years since the Stinney boy, only fourteen years old, had been convicted with no physical evidence and sent to the electric chair. Nobody of color assumed a fair trial or fair anything for that matter.

Harry knew he was gambling the only witness that could verify that Thomas was nowhere near the Sears loading dock was Larry Johnson, and Larry by his own account was one redneck racist "nigger" hatin' son-of-a-bitch. Larry and his buddy Randy Delhomme had run up on Thomas walking home and decided to spend an afternoon having some harmless fun terrifying the boy. No harm done they claimed, a nigger needed to know his place they said. Randy's son Jake would be born later that year and a short six years after that Jake would witness an even more brutal episode. But at this point Randy and his ilk still believed they were in control and that society believed as they did.

Randy Delhomme did a fair bit of work for old man White, which precluded him from being a witness. He had met his son Harry a number of times, so he hadn't thought too much of it when Harry had stopped by his place two weeks ago. What he hadn't expected was for the White boy to come on so strong. Insisting they testify that the nigger boy Thomas had actually been with him and Larry that afternoon.

"You musta bumped your head boy, ain't nobody gonna believe that nigger was with us, what we supposed to say? We were having a picnic? That's just stupid," had been Delhomme's response.

Even though he was only a few years younger than Randy Delhomme, Harry took a respectful tone hoping to gain his cooperation. "Listen Mr. Delhomme that's exactly why they are going to believe it.

Think about it, why would either you or Mr. Johnson lie for this young man? I, and I know my father would consider it a personal favor if you could convince Mr. Johnson to testify, he needs to be there Tuesday morning at nine o'clock."

With a finger in Harry's chest, "I'll tell ya what boy, I'll do it, but it ain't for this nigger. I'll do it cause your old man's done right by me. Oh, and listen you fuckin' owe me so when I come callin' for anything I expect you'll make yourself available... understand."

"Fair enough, but don't let him be late and tell him to wear his Sunday clothes." Harry might have been a good, even great lawyer but he had just struck a bad deal with a man that would never let him forget it.

Overhead the ceiling fans circled with a melodic whump, whump, whump. It was almost nine o'clock and no Larry Johnson, the sweat began to bead on Harry's forehead and he could feel the coffee rising in his gullet. The unfairness of it all rankled him down deep, it wasn't for himself, but looking over at the young man next to him he could see the shining hope in the boy's eyes. Thomas believed in Harry; believed with everything in him that this white man was going to save him. The

bailiff gives the familiar "all rise" command and
Judge Waters robes billowing behind him lets his
gavel ring forth, as the last rap fades the swinging
doors at the back bang open...

Chapter 40

Jake knew that the key to any conversation with a cop was a mixture of respect and a touch of fear, it appealed to their ego and the fact that most of them hid an inner bully. This probably wasn't altogether true, but good luck convincing Jake of that. The second and more important tactic was to mix in just enough truth that the story would hold together especially if someone started spot-checking facts. "So as I was saying Mr. White was supposed to stop by tonight to discuss some carpentry work I been doing on his office and drop a check off. I've known Mr. White ever since I was a kid, he was my dad's attorney and always handled all kinds of stuff for the family. My dad passed a while back and Mr. White I guess is the closest thing left to family I've got around here..." Hurrying on before Ryan can interrupt him, "now not saying he did but I know he liked to have a martini or two in the afternoon... so when he didn't show up after dinner I figured he was up here at the bar. Man, he loves this place, it's the only place he drinks... you know how old guys get, they like their routines. Like I was sayin' he never showed up so I got to worryin' about him, took a ride out to his place... didn't find him so figured this was the next best place to look, and well you know the rest."

This all seemed a bit too convenient to Ryan, "so you figured since he didn't show by midnight you would just make the rounds looking for him? You're a regular Boy Scout aren't you?" Ryan taking out his flashlight and opening the door turns to Jake, "let's take a look at that truck of yours, you sure you didn't hit anything, say like maybe a white Lexus?"

"Awe come on officer," almost a whine, "I told you everything I know but go ahead and look, ain't nothin' there. I didn't hit nothin', I got here a few minutes before you did, besides if I'da hit him would I have stuck around?"

Mistake number one dammit, Jake knew better than to ask a cop open-ended questions. "I don't know that that's a good question so why don't you tell me..."

Walking around the truck, "see, nothin' officer. I told you everything, I was just worried about the old man, he was a friend of my dad's and I just felt like I should check on him."

"Alright the truck looks clean, but listen I might have some additional questions for you, let me get your license and phone number."

"Here's my license, ain't got no phone right now."

After making some notes Ryan hands him back the license. Jake makes a quick exit not waiting to see if there is anything else. Ryan sits in the cruiser replaying the chain of events in his mind, *what the hell am I missing?* He watches Jake execute a quick three-point-turn and head South. *Damn the girl!* He forgot to ask about the girl. Dropping the cruiser into drive he kills the rotating strobes and heads toward the medical center hoping the old man has survived long enough to answer some questions and wondering how the hell he could have forgotten a young girl in the middle of this mess. *Where the hell had she gone?*

Harry spent five minutes in transport to the copter and a short seventeen minutes after taking off from the parking lot the helicopter drops out of the night sky landing gently on the roof helo pad. On the roof of the Catawba Trauma Center Emergency Room the trauma team waits. The transport team jumps out opening the back doors and sliding Harry onto the waiting stretcher as the clock winds down on his golden hour.

Chapter 41

Jake pulls into the McDonalds' parking lot just outside of Chesterton a few miles South of Catawba Medical Center. He slides the truck into one of the spots in the far corner of the lot, turning the engine off he lays his head on the steering wheel. The hot tears on his cheeks leave a salty residue on his lips. He doesn't really know why he is crying, but it occurs to him he really loves that old man probably more than he ever loved his own father.

Maria doesn't interrupt him, her cheek leans against the coolness of the window lost in her own thoughts, trying to sort through the complicated web of feelings assaulting her. Not quite sure how she has become so entangled in the lives of these two men so different from herself. She hadn't been sure what to expect when she had left home, but certainly not this, not tonight, not sitting in a dimly lit parking lot of a 24/7 McDonalds in upstate South Carolina. A fifty something year old, barely concealed racist handyman next to her... no, this hadn't been part of her plan.

Okay, maybe that's a bit harsh, after all

aren't all of us just a product of our environments, and didn't she interpret things based on her own upbringing? And to be sure nobody had made her get in the truck that morning in Florida. No, she had made her own decisions, like it or not, understand it or not, she still believed there must be a reason for all of this. *It wasn't possible that all things were just coincidence and chance, was it? How could that be possible?* How do you explain the dreams she had, or for that matter fear, hope, love and the myriad of emotions she was just learning to deal with? Were they all just chemical reactions? No, she didn't believe that, but so many questions with no answers... She wasn't sure she believed in a God that ruled over everything and had already planned out your whole life for you either though. She had enough friends that went to church to have heard the modern day religious ramblings. None of that really made any sense to her, *how could you have free will on one hand and if everything was planned out and decided already?* She had felt and seen enough to believe there was something bigger out there, some force, call it God or whatever, but she also didn't claim to know what it all meant. The small Bible her mother clutched on the few Sundays she wasn't working and actually made it to Mass didn't offer much in the way of an explanation. She didn't know it but she had a more mature understanding of things than many who sat in a pew every Sunday.

Jake gives his nose a blow, the noise explodes through the cab jerking Maria out of her confused thoughts.

"I don't know if we should go to the hospital or not," Jake says, "I am pretty sure that cop was headed there and I don't want to have to answer any more questions or explain why you were there. Kinda strange he didn't even ask about ya, in fact I thought we were blown when he did that walk around on the truck, but hell it's like he didn't even see ya."

"I know Jake, but I want to see Harry. We have to at least find out how he is doing... what if he, well what if he... didn't make it?"

"Jesus Christ, don't fucking say that, people die when you say that shit." Looking over at her seeing she has started to sob, "look, I'm sorry, I am just upset and I'm worried as hell about all this. I know you didn't have nothin' to do with this. I'll call up there and see if they will tell us anythin', there's a pay phone over there," he says pointing to the far end of the parking lot.

"Ok, I'm just really worried he looked so bad when they carried him up."

"I know, but those guys are really amazing with some of the stuff they can do," Jake says half trying to convince himself.

"Catawba Medical Center can I help you?"

"Yeah, need to check on an old man they just 'coptered in from a car accident, names Harry White."

"Sir, I can't give any patient information out over the phone, privacy rules we have to follow."

"Look, I'm... I'm his son and I'm on my way. I just need to know how he is... please, please, help me," his voice breaking as the lie slips easily off his lips.

"Look sir, I can't tell you anything, you understand, right? But listen, I believe they just took an old man into surgery, I think for his legs, he was in a car accident, do you understand what I am telling you? I can't say anything more than that."

"Oh sweet baby Jesus, thank you, thank you, I'll be there quick as can be," Jake whispers almost breaking down again.

"Park in the side lot sir by the Emergency Entrance. It's the only one open this late, you want to go to the Surgery waiting area on the first floor and sir, Good luck, I hope he makes it." That didn't really make Jake feel any better, he had been on the wrong end of luck too many times. He knew she was just trying to make him feel better, but luck was as real as his truck and fishing pole to Jake and mostly not his friend.

Biting her lip Maria can see Jake leaning his head against the top of the phone, she can't make out what he is saying, but she stifles a whimper when he sinks to his knees hanging the phone up.

"God, I could use a cigarette" Jake is leaning his head against the top of the truck door. "She said they took him into surgery for his legs, she wouldn't tell me nothin' else though. Hell, I don't know what to do."

Sitting on the tailgate Maria turns toward Jake, "will they let us see him if we go up there?"

"I don't know, I could probably talk my way in, have ta say I was his son or somethin' like that, but it might work, it's just that damn cop will probably be there."

They were no closer to a decision or plan when they pulled out of the parking lot, Maria trying to suck the too thick fake ice cream of a strawberry shake through the straw and Jake munching on a cheeseburger with no pickles. He was thoroughly convinced that a special order burger somehow made it fresh. They shared a large order of the skinny salty fries McDonalds was famous for.

Chapter 42

The rear swinging doors of the courtroom banged closed and there was Larry Johnson looking none too happy about the whole affair and Randy Delhomme with this pretty as you please shit eating grin on his face. They marched right up front taking it slow and making a grand entrance. Stopping at the front row behind the railing separating the gallery from the attorney's desks and the rest of the courtroom each trying to out-polite the other.

"Mr. Delhomme, Mr. Johnson, I don't know why you are in my courtroom, but sit down and be quiet," Judge Waters boomed from the front of the court. He was quite familiar with the antics and carrying on of these two having had them in his courtroom on numerous occasions. Although this was the first time he could recall either being here of their own accord. Turning to Harry, "Mr. White do you have any witnesses you wish to call before we turn this over to the jury?"

"Yes your Honor, Mr. Johnson here is going to testify on behalf of young Mr. Jefferson."

And just that simple statement created Harry

White's reputation as a miracle worker, advocate of the colored, and all around brilliant lawyer, was sealed. Larry Johnson warmed to his testimony like a born again backslider at a Sunday morning tent meeting. In the end, if you didn't know better you would have thought he wanted to adopt the young man he was so proud of the fine "Negro" he was growing up to be. Everyone in the courtroom that day knew it was total bullshit, especially DA Hancock who had stormed out almost before the Judge had finished banging his gavel. It had taken the jury approximately six and half minutes of deliberation to find Thomas innocent. It had nothing to do with how they felt about him or even any aspect of the case. No quite simply nobody knew why Johnson and Delhomme had done what they did, but nobody wanted to be on the wrong end of those two either.

Harry was gathering up his papers and getting ready to leave when Randy leans over the balustrade, "don't forget you owe me boy," turning away he leaves Harry trying to convince himself it had been worth it.

Harry had handled hundreds if not thousands of cases in the fifty some odd years since Thomas Jefferson Jeter, many had been more important and complicated but none had meant more to him than that first foray into the fracas of the courtroom. Chronically underestimated by prosecutors because he didn't fit the mold of the typical lawyer. His trademark suspenders, unruly mop, and reputation as a bit of drinker all continued to belie the burning intellect that left even the best of them wondering what had happened. Randy Delhomme had called in a favor or two: an assault, public disorder, destruction of property, they had all been fairly routine for Harry and Randy had never served more than a night or two in jail. That was until the summer of 1981 and a 2AM phone call from a scared and desperate Mr. Delhomme.

The whole episode had been a catastrophe, with the town convincing itself the folks out at the old plantation were devil worshippers. The final straw had come when angry mob had burned a large cross in the yard and several shots had been fired in both directions. You guessed it; it was led by Randy Delhomme and company, men who should have long ago outgrown that type of ignorance. After that the State Law Enforcement Division (SLED), a special branch of the state police under the direct supervision of the Governor and State's Attorney General had been dispatched to clean up the mess. Local involvement was not welcome or tolerated, someone had pulled in

some pretty huge favors to get those boys deployed so
quickly to a town like Peakeville. Harry had always
assumed it had been Judge Waters, who interestingly
enough had become quite good friends with the woman
Sally.

"What you think I don't know what time it is?
You owe me boy, now get your ass outta bed and pick
me up at that service station out 149 and make it
quick... I don't like being out here alone." He had
picked Delhomme up that morning as much out of
curiosity as an obligation. It wasn't everyday
someone could scare the shit out of Randy Delhomme.

"Alright Mr. Delhomme calm down and tell me
what happened."

"Just fuckin' drive! I don't wanta talk about
it, you ain't never gonna believe it anyway."

"Listen, try me, I'm your attorney. I can't
help you if you're in trouble if you won't talk about
it."

He never did get the story out of him, just
bits and pieces that didn't seem to make any sense.
But there was no doubt Randy Delhomme was scared and
not just scared but terrified, not like a child but
full on adult terrified. Combine that with looking
like he had gone more than a couple of rounds in a
particularly brutal bar fight and Harry was sure that

the story would emerge sooner or later. Strangely enough it never had, and Randy Delhomme never spoke about it again either. Almost as strange was the disappearance of Larry Johnson, but no one ever spoke about that either.

A few weeks later the SLED contingent packed up and left town, case closed, no explanation, no press, no nothing. An uneasy peace settled on Peakeville, the folks out at the plantation kept to themselves and the fight seem to have gone out of the town. It was about a month or so before the town even realized the plantation was empty. A few of the braver souls had actually driven out to look around, word passed quickly the place was locked up tight, no furniture, no animals. The fields just recently filled with vegetables and corn had been tilled under and not a soul was to be found. Jesse Thompson, the local mail carrier, confirmed there wasn't even a forwarding address and admitted to taking a look around himself last time he was out that way. Drinking his morning coffee at McElroy's more than a few folks heard him say, "I won't be going back neither, felt like the place was watching me, it might be empty but that don't mean there ain't something out there if you follow what I saying."

It was a comment from that first night that had

set Harry off earlier in the week something about how Maria had described her dreams that triggered a long forgotten memory of Randy Delhomme's ramblings. He had chalked most of it up to shock or being drunk, but now thirty plus years later it seemed oddly familiar.

"They was waitin' for us, no way they coulda known we were comin', but sure as shit it was like they knew everythin' before we got there. And that witch, fuck me, when they took Larry I heard her clear as day, I swear I did, do you hear me, she told him she fuckin' told him."

Harry was pretty sure he did not want to know why they had headed back out there after burning a cross in the front yard a few weeks earlier. It had triggered an exchange of gunfire and within a few days the arrival of SLED after all. Harry, trying not to set him off again had to ask, "what did she tell him Randy?"

"Oh Jesus, sweet Jesus, how could she know? She told Larry she'd seen us in her dreams, knew we were coming, then she started sayin' sometin' about how they had sometin' special setup just for him." His voice breaking into a sob, "I couldn't help it I just ran, I could hear him screamin' for me and I knowed I shoulda tried to help him, but, but, I just

171

couldn't... got lost in the woods... oh Jesus this can't be happening..."

Randy Delhomme had rambled on like that for a good half hour or so, Harry hadn't understood most of it and had filed it away figuring Randy would sleep it off and probably not remember most of it the next day.

Randy Delhomme had been fifty-two years old that night and in the twenty-seven years he continued to live and reside in Peakeville he never spoke of it again. Although he was still an acerbic, racist, miserable son of a bitch, he never actively went out of his way to mistreat another person black, white or otherwise.

Chapter 43

Having been briefed by the flight medics enroute the ER docs were barking orders even as they rolled Harry in. The legs were an obvious problem, but since he was unconscious they couldn't ignore a potential brain injury and the swelling on his left side was a visual indicator of some type of internal issue. This combined with an elevated heart rate and dropping blood pressure was pointing to injuries to the spleen, but again, no assumptions especially for a patient his age.

Normally a physical exam followed by a trauma series of x-rays or specific CT scans would have been the way to proceed. But with an unconscious patient having serious issues, and no immediately identifiable life threatening injuries hard data became more important than speed. The trauma team had decided to move forward with the new helical CT scanner that had been installed earlier in the year and do a complete body series. This would achieve the most diagnostic data in the quickest manner, and then they could build a plan of attack.

Starting with an immediate CT of his brain and

abdomen would give them a better idea of which order to begin treatment. Of course any noticeable swelling or bleeding in the brain would have to take priority, but a ruptured spleen would kill him just as rapidly. To the normal person his crushed legs would have seemed the most serious injuries, but trauma physicians know it's often the injuries you don't see that cause the most damage.

Harry had spent more than six hours in surgery, the priority had been his spleen and the surgical team had managed to avoid a total splenectomy. Partially saving a portion of Harry's spleen and stopping the bleeding. Additionally, it had been decided to proceed with the repairs to both tibias, and the left femur as he seemed to be tolerating the anesthesia and his vitals had leveled out with the multiple units of blood he had been given. There was some question how long he would be in therapy before he might walk again, but with weeks of recovery ahead and plenty of opportunity for complications that was the least of anyone's concerns.

The simple fact was that as bad as his injuries were Harry was a lucky man. Oh, there was going to be plenty of pain and a long road to recovery, but he was alive when he probably should not have been.

Deputy O'Neill had left his card with the young

nurse at the ER desk and she had promised to pass it on to the surgical charge nurse when she went off shift. There really was nothing more he could do here, fact is, with the exception of this Jake character and the girl, let's not forget her again, this was a pretty straightforward MVA. Well, probably a DUI also once they got the toxicology reports back. It would wait. Mr. Harry White wasn't going anywhere anytime soon.

Jake and Maria had camped out in the surgical waiting room. Jake had told them he was Harry's son, no one questioned him, maybe because he seemed so distraught. Even in today's world of extreme patient privacy and safety everyone seemed genuinely concerned about the old man and was quick to reassure him everything able to be done to help him was happening. The reality is Harry was alone in this world and Jake really was the closest thing to family.

Harry was moved to ICU later that morning groggy but finally fighting through the fog to regain consciousness and make some sense of the immense pain he felt everywhere. The doctors had told Jake he might have some short-term memory issues as a result of the accident but there was an excellent chance things would come back to him over time. Jake didn't want to leave without at least seeing him once and letting Harry know they were here.

Maria waited in the vestibule outside, there was no version of this story where she passed for family or that would have made sense. Never mind that Jake was nervous enough as it was. The old man seeming to have shrunk, a smaller version of himself lay in the bed covered by the thin blanket. His eyes closed as the monitors softly beeped and tracked any number of things Jake didn't understand.

Jake takes his hand, the papery skin seems so fragile and crinkly, holding back the unbidden tears he whispers Harry's name softly. The old man opens his eyes trying to focus, like when you've been sleeping late on a cold Saturday morning and don't want to really get up so you lay there trying to recapture a glimpse of the last dream. Of course it's always just out of reach.

It's just a croak, but it's enough, "Jake, son glad you're here..." and with that Harry falls back asleep. Jake wipes his eyes with the back of his leathery hand and strides out of the room.

"Let's go, we have work to do," as he passes Maria.

Chapter 44

Larry Johnson had not disappeared into thin air that night, neither had some fantastical nefarious spirit world ingested him. No, he had been given a choice. It would be many years before the Federal Hate Crimes statutes would be enacted in 1994 and further strengthened 2010. However, there were plenty of charges with which to put him away and there was no doubt the Governor would assign the top prosecutor in the state to this case. The alternative: decide that evening right then and there to come under the mentorship of the school and their teacher Sally for a period of no less than five years. The state would consider it a work release probation, no trial, no jail time, no questions.

The group known as the Juxa Corporation had been working on building a number of campuses, the plan had been to make the South Carolina operation the headquarters, but it was clear now another location would have to fulfill that role. The campus in Pennsylvania was probably closest to completion and the proximity to New York City and the Northeast corridor allowed for a more tolerant and open-minded environment. It would be here Sally's dream would take root and grow and Larry Johnson's transformation would become iconic within the Juxa Corporation's evolution.

Unfortunately, Randy Delhomme, his son Jake, and ultimately Peakeville would never experience an awakening or even the residual benefits of its proximity to the school. No, it would fade back into obscurity consigned to a legacy of hate, intolerance, and ignorance.

It was early Monday morning and Harry didn't hold out much hope of tracking down Larry Johnson, in fact he wasn't even sure where to start. A couple of calls to Columbia had given him a place to look though. The files dealing with the school incident had been sealed by the prosecutor's office. But all the non-microfiche records had long since been transferred to the basement record room of the Clerk of Court's office and that was somewhere he still had excellent connections. This was South Carolina after all and the "good ol' boy" network was still alive and well. A couple of calls and some good natured ribbing and he had secured a couple hours "alone" in the basement file room. He hadn't mentioned what case files he was looking for, just that he was thinking about writing a memoir and wanted to review some of his early work. He had tried enough cases at the State Supreme Court level that this wasn't much of a stretch. Finding the "school" file, peeling the security seal and getting out undiscovered was going to be the real trick.

Tammy Jensen let him in the side entrance a little after ten thirty. She gave him a nonplussed look, insinuating that if some old fool wanted to dodder around in the archive stacks she wasn't going to waste any time worrying about it. He was counting on that and had no problem playing up the "old fool" act for her either. He wasn't interested in piquing her curiosity, he wanted the place to himself for as long as possible.

The long rows of shelves were stacked high with file boxes marked with case numbers, dates, names and fortunately there did seem to be some sense of order, but the sheer number was pretty overwhelming. Harry knew just what he was looking for though and, as luck would have it, the three boxes occupied one of the lower shelves. He hadn't thought about it, but he wasn't sure he could have lifted them off one of the higher shelves. Harry moved the boxes one by one over to one of the many long tables lining the center of the room. Before the internet and the transfer of most everything to searchable law databases these basement archives would have been full of paralegals, junior associates, and even an old timer like himself digging through case law and making copious notes on their yellow legal pads. Not today though, just one lonely stooped figure scribbling furiously in the shorthand he had developed himself. He wished he had more time and but he knew it was the one commodity he did not have enough of.

The first box and half the second one contained all the SLED files detailing the incidents at the school. They included the on scene officers' reports, local interviews, and directives from the Governor, Attorney General and the Division Headquarters. Harry spent a half hour skimming before pulling himself away, it read like a barely believable novel, but it wasn't what he was looking for.

The balance of the second box contained a number of letters and appeared to be the Governor's personal correspondence. It was here Harry found his first pearl, a letter from Sally, the leader of the school printed on Juxa Corporation letterhead. Harry made some quick notes knowing he could pull all the corporate information he needed off the state's database of corporations. Finally the connection nobody had understood, he had always thought it was Judge Waters who had intervened, but here it was. The

Governor had served in the Air Force with this woman's father, in fact had been his second in command at Howard Air Force Base in Panama during the Second World War. *Sweet Jesus, how had nobody picked up on that,* he wondered. Well the swift response made a great deal more sense now. Harry needed more though he needed to know what had happened to Larry Johnson. People just didn't disappear into thin air with a whole contingent of state police watching.

The treasure was in the third box, as Harry began sorting through the folders one dog eared file stood out. Simply marked L. Johnson it was more worn and much thicker than the rest. Gently laying it on the table he knew this is what he had come for. Finally, some answers for what had happened that dark night thirty odd years ago. *It wasn't possible was it?* Harry had never even heard of a "Work Release Pardon" before, wasn't even sure if it would legally stand up, but here it was. They had charged Larry Johnson with attempted murder, drawn up an arrest warrant and then this "pardon". *It didn't make any sense, how could you pardon someone without a conviction? This type of subterfuge just didn't happen in the modern legal world.* But here it was with the Governor's signature clear as day, he had seen it enough to know, and on the other margin Larry

Johnson's barely legible scrawl, which he had seen plenty of as well.

Digging back into the folder he found a series of status letters from the Juxa Corporation detailing the program and progress Larry Johnson was making. *It was simply remarkable, why hadn't anyone heard from him? Randy Delhomme had never even mentioned him again.* The letters, all from an address in Northeastern Pennsylvania, had ended in 1987. There was a final notation showing the file closed shortly thereafter. Harry jammed his notes into his briefcase, labored up the back stairs and slipped out unnoticed. He felt no need to inform Ms. Jensen of his departure.

What do now though, he had already promised to meet Jake for breakfast the next morning, but he really needed to put these final pieces in place, *could it wait another day?* He figured if he left right after meeting Jake he could be in Pennsylvania around midnight. A couple of days to snoop around up there and then back to update Jake and Maria, thinking beyond that was pointless.

Chapter 45

The Starbucks was only half a block from the medical center. Jake pulls the truck into a spot right out front and lets out a long sigh. "Ok, here's what I'm thinking - the bone doctor, I can't remember his name, but he was the tall bald one. Anyway he said Harry will probably go home with a wheelchair and a walker and may even need help with stuff around the house. I think they have nurses come out to do stuff for them also." Jake was a mile a minute, "Probably be another week or so they said, if we start today should be plenty of time, I know we can build one of those ramps at the house and the office so he doesn't have to do the steps and the bathroom is on the first floor at his house so we can make sure that's setup for him too... what?"

Maria smiling says, "nothing, it's just good to see you so... I don't know... energetic maybe? But let's go inside I want a frappuccino and you can tell me how I can help."

Jake gives her a look just to make sure she isn't teasing him again, "sure let me get my pencil and I think there is a pad in the door over there."

Grabbing his carpenter's pencil, already whittled to a short stub, he heads to the door, "well, you coming or what?"

Thirty minutes and a grande caramel macchiato later Jake has sketched out ramps for both the house and the office. There is also a list of items they will need for the bathrooms. Jake will do all the carpentry work for the ramps while Maria works on adding a series of suction based handles in the bathtub and an adjustable showerhead with a long hose. This way Harry can sit on a shower stool while still having control of the water. Jake is pretty sure Harry is going to be adamant about his independence and not wanting some nurse in his house bathing him. Well, unless they can find him some young pretty blonde one.

Whatever else it was, Peakeville was still a small southern town that knew how to rally around its own. By the time Jake and Maria had made their way to Sanders with a pretty significant list of materials, old man Sanders already had a crew together and one of his delivery trucks standing by. He took Jake aside and told him, "Son, anything you need let me know, I've got plenty of help if you need a couple of boys to work with you. Harry White means a lot to this town and we know how take care of our own."

"Yes sir, I appreciate it sir. I'll let you know if we need anything," Jake replied.

Strangely enough the dichotomy represented in old man Sanders didn't hit Jake right away. The town had a soft spot for its own but God help you if you weren't from here though. Easy enough to chalk all the help up to good Christian charity, but that wasn't really it was it? No more like, you are like me and I am like you and we are the same. So I'll protect your right to white ignorant bigotry and you'll look the other way at mine, and in doing so we will all feel good about ourselves. It was a perfect system working in a perfect circle. Just don't step outside the lines, don't question the imperfect order it represented, and don't point out the obvious fallacy represented by the blatant hypocrisy of it all. Within this fragile equilibrium lay a multi-generational lie stretching back over time. The self-actuated belief that they were good people, that their prejudice was justified and even ratified by their God and wasn't this evidenced by all their good deeds?

It took three days to build out the ramps at both the office and the house, well four if you counted Sunday. But no one in Peakeville worked on a Sunday whether you did church or not. Jake had taken

Mr. Sanders up on his offer of help. Leveling off the joists and setting the footers was much easier with a couple of people working together. Maria had been busy cleaning the house from top to bottom and Jake had taught her how to use a few basic tools so she could change out the showerheads. All in all the work had gone smoothly and Jake had surprisingly found himself comfortable working with and directing a small crew. Every evening they had cleaned up and headed over to the medical center to check on Harry. He had been sleeping most of the time, but by the fourth day had been awake enough to begin asking some questions and generally become a pain in the ass for the nursing staff, affably of course but still a pain in the ass. They moved him to a private room late that afternoon. The doctors were projecting another six days in the hospital presuming his physical therapy progressed and appropriate homecare could be set up in Peakeville for him.

Jake hadn't pressed Harry for any information. He was happy enough to have him talking and spent most of Tuesday night updating Harry on the projects at the house and office. For a man his age and with the severity of his injuries Harry was recovering remarkably well.

Wednesday evening Jake stepped off the elevator

on 4 West, the Med/Surg floor, visiting hours ended at eight so he only had about forty-five minutes to spend with Harry. It had been almost a full week since the accident and the days had flown by. They had finished the last of the projects up today, sealing the new ramps, installing the new door thresholds, and completing some basic painting and cosmetic work. Neither the house nor the office had looked this good in years. As much as Maria loved seeing Harry she had begged off exhausted after three straight days of cleaning and painting. He heard animated voices from down the hall and then Harry's reedy laugh echoed from his room. Jake picked up his pace, *who the hell was the old man carrying on with now?* Jake pushes through the door and pulls up short... *Fuck me*, he thinks, *Deputy Ryan O'Neill*.

"Come on in Jake, I believe you know the good deputy already," Harry motions him in. Jake shakes the deputy's hand, albeit rather tentatively. "Young Ryan here was just filling in some of the blank spots in my memory from the other night. I guess I am pretty lucky you two boys came along when you did."

"Umm, yes sir, I guess so, but it was the deputy that got everyone moving, wasn't much I could do there. Those EMT and rescue guys were pretty amazing sir."

"Well, Ryan was just filling me in on the possible charges and paperwork he is going to have to do, what do you think about that?"

Jake was seriously uncomfortable with the line of questions but played along. "Well sir, with how messed up your car is and how bad your insurance is gonna screw you over on the premiums... I guess I figure you got enough pain without a couple traffic tickets on top of it all."

"Funny I was thinking the same thing. Of course if we take it to court and I have to roll up in my wheelchair like old Raymond Burr in "Ironside" I'll be forced to teach the young deputy a lesson or two in courtroom drama..." Dead silence ensues, "I'm just kidding, you two try not to look so serious," he laughs again.

Jake gives a wan smile still not sure about this turn of events, and not sure exactly what Harry has told the deputy, he is terrified it doesn't match his own story from the night of the accident.

"Well Mr. White I won't be issuing any citations, even though it might interesting to watch you operate in court. Sergeant Jeter already warned me about that, I guess lesson learned, right?"

"Young man, I can guarantee you it won't be happening again and I think my future days of driving are limited anyway. Right now I just want to get back to walking and get out of this hospital bed. After that I plan on fading into the memories and ramblings of an old man."

"Well, I'll be on my way then, hope you have a full recovery sir, you're lucky to be here," he shakes Jake's hand and gives him an almost imperceptible nod on the way out the door.

With a deep breath Jake says, "Jesus, Harry what did you tell him? I went round and round with him that night, he was convinced I had something to do with the whole thing."

"Nothing to worry about Jake, I let him know your dad and I went way back and you were pretty much the closest thing to family I had left around here, seemed to satisfy him. Son, you know that's how I feel too... to be honest your father and I were not close, I was his attorney, but he never let his guard down and we didn't see eye to eye on a great many things. When this is all finished I need to talk to you about what that means, how your father and I came to be involved with each other and you and I have some decisions to make."

"Ok sir, I don't know what you're talking about as usual, but whatever you say I'll do."

"Time enough for that later, tell me how the

projects are coming, if I remember correctly you had some of Sander's boys working with you, how did it go?"

Jake jumps right in telling Harry about all the projects they finished up today, Maria had even repainted the kitchen and stripped and polished the linoleum floor while he and the Sanders boys had sealed the ramps and decks for both the office and the house. Jake explained how he had set each of them up with specific tasks making sure they completed each one properly. Glancing over he sees Harry has drifted off, a small smile still on his face, bending over he gently covers the old man and holds his hand tenderly as he quietly says goodbye. He doesn't fully understand the emotions in his actions, but it feels right and he tries to blink away the filmy moisture of impending tears as he heads for the elevator.

Chapter 46

The doctors released Harry the next Saturday after ten days in the hospital. He was a long way from recovered and would have physical therapy in his home three times a week until he regained the ability to walk with just a cane supporting him. The doctors had told him it would be months at a minimum. They had also insisted on having a nursing service visit daily to provide dressing changes and monitor him for infection until his first set of follow up visits in two weeks. It was going to be a long, busy and infuriating few weeks for Harry until he regained some sense of privacy and independence.

Harry lived in a stately but not ostentatious rancher on the North side of town. His place was tucked into one of the smaller but upscale neighborhoods a long way from the clapboard mill houses of the West side where Jake had grown up. He had eschewed the older southern mansion with its massive magnolias his father had owned in the center of town selling it shortly after his parents had passed away.

Most small southern towns had the same basic

layout, the mills were almost always located near water, be it a stream or pond and the mill houses would be clustered around in a series of smaller streets compromising that particular mill's working class neighborhood. It wasn't uncommon for even a small town like Peakeville to have two or even three mills. The center of town was built around a single broad thoroughfare or main street. It seemed most towns were designed in much the same way, one end anchored by the local government including a courthouse, police station, post office, utility offices and most of the local professionals: attorneys, accountants, and the like. In fact Harry had converted a small but beautiful home two blocks from the courthouse into his office many years ago. The center of town consisted of the merchants, banks, barbershops and the occasional restaurant. Anchoring the far end of main street would be the First Baptist Church and the local gentry residing in their stately southern mansions with massive columns, huge front decks and balconies each competing with the other for position. They were owned by founding families with names like: White, Brown, Jeter, Jackson, Alexander, Jordan, and Baker. They represented the power and wealth of these little towns and even in this "enlightened" age they grasped tightly to their family positions managing to maintain a firm grip on the majority of property and wealth. The term the "New South" had been used in various forms since the Civil War but there was nothing new about the consolidation of wealth and power by these ruling families. The continued economic subjugation of working class whites and the just under the surface racism, was alive and well in these small towns. It seemed they all had a bypass these days, dotted with Wal-Mart, The Dollar Store and fast food chains. These further propagated the myth of progress and wealth while really just managing to cater to the lowest economic denominator. No, there was nothing really "new" in Peakeville.

Harry understood the intimacies of these small southern towns better than most. In fact it was one of the reasons in particular his family and he had chosen to stay here. Unwilling to abandon this town completely he and his father before him had been a bastion of hope and justice for those less fortunate around them regardless of race or economic status. The task wasn't complete, but Harry knew he was reaching the end of his tenure and for whatever reason the Lord had not seen fit to bless him with any progeny to carry the torch into the twenty first century. Jake was to be his final project, his enduring testimony, if you will. If a man of integrity, honor, fairness, and compassion could rise from the ashes of Randy Delhomme then maybe, just maybe, there was some semblance of hope for the future. Harry understood that although it may have appeared at a national level real change had occurred, after all who would have believed fifty years ago that today an African American would sit in the White House, no one of course. The reality however was as long as discord and intransigence existed at an interpersonal level, the very foundation of this great country would still be in jeopardy.

Harry had no illusions about the forces arrayed against him, the accident, if you could call it that, combined with the almost unbelievable discovery in Pennsylvania had provided him with a much clearer understanding of the true magnitude of the problem. He hadn't understood Maria's role until that afternoon. *How did the good Book say it, "A man who has no experience with the miraculous will not believe if he cannot see it for himself,"* and so Maria was not only necessary but a lynch pin. He didn't question the why of it, nor did he concern himself with his particular role. His only focus now would be reaching through the years and finding the thread that would tie this altogether for Jake and just maybe provide the lifeline that could save his wayward and broken spirit.

Chapter 47

It was decided Maria would move into Harry's guest room; he of course protested vociferously but neither one of them was having any of it. He needed someone to keep the house clean, prepare meals, and general watch out for him. There wasn't a better option and Maria insisted finally feeling like maybe this was why she was here. Harry knew better but kept his peace and the simple fact was he enjoyed her company. She brought a youthful spirit into his existence and a contagious positive energy you couldn't escape. Never mind the young lady was becoming an excellent cook in her own right mixing the southern comfort foods of Jake's mother with the spices and flavors of her Mexican heritage. Combinations of chili powder, garlic, cumin, and the pungent Mexican oregano elevated the roasts and sauces of traditional Southern cooking to whole different experience and Harry loved all of it.

Harry had insisted they both have cell phones on his plan, pointing out if he ever needed either of them there was no way for him to reach them. As usual there was no arguing with Harry when he had made his mind up. It solved a major issue Jake had been struggling with since completing the renovations on Harry's place. Old man Sanders had spread the word about what excellent work he had done, self-serving sure, since his boys had helped out. But the fact was he was getting a few calls a day asking how to reach Jake for work. They had quickly worked out a deal, Jake would purchase all his materials at Sanders' place and the old man would continue referring him all the work he could handle, oh and Jake would employ his two boys at a flat hourly wage as well. And right then "Jake's Carpentry & Home Repair" was born.

It had been three and a half weeks since Harry's release. He was enduring the three times per week physical therapy sessions and had passed his two-week check up with flying colors. He had busied himself at his home office setting up a simple corporation for Jake and walking him through understanding what he would need for insurance, work orders, and basic bookkeeping for his invoices. It was a new world for Jake, but he caught on quickly and Maria was able to help keep his ledgers and bills organized for him. Summer was running on towards early fall and the three of them were quickly falling into a comfortable routine, but Harry knew he had been avoiding discussing his trip to Pennsylvania with the two of them. Things were going so well... *Why disrupt it? Did it really matter? Wasn't this success after all?* Harry asked himself. Jake was working, it had been at least two months since he had last smoked, he no longer drank at all. In fact he was as focused and positive as Harry had ever seen him. Why jeopardize this progress with unbelievable stories from the past? *Maria hadn't had any dreams since the accident, wouldn't it be better to just leave things be?*

Harry knew it was all wishful thinking, he wasn't naive enough to believe in fairy tale happy endings, whatever forces had been at work creating this confluence of events and people had not just abandoned the effort. No, he was sure things were in play that they just were not aware of yet.

That was the problem with being a wise old man, you tended to be right about things even when you would have preferred not to be. That was also the same day the letter had arrived from Pennsylvania addressed in the spidery scrawl of Larry Johnson.

Chapter 48

Molly had fallen into a comfortable routine over the past weeks getting up early to catch the number two bus downtown to the Wolfson campus for classes. Most days she would pack a lunch and find a quiet spot to eat while reading over her work. Other days she would take a quick walk across Third Avenue for a sandwich at Subway. She had been worried she would be the only older person among a bunch of kids, but she had been surprised at the variety of people she had seen on campus. No, she definitely wasn't the only one getting a late start. She hadn't developed any friendships, choosing to focus on what she considered her mission, besides, there was more than enough social interaction at Pete's in the evenings.

It wasn't just the acquisition of knowledge that was driving her, she felt a growing sense of empowerment, a belief in herself that hadn't existed before. Molly had always found herself settling, never really believing that the world held any opportunity for her. Why would it? She was just a simple girl from the Carolinas, nothing special about her. The loss of Jake had been a watershed moment for

her, not so much because he had left, but because she
had finally taken a look at herself and realized that
she was only powerless because she allowed herself to
be. There would never be another ending to her story
if she never took responsibility for herself, if she
never stopped playing the poor victim of
circumstances. Circumstances she now realized she had
been creating for herself. Of course it hadn't been
quite that simple, she had really loved Jake. That
made the loss all the more impactful combined with
the remonstrations of Pete. She had been lacking a
level of maturity in earlier relationships, but now
she had finally arrived at a place where she could
look with some honesty in the mirror and have a
candid dialogue with herself.

Part of redefining herself was also the
realization she didn't have to settle in
relationships. She didn't need a man to complete her,
she was okay. There wasn't something wrong with her
just because she wasn't in a relationship. The
freedom this understanding had brought to her heart
had been so overwhelming she had tried to explain it
to Pete. That had been hopeless, he had been a good
sport about it, but it just wasn't something she
believed a man was going to understand. She was
finally understanding the truly oppressive social

conditioning that said her value as a woman was defined by her figure and whether she was able to keep a man happy. Conditioning based on the warped misogynistic beliefs of an unenlightened Bible belt mentality still rampant in the small Southern towns like the one she had grown up in. She had escaped the gropes, the overly zealous hugs, and the constant barrage of thinly veiled comments most teenage girls suffered through from the adult men in their lives, be it a church deacon, a friend's father, or a teacher. She had escaped, leaving right after high school not knowing how to explain it to her mother and pretty sure her mother wouldn't have understood having long ago accepted it as her own reality. She had left but not really escaped, she carried the emotional damage and baggage with her.

The relationship with Jake combined with the healthy support of Pete had finally enabled her to shed some of the residual conditioning of her early life. Jake in many ways had become an iconic representation of that early oppression. It wasn't so much that he was himself that way, but in leaving he created the opportunity for awakening. He had provided the shock her psyche needed to finally begin to see things clearly. Although his actions had been cowardly and self-serving he had done her a favor and now she finally felt she was on a path of her own

design.

Chapter 49

Thursday August 17th had been your typical late summer day in Peakeville, plenty of sunshine with temperatures in the high eighties and the requisite late afternoon thunderstorm. The sun came back in time to dry the grass off and chase the clouds West into the burgeoning twilight just beginning to be pricked by the early stars of the summer constellations. The darker hollows and shadows were already harboring lightning bugs and the deep croaking of frogs warming up for the evening symphony had started in the ponds, and as always seemed to be the case a lone whip-poor-will's quavering call echoed somewhere in the distance.

Maria was in the kitchen finishing up a batch of fried chicken in a cast iron skillet she had salvaged from Jake's, the green beans simmered quietly on the stove and her first attempt at homemade biscuits were rising in the oven. Jake had shown up about a half hour ago and was out on the front porch sharing an RC Cola with Harry, she could hear their voices drift in and out as Jake related news from around town and the details of his current project. They had slipped into a comfortable routine over the past weeks and she had not felt this at peace in a long time.

Granted, it was a strange trio she found herself in, the old wise attorney, the fifty something burnout making a miraculous comeback, and the eighteen-year-old runaway Mexican girl. Definitely not what anyone would have expected, yet they each had something the others needed and so it worked. It hadn't occurred to her at the time but at its core it was about companionship, mutual respect, and looking past what society considered irreconcilable differences. Once you dropped the labels, the prejudice, your own pre-conceived notions and met people at an elemental level it was pretty amazing what was possible.

The biscuits were an unmitigated success, Jake had eaten three of them and even Harry managed to down two slathering his with butter and honey. He had said it was the only way a respectable southerner would eat a biscuit that good. With the table cleared and the coffee brewing, Maria fetched three small plates for the peach pie Jake had brought from McElroy's, first one of the season he said. She hadn't ever tried peach pie but she loved anything with ice cream so she was sure it was going to be excellent.

With the coffee poured and only the pie crumbs remaining Harry cleared his throat announcing it was finally time, maybe well past time to tell them about his trip to Columbia and Pennsylvania. "Now I want you two to just listen so I can get this all out, I know you are going to have questions and Maria you probably won't know some of the people in this story, but let me get it all out before I start answering any questions, and then I'll read you this letter." He held up Larry Johnson's letter up for them to see. They both nodded in agreement not saying a word, the quiet peacefulness of the evening now somehow fraught with a tension they all could feel.

Harry brought them up to speed on his search through the records in Columbia, telling the story of the late night run to pick Randy Delhomme up and the babbling explanation he had given. Jake was dumbstruck, never having heard any of this and honestly amazed his father had never told anyone, not even him. Harry turned to Maria, "it was your description of the dreams that triggered the memory for me, it just seemed so familiar," he explained.

Maria of course knew none of the story at all so Jake and Harry had to start at the beginning telling her about the school and the craziness that had ensued. Jake even humbly explained, for the first time to anyone, his own role in creating the hysteria that had gripped the town, "God I was young and stupid wasn't I?" no one disagreed.

Harry went on to explain the disappearance of Larry Johnson and his search through the sealed records in Columbia and how he had finally found an explanation for everything in the final box of letters. "You can imagine my surprise, I mean you two need to understand these kinds of things just don't happen. I mean this is the United States of America and we have a, well, had a Governor basically make a person disappear. It's just unbelievable really not like some of these crazy movies make it seem. Anyway, I couldn't leave it there so I decided to drive to Pennsylvania to see if I could track down this Juxa Corporation and maybe someone who remembered Larry Johnson. I know, I know, a long shot after all this time. I should have told you before leaving, but I got caught up in the mystery of it."

"So this all started that morning after breakfast," Jake asked.

"Not exactly, I had already been to Columbia the day before, and I know I should have told you about it there at McElroy's, but you didn't seem yourself and were pretty out of it if you will recall

Jake."

"Yeah I know, not sure what was going on with me that morning, but working on your deck that afternoon really seemed to set me straight."

Breaking in Maria asks, "Can we get back to the story, I want to know what you found..."

Looking around seeming almost afraid he will be overheard Harry lowers his voice... "What I found was Larry Johnson..."

Chapter 50

The main campus was nestled in a small valley
town named Bethany in the heart of the Pocono
Mountains of Northeast Pennsylvania close enough to
the Interstate 95 corridor to provide good access to
the urban centers of Washington D.C., Philadelphia
and the greater New York City area. Even so, it was
still remote enough to provide both security and
privacy. Bethany, a collection of small horse farms,
artists, and intellectuals looking to escape the
city, it was the perfect setting. The Juxa
Corporation had purchased the main seventy-room
three-story mansion off John Strongman of Woolworth
fame, as well as a collection of out-buildings
dotting the property. The original home had been
built in 1908 and renovated into a three story
mansion in 1929 -1930. At the time it was also a
large working farm encompassing seven hundred and
fifty acres with a number of large stately barns. The
Property had been parceled out since the original
family had sold it in the mid 1960's. Two main
parcels remained: the main house and buildings now
belonged to the Juxa Corporation's Institute of

Higher Learning. They had also purchased a number of parcels surrounding the property and the original barn complex had been renovated and was now a high end assisted living center named Bethany Village. Interestingly enough the two centers worked well with each other and many of the Institute's teachers and students would give seminars and lectures at Bethany Village from time to time. The institute also made its pottery, art, and music studios available to residents of the Village creating a very positive, cohesive synergy between the two groups and by extension the surrounding residents. Lessons had been learned all those years ago in Peakeville.

The main building was the Institute's administrative offices, library, classrooms, main kitchens and dining rooms, as well as a limited number of residence suites for selected members of the management team and visiting teachers. The outbuildings were a collection of music, art, and pottery studios, a small dormitory, yoga room, a gym, woodworking shop and a maintenance building. There was also an extensive set of gardens, a small orchard, a working farm and a chapel rounded out the campus. Of course Harry didn't know any of this when he pulled up to the Hotel Wayne in Honesdale, Pennsylvania, the neighboring town and only hotel in close proximity to the address he had scribbled on his yellow legal pad. His GPS system told him he was within a few miles from Bethany and hopefully some answers.

Early the next morning Harry grabbed a quick coffee and a couple of "nutty" donuts at Day's Bakery across the street from the hotel. The place looked like just another one of the older quaint homes on the street, but when he had checked out, the front desk clerk had assured him he wouldn't regret the stop. The girl at the counter had convinced him to try a couple of "nutty" donuts, apparently a local specialty. He wasn't quite sure what a "nutty" donut was but after one bite he was sure they were habit forming. The soft doughy inside combined with the occasional crunch of nuts all smothered in a light glaze was amazing. He was alternating bites with sips of the hot sweet black coffee as he headed up Route 670 toward Bethany.

Harry didn't quite know what to expect, he probably should have done a little research on the Internet, but mastering email was about as far as he had taken his tech skills. Now that he was here though he wished he was a bit more prepared. As he pulled into Noble Lane and approached the complex a bronze sign with a nine pointed star type symbol stated: "The Institute for Higher Learning" and just under in smaller letters "A Juxa Corporation Project". Harry had arrived. He parked the car in the front parking lot across from what appeared to be the main entrance, the grounds were immaculately manicured and the buildings gleamed almost as if they had a new coat of paint just that morning.

Brushing the shards of sugar glaze off his shirt Harry pushes himself out of the Lexus adjusting his suspenders before opening the back door for his sport coat and portfolio. Walking up to the front door he continues to marvel at the immensity of the property, how was it possible they had left Peakeville in the middle of the night like a band of gypsies and now this?

The front door opens silently before he can push it and he is greeted by a young man in white linen slacks and short sleeve button down shirt, "Mr. White, if you will follow me please." The young man leads off down a hallway with Harry trying to keep up, too stunned to say anything and trying to take in the large black and white portraits on each side, many of them dignitaries he recognizes. He finds himself in a large sitting room, floor to ceiling windows look out at the gardens abloom with late summer flowers. "Mr. White, may I bring you coffee or something else to drink?" the young man inquires.

"Uhh, yes, yes, coffee please, I'm sorry, where are my manners, yes please, thank you," he stammers.

"It is no problem sir, I think you will find everything you need here," as he points to a side board set with a freshly brewed pot of coffee, cups and utensils. "If you will please wait here sir someone will be right with you."

"Yes, thank you young man, I appreciate it," says Harry finding his composure and heading toward the coffee. The young man has already silently let himself out. Harry pours a cup and opening the blue sugar bowl plucks out two cubes, slowly a smile spreads and shaking his head he murmurs, "that's got to be a coincidence."

"Good morning Harry, it's been a long time, I am glad you finally came, I've been waiting for you," says a balding, older, but radiant Larry Johnson.

Chapter 51

"Wait, wait, wait... you are telling me they built this giant school place up there, and they knew you were coming and then on top of all that, fuckin' Larry Johnson was there, seriously?" exclaims Jake shaking his head, "how is any of that possible?"

"Jake, son, I know this sounds incredible, and honestly, I wouldn't believe it myself if I hadn't been there. But, why are you so upset by this, what are you so worked up about?" Harry asks lowering his voice.

"After what they did..." Jake catches himself stopping mid-sentence as he looks at the others and drops his head into his hands. "We deserved this didn't we Harry, we did this to ourselves, this little town with our, our... I don't know," Jake looks up, tears in his eyes, "it could have been so different, we could have been so different, I could have been so different..." his voice drops to a whisper. "Oh Jesus Harry I did this, me and that idiot Jimmy, we started the whole mess that summer."

"Jake, son, let me tell you the rest of the story and maybe then you will see that although things could have gone much differently and you are right we failed as a community maybe things ended up on a better path in the long run," Harry says patting him on the shoulder. "But first let me tell you about Larry Johnson, he is older than I am, but well preserved if you will. He left here that summer with the folks from the school and became the personal student of Ms. Sally, that's what they call her up there. Anyway, he is a senior member of their staff and a bit of a celebrity. You see he was the first outsider, the first student to fully go through the program and achieve success."

"Harry, you keep saying the school, what does that mean? Do they like teach classes and stuff?" Maria interjected.

"Well, they call it the Institute for Higher Learning, but from what I was able to gather it's not like a college in the traditional sense, they take students on a very selective basis and there are classes but the focus is not on increasing knowledge of a specific subject but on the development of one's self. If I understand correctly, in a nutshell, it's this: 'when a man begins to make efforts to live consciously, you could say that his real life as a man on earth begins... he begins to act instead of react — he begins to participate in his own destiny,'" Harry recites it almost as a chant. "I'll tell you that this affected to me so deeply I had to memorize it before leaving there. It's inscribed on a plaque at the main entrance; apparently it's a quote from Ms. Sally. There is a lot more to it of course, but they teach you how to raise your self-awareness, how to achieve harmony between the three centers, intellectual, emotional and physical. Larry explained to me that they help you develop this technique of 'objective self-observation' as a means of becoming fully aware. I've got to tell you it's really intriguing stuff!"

"Harry, I don't understand any of this really, I am just a simple redneck from a small town, what does any of this have to do with us, well, me anyway?" Jake asks plaintively.

"Well son, I think it has everything to do with us and I guess that's the point. We missed our chance once and I think we are being given another opportunity. Ask yourself this Jake... are we... all of us..." Harry makes a broad gesture with his hands. "Are we the way we are by our choice? This is what struck me about Larry, Jake, he was Peakeville if you will, he embodied what our little town is all about, but Larry opened his eyes, he embraced the concepts this Ms. Sally was teaching and in doing so he was able to practice this self observation they talk about. He told me the first time he had a real breakthrough really and saw himself for what he was it almost killed him, but he says that was his first step to self-awareness. He said it was only then he began the real journey to become a conscious being able to participate in his own destiny. Jake, it's the opportunity to become what the universe, God if you will, intended us to be, not stuck in the die cast by our parents, society, friends, and most of all our own weakness. I have books I need to read, there is so much to learn but Jake, we have the power inside us; it's just a matter of learning how to unlock it." Harry grows silent for a moment and then softly, "...I just wish I had more time..."

"You make it sound so easy..." Jake trails off.

"No Jake, it's not easy, nothing worth doing is..."

"You and your little pearls Harry," Jake smiles, "I keep meaning to write them down. Okay, I still don't really understand it, but what now?"

"Well that brings me to this letter I received today from Larry... Jake, I'll just cut to the chase, he wants you to come to Pennsylvania to see him... and he wants you to bring Maria."

Jake explodes, "No fuckin' way Harry! How am I

supposed to do that? I've got jobs lined up and well, you can't be alone yet... No way in hell I'm driving up there!"

"Settle down now Jake and let me finish. They are having an open house over the Labor Day weekend and you can spare the three days. I'll be fine by myself for a few days and I am already getting around better with the walker, I want you to go son, it's important..." It hangs in the air between them.

"Yeah well, I'll think about it but no promises, I don't know what the point is anyway," standing up Jake drops his cup in the sink and turns, "I'm headin' home I'll stop by tomorrow and we can talk some more."

"Alright son, see ya tomorrow."

Maria follows him to the door, "Goodnight Jake..."

"Goodnight" he grumbles heading for the truck as she turns back inside and rejoins Harry at the table.

Outside they hear the gravel spray as Jake spins his tires leaving... "He'll go, don't worry... I already dreamed about it, just didn't want to say anything to make him worse..." she says with a wan smile, "and yes I am going with him."

Harry looks up, "I didn't tell you earlier, but

they knew I was coming, even greeted me at the door by my name. Scared me to be honest. Even after listening to you describe the dreams and all, it was still unnerving to experience firsthand."

"Well, you aren't going to like this then Harry... I uh, dreamed your accident, I think maybe before it even happened."

He smiles, "no that's fine, I would have died out there if you hadn't, and Maria I tried to, I don't know really how to describe it... but reach out to you when it happened. At least I think that was what I was doing, it's still a little fuzzy. I'm tired, time to turn in, good night Ms. Maria."

"Goodnight Harry."

Chapter 52

Jake knows he isn't going to get any sleep tonight. His mind is turning over on itself, *why why why...* Harry just couldn't leave it alone could he? The old man just had to keep pushing, had to get to the bottom of it all. *Well, just fucking great, now what was he supposed to do?* He didn't need this shit, he had a perfectly fine thing going before he picked up that crazy girl and got mixed up in all this shit. *They were all batshit crazy*, he thought. Even more so if they thought he was going to drive to Pennsylvania to meet with some old asshole his father used to run around with. *Why couldn't they just leave him alone?* He hadn't asked for any of this.

Jake pulls in to Bob's Bar, his old watering hole. He hadn't been here since he had come back to town and right about now he thought a cold one and a cigarette sounded damn good. *Jesus, they even had him convinced to stop drinkin' and smokin' like some fuckin' church deacon.* He can hear the jukebox, as he gets out of the truck, loud enough to mask the ticks and pings that usually soothe him. Pushing through the door he takes a deep breath of the smoky air, drinking in the vibe, the smells, the noise, the atmosphere, that is the bar. Bob's is about two thirds full tonight and Jake figures he knows most of them. His eyes adjusting to the dim light he spots Jimmy and the usual crew down at the end lounging around the pool table, no doubt telling the same stories as always. Hell a year ago they had partied there on the night he had headed for Miami, he and Jimmy holding court retelling every tale from high school. He heads that way, it's good to be back, signaling Carol behind the bar to bring him two, she nods already knowing his standard order.

"Whoa, look at this mother fuckin' spic lover rollin' up in here like he owns the place..." Jimmy bellows out. "Boy, you better turn your shit around, you done shamed ya daddy's memory..."

Jake can't believe it, "What the hell are you talkin' about Jimmy?"

"Oh hell no buddy ro you don't get to act like you're one of us... hanging out with that little spic slit and the old man like you're something special, you fuckin' forget what side of town you growed up on?" Jimmy slurs poking him in the chest.

"Get outa my face Jimmy, I'm just here to say hello and have a couple cold ones, just chill out." As he turns to take the long necks from Carol Jimmy pushes him in the back.

"Don't turn your fuckin' back on me asshole, Ill whip your ass for ya..."

Jake sets the beer down, "What the hell Jimmy, I didn't come in here for no trouble, hell we've been friends forever."

Jimmy is right up in his face, "well looks like you got it anyway don't it... and I don't need no spic lovin' turncoat frrr..."

Jake can't believe it, it's like he is watching a slow motion replay of himself, but Jimmy is already falling to the floor as Jake tries to shake the sting out of his fist, he hadn't even thought about it, he had just cold cocked the loud mouth. Turning to Carol he tosses her a twenty, "Sorry about the mess..." and walks out, he misses the smile on her face and the stunned looks of what had once been his boys.

Jake starts the truck dropping it into drive and heading back toward Main Street, the windows are rolled down and the scents of a Carolina summer night surround him. He can smell the fresh cut grass from Mr. Simpson's mansion, the night jasmine Mrs. Brown loves so much. Further on are the mouthwatering scents of old man Jackson baking pies and rolls for tomorrow's diners at McElroy's. This was home, and yet Jake felt like he was on the outside looking in,

221

like somehow he was moving past this sleepy little town stuck in time.

Reflecting on the scene at the bar he struggles with what happened, *why would Jimmy have been so in his face? Sure, Jimmy was an asshole and drinking only made it worse, but this had been different, Jimmy had been genuinely angry and there had been real hate in his eyes. Jesus what had gotten into him, there was never a situation where he would have just cold cocked Jimmy*. Fact was Jimmy had always scared him a little, he would never admit it, but it was always there in the background, but not tonight, *what was different?*

Jake already knew what was different, it was now just a matter of admitting it to himself and coming to terms with what it meant. He leaned back against the seat as the truck cooled, the ticks and pings speaking their familiar refrain. He didn't remember turning in, but the ghostly blue light of the street lamp bathed the truck while his father's house stood nearby in the shadows. He hadn't been thinking about it, but the images of his childhood returned suddenly, the knowing smile of his father across that pine glade as he pulls on the rope...
"That's right Jake, this is your legacy son... this is who we are... this is who you are..."

It's only then the tears come, finally breaking through, head down on the steering wheel heaving sobs wracking his whole body, Jake can no more stop it than he can stop the setting sun or waves on the beach, he is consumed. You can't manufacture real anguish, it can't be summoned like the tears of some actress in your favorite movie, it comes from the soul; it's real, it's naked unfettered and all-encompassing and tonight it has Jake tight in its grip. These are not the sobs of a soul sorry for itself. No, this is the realization of a lost life, lost opportunity, the stain of prejudice and purposeful hate that pollutes every aspect of a man. Jake lets it all out, the anguish of self-realization, the grieving that comes with self-awareness is the only pathway to recovery. A man must face himself before he can move beyond where he is, before he can wash the dirt of his existence from his soul. For we are perfect in our creation and it is our own doing that creates the evil caricature we become. Man does not have the capacity to destroy his soul only to pollute it and only with that realization can he begin to heal himself.

Chapter 53

It has been a long time, well at least a few months, since Jake has woken stiff and cold in his truck and it sucks as much as he remembers. *Jesus, what a fucking crazy night* he thinks, stretching and working the kinks out of his neck. He heads inside to grab a hot shower and a change of clothes. He needs to head over to Harry's and apologize for blowing up at them last night. His frustrations he realizes now had nothing to do with them. *God, it's a beautiful morning, but damn if his hand doesn't hurt like hell* he thinks with a rueful smile reserved just for himself. Closing the back door behind him he switches on the kitchen lights and starts a pot of coffee brewing then heads upstairs shedding his clothes as he goes.

The hot water cascades over him washing out the last of the soreness from his ill-advised truck slumber and Jake does not miss the symbolism of the moment the cleansing of the poison that's been a constant part of his life up to this point. Only problem, he has no idea where to go from here, the events of last night were cathartic, freeing, and for a man like Jake completely overwhelming and like all moments of self-realization demanding of a next step, but what? The three shotgun blasts in rapid succession jerk him out of his reverie and have him diving for the floor... *Jesus, what the hell...*

Jake hears the truck roar off before he can make it to the upstairs window, not thinking that might not be the safest move. Pulling on his jeans, a T-shirt and pair of tennis shoes he heads downstairs, strangely more curious than scared. Yes, something has changed in him since the confrontation with Jimmy last night, he can feel the fear he has lived with just beneath the surface slowly receding and being replaced with a calm steadfastness he doesn't recognize. The front two windows have been blown out and the mailbox is barely hanging on, Jake dials up the locals and asks them to send a car over. He is still sweeping up the splintered glass when Sergeant Roy Thompson knocks on the door jamb, "Shit Jake, you got quite a mess here..."

"No fucking kidding RT" he replies... Jake and Roy have known each other since grade school. Roy grew up three blocks over and had wanted to be a policeman as long as anyone could remember. Roy's dad had been killed in Vietnam and he had been forced to grow up fast taking care of his mom and three sisters; it had just reinforced his desire to be a cop. But it hadn't changed the "mill town" mentality he had grown up with.

"So what do you think Jake? Gang bangers pissed you're holed up with one of their chicas?"

"Are you fucking serious!? You know damn well this wasn't some gang banger over here in mill town with a shotgun." Jake lets disbelief seep into his voice, "you and I both know who did this and it's pretty typical for him when he's pissed off."

"Well Jake, unless you saw someone or something I am going to have to write it up the way I see it, and I see a local boy holed up with some little young chica on the wrong side of town. It's not safe over here for her kind," looking around then at Jake with a low chuckle, "or for you either now that I think about it. Next time you might want to think about who you take up with." He quips as he turns to leave.

"So that's how it's gonna be? Thanks RT, I appreciate the help... no really," Jake says.

"Not a problem Jake, always happy to help a citizen," he chuckles again walking down the front steps.

Jesus Christ, please tell me I wasn't like this, Jake muses to himself, knowing full well he was just like this and worse, in fact he had been just like this to Maria when he first met her. With his breakfast plans shot he heads over to Sanders for a couple sheets of plywood to cover the windows until he can get new glass ordered.

Jake pulls up to the contractor entrance waving to Danny as jumps out of the truck, "hey buddy, need two sheets half inch ply, can you load them up for me?"

"Yeah, no problem... Old man Sanders is looking for you, wanted me to tell you to head up front, he needs to talk to you..."

Shit here we go... now what, Jake thinks? The mess from last night and probably this morning were already making the rounds. Peakeville was just too small to have any secrets. "Ok, thanks Danny..." Popping his head into the office, "You needed me sir?"

Dropping his glasses on the desk and rubbing his temples Sanders says, "come on in Jake, close the door will ya?" With a deep sigh, "now listen Jake, I heard about last night and everyone with a scanner is already talking about your house gettin' shot up this morning..." Jake starts to interrupt, "Now just let me finish son, you and your buddies were more than a pain in the ass growin' up and well honestly, I am sure being Randy's son didn't help none, but Jake you seem to have gotten yourself together and from what I hear and what my boys tell me you are one helluva carpenter. More than that you seem to genuinely care about Mr. Harry. So listen son take my advice stay away from Jimmy and that crowd, I don't want anything to happen to you and I certainly don't want my boys mixed up in any of this mess."

"Yes sir, I understand and sir I appreciate everything you have done for me these past few months. I don't know what happened last night, I know how Jimmy is, but I just couldn't stand there and let him run his mouth..."

"Jake I don't need no explanation, little Carol was at McElroy's this morning telling everyone what you did, and believe me most of us understand completely... But son there ain't no reason to go poking a beehive if you don't absolutely have to, you understand what I'm sayin'?" Not waiting for answer, "good, now get out of here."

Jake turns to leave, "I hear ya sir... I'll be more careful."

"And Jake, this town ain't all bad son, some of us are trying to change..."

Chapter 54

It's almost lunchtime before Jake has the plywood cut and tacked up over the two holes in the front of his house. He finishes the rest of the cleanup and turns his attention to the mailbox. *Jesus, what a mess,* he thinks. *What the hell, let's just reattach the mailbox, buckshot holes and everything,* his own personal statement of resistance. Jake had no intention of provoking Jimmy and his crew, but he also wasn't going to back down either, right was right and he was through being intimidated by the likes of Jimmy Sewell.

Pulling into Harry's driveway around noon he sees the physical therapist on his way out and waves. It is a pretty amazing job they are doing getting Harry back on his feet. Jake had watched one of the sessions and was impressed, they were so supportive but still able to get you to do so much more than you thought you could. Harry was always complaining that they enjoyed torturing him, but you could tell he really appreciated it and he was working hard to get himself well.

Jake is just in time for lunch, Maria is making

a plateful of egg salad sandwiches, not the creamy supermarket egg salad either. No this is chunky and has chopped bread and butter pickles, onions, and celery in it with just a touch of fresh chopped cilantro, another variation on one of his mother's signature recipes. Pretty amazing that she was able to even find cilantro in Peakeville now that he thought about it. The tea was cold and sweet, Maria still couldn't believe how much sugar was in it, but Harry and Jake insisted the ratio of one cup per gallon was accurate. Fresh sliced tomatoes Jake had picked up at the farmers market completed the simple lunch. There is an awkward silence at the table until finally Jake can't take it any longer, "listen, I am sorry about last night, I lost my cool and took it out on y'all."

"Hmmph, I heard you took it out on big Jimmy Sewell," chuckled Harry.

Stunned Jake says, "well, I guess news travels fast round here..." Taking another bite of his sandwich he looks at the other two trying not to laugh at him, "What are you two grinnin' about, it's not the least bit funny!"

They are undone, breaking into uncontrollable laughter, it really isn't funny but the built up stress finds an outlet in its own way. "Oh, and I suppose you two think that jackass shooting up my house this morning is pretty hilarious too?"

Harry sets his napkin down, "Jake, what are you talking about? Who shot up your house, are you okay?"

"I'm fine, blew out the front windows and did a number on the mailbox though. My guess is Jimmy being Jimmy, gonna take him a long time to get over being put on his ass by the likes of me I'm afraid," Jake sighs.

Shaking his head Harry asks, "are you sure it was him, did you actually see him?"

"Nah, didn't see him, but his truck is one of those big diesels and it sounded like him taking off, besides this is just the kinda thing he would do... called the cops and RT, I mean Sergeant Thompson as much as confirmed, although he won't be any help, told me it was probably gang bangers pissed off Maria was stayin' at my place. Of course that don't make no sense, especially since I don't think we even have any gangs here do we?"

"Jake if this is my fault I can find somewhere else to stay, I don't want to cause you or Harry any problems..."

"Oh hell no, we aren't letting some ass like Jimmy Sewell get his way, you're not going anywhere, I'll be damned if I'll let some redneck ass bully me," Jake is getting pretty worked up again.

Harry lets a low chuckle go, "well Jake that's pretty poetic," laughingly, "yep, just about right I would say..."

"What's so funny old man?"

"Well Jake, if I recall correctly, and I do, this is pretty similar situation to, albeit on a smaller scale, a certain summer, say about thirty or so years ago. I mean think about it, some folks a bit out of the ordinary, begging your pardon Ms. Maria, come into town acting a bit different than the average person here and some down home trouble maker starts up with them. Hell, even shoots up their house, that ringing any bells for you?"

Jake can feel the heat creeping up his neck the scarlet tinge betraying his embarrassment, "So Harry you saying I deserved this cause what Jimmy and I did all those years ago?"

"No, no, no, Jake that isn't at all what I am saying, no one deserves this, and that's really my point, not you, not those folks out there at the old plantation, not any of the people that have ever been mistreated for no other reason than they were somehow different."

Quietly, "no, not even that fella my pa hung from that tree all those years ago..." and the tears start...

"Jake, son what fella? What are you talking about son..." asks Harry reaching for his hand.

Jake tells them the story of that evening long ago standing in the pine grove watching his father and Mr. Sewell lynching the black man. He remembers it like he was standing there, the pungent smell of burning pine pitch, the sour odor of spilled beer, and the jeers of the men gathered round cheering his father on. The most searing memory of all the wisp of a smile his father had given him across the clearing, yes he remembers it all. Head in his hands he tells the whole tale, looking up he says, "I know now, I guess maybe I always knew, my daddy lynched that man that night, I was six years old, I didn't want to believe they killed him, guess I couldn't believe it. Oh sweet Jesus and then I follow right in his footsteps and become as big a son of a bitch as he was..."

"But Jake you never killed anyone did you," Maria asks...

It stings that she even has to ask, but he knows where it comes from, "No, no I didn't but don't you see that don't really matter, neither did any of those men that stood in that circle watching my dad... but none of them stopped it, none of them said

233

anything, none of them said NO. I'm finally figuring this out, and I'm not the smartest guy around, but if you let it pass, if you look the other way, if you don't stand up and say no, aren't you just as guilty as the one that does it?" Hanging his head, "...and honestly more times than not I was the one running my mouth, or starting shit, hell, I'm no different than Jimmy we both did as much as the other..."

Pleadingly Maria says, "Jake don't say such things, you are nothing like him..."

"Oh but I am Maria, I am, I even did it to you and you know it's true..."

Harry cuts him off in his courtroom voice, "well now we have it don't we? So Jake what are you going to do about it?"

Chapter 55

Jake had come to the realization that the only
way to have any kind of peace in his future was to
finally face his past, all of it not just the legacy
of his father, but to also finally take
responsibility for the state of his own life. Jake
didn't have all the right words or even know how to
necessarily express himself yet, but he knew that
there was no one to blame for his life, not his
parents, not fate, not lady luck, the only thing that
had conspired against him was himself. He had told
Harry he would go see Larry Johnson, it scared him
more from a lack of understanding and admittedly
shame for his part in things, but he would do it. How
better to close that chapter of his life than
confronting it head on.

Harry had called Dan Silvers, the Chief of
Police. Dan had been a rookie deputy thirty years
earlier and remembered quite well the mess with the
school. It didn't take too much prodding from Harry
to gain his cooperation in shutting down Jimmy and
his crowd. Mention discrimination, local violence,
and SLED in the same conversation and it was amazing

how attitudes changed. No matter how they really felt no one wanted a repeat performance of those few weeks one long summer many years ago. Peakeville may have been stuck in time, bypassed by prosperity and opportunity, but it had a collective memory. Fact was nobody wanted to revive the stigma of cross burnings, intolerance, and racism. So the word was passed to Jimmy and his boys, most likely through Sergeant Roy Thompson, that there better not be a repeat performance of the other morning because nobody would be looking the other way this time. The days of being able to act with impunity were over.

Jake didn't relax though, it wasn't because he didn't trust Harry or the Chief, but he knew Jimmy well enough to know he wasn't likely to just shrug his shoulders and move on. He probably wouldn't come at him head on, but if the opportunity arose he would definitely take a cheap shot, so it didn't hurt to watch your back. Jake might have had a revelation or two about his life, but it sure didn't mean his old life was just going to disappear. He might be facing his demons and moving on, but his demons and all they represented were still alive and well. Jake had come to the crux of it, the realization that when a man decides to change his life, he controls himself, his actions, his view of things, but the rest of the world is not obligated to give him a pass or necessarily forgive his earlier transgressions. It takes time to rebuild trust, reputation, integrity and that's with the folks open minded enough to believe you and patient enough to wait for the proof of your words, the deeds behind your promises. What Jake would find out, like all people that embark on this journey, is you can only do what you can do, you can only change yourself. Maybe most importantly you have to be the one to define who and what you are, your affirmation comes from doing what is right, not the accolades of those around you. The reality was there would be folks in Peakeville supporting him and there would be just as many, if not more, saying he turned his back on his own and had started thinking too highly of himself.

Jake had agreed to drive up to see Larry Johnson over the Labor Day weekend and Maria would go with him, she had insisted, but with three weeks left in August it might as well have been a lifetime away.

As is usually the case when a person has an epiphany about their past, be it behavior, addiction, or any other number of real or perceived shortcomings, there is an overwhelming desire to make things right. To undo the past, make up for lost time or missed opportunities. These are key steps in the

well-known twelve step programs, the cataloguing of
wrongs and the effort to make direct amends where
possible. Jake was not specifically aware of the
steps, having never graced the door of an AA meeting,
but the steps were a reflection of a deep-seated need
for forgiveness. It is human nature to rationalize
our bad behavior with phrases like "original sin" or
"it's just our nature" or everyone's favorite "the
devil made me do it". And of course there is
corresponding need to seek absolution, forgiveness
and it is just as often shrouded in rituals like
confession, penance, animal sacrifice, and the ever
popular need to spend time in some personal
purgatory.

Jake didn't have any particular insight into
any of these customs, rituals or beliefs, his
religious background had consisted of the vitriolic
sermons of Reverend Dan Richards and the
remonstrations of his prayerful mother. Neither of
which had much impact after that fateful night he had
stood trembling at the horror his father was so
casually perpetrating on another human being. Jake
wasn't consciously aware of it, but his young mind
had decided that no real God would have allowed
something like that to happen and so the
remonstrations of Preacher Richards had fallen on

deaf ears afterwards.

Jake had a fairly short list of people he was interested in talking to, his new found sense of remorse and self-introspection didn't necessarily extend to throwing himself on the mercy of those he had wronged over the years assuming he could even remember most of them. It wouldn't have surprised anyone who knew him to find Annie Tildon, Molly and Maria on that list, and in a new found sense of nobility he figured he probably owed this Ms. Sally at the school an apology for the stupidity of that summer years ago. He also figured since Larry Johnson was still there, and he really hadn't known anything about it anyway, he could be forgiven for not bringing his father's part in all that, up. This had all seemed like a much better idea when he had been talking it over with Harry the other night.

Chapter 56

Standing on her porch, the Saturday mid-morning sun prickling his neck and just beginning to dry the dew from the perfectly manicured lawn, Jake was having second thoughts. It had taken some digging to even find her and he had finally needed to enlist Maria's help using Harry's office computer, but here he was on Annie Tildon's porch, actually Anne Tildon-Jessup's porch. Her Facebook page hadn't given him a lot of information, but enough to make some inquiries around town and track down an address over in Rock Hill right on the border with North Carolina. Now here he was feeling like that fifteen-year-old boy from so many years ago that had screwed it all up.

There are moments that we remember clearly, a slice of time frozen and preserved just waiting to be recalled, and this would be one of those moments. As the last chime of the doorbell faded and the front door opened time stood still for Jake. He could hear the hum of a neighbor's lawnmower intermingled with the oh so familiar sounds of his truck cooling, the faint smell of bacon as if someone had made breakfast with the windows open only a short time ago, somewhere close by kids were playing their high voices floated in and out and there was Annie Tildon standing behind her screen door drying her hands with a dish towel. The blue of her eyes as bright as he remembered, the bridge of freckles, the dimples, she had grey in her hair now, but she was still the Annie he remembered.

"Jake, Jake Delhomme? My God, what has it been, thirty-five, forty years?" Her voice was deeper, softer, but like a favorite old song you haven't heard in a long time achingly familiar.

"Yes Annie, it's me, I uh, hate to just drop in like this, but can we talk for just a minute or two?" he stammers.

"Well sure Jake," turning she raises her voice slightly, "honey come here, I want you to meet an old friend I went to high school with." John Jessup is tall, a bit more than six foot, and solid not like a football player, but he has an air of substance to him. He is comfortably dressed in an old pair of khaki cargo shorts and a University of North Carolina tee shirt. His black hair cut short but with the grey showing through on the sides, angular jaw, and grey green eyes that seem to take everything in but with none of the playfulness of Annie's. No, John Jessup may seem like an easygoing fella on the surface but just below is a seriousness more sensed than seen.

Taking Jake's hand in a firm grip and with a measured clipped tone, "Please to meet you, John Jessup."

"Uh, thank you, Jake Delhomme... I appreciate you both taking some time to see me..." Jake nervously adds, he as a habit steers clear of serious guys like Jessup. As Annie leads the way to the kitchen Jake is having second thoughts about this whole thing, *what the hell was he thinking coming here?*

"Coffee Jake," she asks, "I was just brewing a fresh pot."

"That sounds great... thanks," he manages to get out.

For one long awkward moment the three of them sit at the kitchen table, the sun filters in through the windows and the coffee pot gurgles and chortles, the neighborhood sounds are muted now but still come and go in the background.

"So Jake, what brings you over this way this morning?" Annie asks breaking the silence.

Her voice releases the spell and Jake's not sure where to start, "Well Annie, this probably won't make a lot of sense after all this time, but I needed to come to say sorry for being so stupid and hurting you." He can feel Jessup start to bristle next to him, turning to John, "listen Mr. Jessup, I know that sounds bad, but I was stupid kid in high school and ran with a bunch of redneck jackasses back then; well I guess I still did up till bout just recently. Anyway, I was stupid and said some really hurtful things to Annie here, she trusted me and deserved much better from me than I guess I was able to give." Turning back to Annie, "I need to say I am sorry for letting you down, for not being the person I should have been, anyway, I am trying to make some things, well, a lot of things right and I felt like I needed to start here." Having said it Jake takes a deep breath, not believing he got it all out.

Jessup is staring at him rather incredulously, "you mean to tell me you're here forty years later to apologize to Annie for being a jerk in high school, are you serious?" Turning to Annie, "Honey, do you know what this fella is talking about, cause that seems a tad, I don't know, well, odd to me?"

"I do..." and turning to Jake, "Jake, that was an awful long time ago, we were just kids so why now? I mean I understand you said you are trying to set some things right but... well we were just kids back then."

Jake is struggling now, he had no idea this was

going to be this difficult, it had all made sense when he had worked through it in his head, now he was beginning to wonder if it was all just one big stupid mistake. *Was he the only one that cared about his mistakes?* It had never occurred to him that Annie would not have attached the same significance to that sweet summer of teenage love as he did. But clearly sitting here it was beginning to sink in that he allowed that moment of personal failure to become a defining moment in his life and she had simply moved on.

"How do you take your coffee Jake?" John asks from the counter. Jake hadn't been aware of him getting up from the table.

"Uh, black is fine thanks," and turning to Annie, "I know it was a long time ago and we were just kids, but I'll explain it if I can. I guess I go back to that as one of the first times I can remember knowing what was the right thing to do and deciding not to do it. I mean I hurt you for no other reason than to show off to my buddies, I regretted it right away, I mean right away and ever since, but it was too late. It seems like I have been making that same mistake over and over again in all kinds of things. Look, I am not asking for any sympathy and honestly I am not sure I really expected you to even see me, but

I had to do this for myself. I had to start being accountable for things I have done, the people I have hurt and generally for being an ass for a lot of years." Jake takes a long sip of his coffee before looking up both Annie and John are staring at him. Rather self-consciously he asks, "What...?"

John manages to answer first, "Well Jake..." shaking his head and with a smile, "that's probably one of the most forthright, honest, and introspective statements I have heard in a long time, and I hear plenty of them."

Annie pats John's arm explaining, "Jake... John is a psychologist, he practices in Charlotte and teaches over at Winthrop."

"Oh..." is all Jake can get out... "um, I gotta be honest, I'm not sure what that means."

They all start laughing at once, it may be the most relaxed and real moment Jake has had in a long time with anyone other than Harry and Maria, and it feels good. "Jake, all it means is I do counseling where I help people work through their problems and issues, you know things that are bothering them or keeping them from being happy," John explains.

"Dang, I should have come to see you a long time ago..." Jake laughs, "So you're a shrink?"

"No, no, no that would be a psychiatrist,

although they don't appreciate being called 'shrinks'. I am a psychologist, we do counseling but we don't use any medications and we aren't doctors."

Annie pats his hand like an old friend, "Jake, don't you know I forgave you a long time ago..."

They spend the next three hours catching up, forty years is just too much to compress into a few hours over coffee, so the highlights will have to do but even so the time passes quickly. Jake regales them with his stories of the Northwest with its towering firs, snowcapped peaks and days upon days of rain. He recounts his harrowing early winter trip through the Rockies, followed by tales of hot Miami nights, Cuban food and sweet creamy coffee. He leaves out the drinking and the heartache, but there is an obvious background story that neither Annie nor John miss. Jake is a natural storyteller and the embellishments are obvious but innocent, but he holds back the story of his trip home and Maria. John and Annie for their part met in college and have been together ever since with three kids, two grandchildren and another on the way. Winter vacations in the North Carolina mountains, summers at Myrtle Beach, it's the prototypical successful southern life. There is no debate Jake's life was by far more adventurous, but he laments the stability and family the two of them have created, knowing it is far too late to embark on that path himself. Morning has crossed into midday and Jake takes his leave with promises all around to keep in touch, everyone knowing full well it won't happen.

They watch him back out of the drive, waving together from the front porch, as they turn inside Annie leans into John her head on his shoulder, "thanks babe, I love you."

"Love you too honey bunny, next time I say we charge him a copay," John quips with a smile. "I'm kidding sweetie, I still don't quite understand it, but that was as courageous as anything I've seen in all my years of counseling, and to have come to the conclusion himself is pretty remarkable."

Chapter 57

Jake knows, in spite of the promises to visit and the invitation to come back anytime, he won't be seeing Annie again. He is at peace with the thought of her, gone is the anguish he has so recently felt, the recriminations waiting for just the right moment to hobble him, and maybe most importantly of all he has faced down one of his long time demons and come out the other side.

Jake is almost back to Peakeville before he notices the red Chevy pickup in his rearview mirror, there isn't any doubt as he knows well enough it's Jimmy's truck, only question is how long he has been following him. He had tried to tell Harry that Jimmy would not be warned off so easily, well here he was now close enough to see the grin on his face and the double bird salute he was raising. Jake makes the left turn onto Orchard wondering if Jimmy is going to follow him all the way home. He doesn't, gunning the big diesel dually and heading further up Mill Street, but Jake knows it's just a matter of time.

His cell rings just as he is pulling into the driveway, it's one of the Sanders boys, the windows have come in. *No time like the present,* he figures and tells them to bring them over. With their help it shouldn't take more than a couple of hours to frame them in, he has already done all the prep work. They are pre-hung so just a matter of making sure they fit and shim up properly before nailing them in and reapplying the molding. He had gone the extra dollar and ordered the four hundred series Anderson Casement Bow Windows, one for each side. They had to be custom ordered to fit and had been shipped from the company's factory in Minnesota. Jake liked the thought of these special windows coming all that way for his little house in Peakeville and figured if he liked them he would replace all the windows with Anderson. Pride of ownership was a new concept for Jake, but the old home was finally starting to feel like his place and no longer his parent's house. *Hmmm, well they looked mighty fine...* pretty eyes on an old lady's face was the mental image that kept coming back to him. *Definitely going to need to give the old lady a face-lift all the way around,* he thought. It would be a good project for the cool dry fall days ahead. He needed to hurry up and grab a shower. He was due over at Harry's by seven o'clock, it was a big night ahead, Harry's first trip out for something other than a doctor's appointment since the accident. Maria had convinced him that Harry needed to get out so they were heading to El Casa Robles for dinner. Jake and Maria had become regulars on most every Saturday night, but this would be Harry's first time. Jake hadn't ventured much past the Carne Asada Platter, but on rare occasions Maria was able to talk him into a taste of something new. Most times he would scrunch up his face sending her into a fit of girlish giggles.

Jake pulled into the circle drive, parking the truck and pushing the clicker to open the garage. He backed the 1998 Buick Park Avenue out, closed the garage and headed up the front steps. The big four-door sedan had been in the garage since Harry had bought the Lexus over a year ago. Jake had put a new battery in and had it down to Jackson's garage for a full service and tune up the week Harry had come home. No way would they be able to drive him to doctor's visits or anywhere else for that matter in Jake's old truck. The Buick was a big beast but it was comfortable and ran like a top. Harry had been driving Buicks for twenty plus years and traded for a new one religiously every four years. He had kept this one figuring it would be his last and it was, till he had gotten a wild hair and bought the Lexus last year.

Jake let himself in the front door calling out for Maria and Harry. He was running about five minutes late, but for him that was pretty close to on time. Closing the door he turned back into the hall, Harry was standing there cane in hand with a well, what are we waiting for look, Maria is behind him sporting a big grin. Harry starts for the door, "well, let's go boy, I don't have all night to wait for you, I got a dinner date with this pretty girl!"

Jake shakes his head grinning, "Harry, you're not using your walker!"

Maria chimes in, "nope, we have been working hard this week, and Harry wanted to surprise you."

"Alright, alright, let's not make too big a deal out of it!" Harry exclaims.

Jake gets the door, "Well I think it's great, tonight's a celebration then, maybe I'll go big and get the carne asada..."

"Oh my God Jake, that's all you ever get, Harry he won't even try anything else," Maria says rolling her eyes at him.

"What? I am a steak man, always have been..."

"You're a chicken!" she retorts. "Actually, Harry they have a great chicken mole` you should try, Ms. Rosalita makes it and it's as good as my mom's. I'm having the tamales de Puerco..."

"Wait, wait... pork right!"

"You got it Jake, Harry I have been trying to teach him the basics, pollo, puerco, carnitas, and of course carne asada, so at least he can work his way around the menu."

Harry laughs, "Well, that's pretty ambitious of you young lady, although I can't say I ever remember Jake here having any problem working his way around a menu."

Jake pretending to be hurt, "Alright that's enough you two, let's get out of here I'm hungry."

Chapter 58

The Mole` was as good as Maria promised, and Jake, to no one's surprise had the carne` asada with rice and beans but he had also downed two orders of the guacamole appetizer. There was just something about the combination of creamy avocado, finely chopped onion, tangy fresh cilantro and fresh squeezed lime that Jake couldn't get enough of. Especially when matched up with the thin, still warm from the deep fryer, salty tortilla chips. It was something Molly had introduced him too, he hadn't shared that or much of anything else about his time in Miami, but tonight it brought back sweet and melancholy memories.

Maria was in the back talking with Ms. Rosalita and the girls, she might as well have been one of the three nieces working here. Like many immigrant families Juan and Rosalita Martinez provided a safe haven and a job for any of their family that made it to this part of the United States. It was no different than the Vietnamese families and their nail shops or the Chinese families and their take out restaurants. Sure, it was a cliché but one that worked and provided opportunities for people to bring their extended families to the States. More than that though, and something completely missed by the "Jakes" of the world, it gave them an opportunity to work, to earn their way, to give back to this great country they now embraced as their own. Jake had for years missed the irony that those who seem to appreciate most the opportunity this great country offers, are those who have come here from somewhere else.

"Alright young man, a penny for your thoughts," Harry says. He sure did seem to spend a great deal more time thinking about things lately.

"Oh, well umm, I was just thinking 'bout this woman I spent some time with down in Miami... Molly. She really loved places like this, introduced me to that avocado mix and this sweet caramel coffee drink." Jake lets a small smile slip, "Which I will deny completely if you decide to mention it old man..."

Harry playfully puts his hands up laughing... "Who me? Jake you're kidding yourself if you think we don't already know about your Starbucks habit."

Jake laughed along with him, "Yeah, I guess it's kinda tough to keep a secret round here with you two always pokin' into a man's business." Turning serious again, "I really did care for her Harry, she was... is a good woman and I pretty much shit all over her. I picked up that morning, left her sleeping in the bed and headed out didn't say a word, didn't call her, nuthin'." Shaking his head, "for sure not proud of that moment. Got drunk up near Tampa that afternoon and didn't even make it out of Florida the first day. Hell, I'm not even sure why I came that way instead of takin' ninety-five straight up. Picked Maria up," nodding back toward where she was standing "Maybe that's why, I don't know. She was just walkin' down the road. Shit, it was like I had no choice Harry, before I knew what I was doing I had pulled over and she is leaning in the window." Looking around Jake pulls his chair in closer to Harry, "She looked right at me Harry and like she had known me my whole life and says, Jake? Like she was surprised to see me there, but not really if you know what I mean... Scared the shit out of me and next thing I know we're riding down the road. That missing time thing with her really weirds me out sometimes."

Harry nods, "I know Jake, I struggle with it too, just can't seem to figure it out. I don't mention it to her, I think she already knows, but as strong as she is she's still a young girl and I worry about the toll this all going to take on her. It's one of the reasons I wanted you to take her to see Larry, maybe there are folks up there that understand this, can give her some answers, cause Jake sooner or later she is going to want to know why she dreams like she does."

Leaning in again Jake whispers, "did she tell you about the young fella in the diner when we stopped for somethin' to eat?" Shaking his head, "Harry that was deep heavy shit, I'm telling you she looked right at him and knew he was minutes away from dying in his pretty little BMW. Never said a word to him though, just looked right at him and that was it..." With a worried look Jake asks, "you think something is going to happen to her Harry? Like something bad?"

"No Jake, that's not what I am saying, but it doesn't seem likely her only purpose is to help you and save me now does it?"

"No, I guess not Harry, honestly I don't even know what to think about this stuff... God, I love these chips," as he dips another in the diminishing bowl of fresh salsa. "Harry what should I do about Molly? I think about her all the time, but what could I ever say to her that would make up for leavin' like that?"

"I don't know son, I think the first thing you

need to focus on is making sure you have yourself figured out and straight. Wouldn't be fair to this girl or any other for that matter if you weren't really ready to make some changes in your life. Jake, I've known ya since you were a boy, watched ya grow up. Wasn't any of my business how your pa raised ya, a man's children are his own business, but I watched you drift into his habits and ways early on." Patting Jake on the arm, "I know in many ways you were just living the example your father gave you, but I also think there comes a time in a man's life when he has to decide who he is going to be and what he stands for. Listen, not everyone gets it or can make the choice, I knew your pa for his entire adult life and he had a chance back on that night out at the old plantation to come to terms with his life but he didn't do it and he died bitter and full of hate because of it. So now thirty years later here we are and you're getting the same chance, only question is what are you going to do with it?"

"Harry, when I was six years old I watched my dad and a bunch of his buddies lynch a n... a black man up in those pine woods south of the Stewart farm, you know the place I'm talkin' about?" Harry nods, "Well I promised myself I would never be like that, but I ended up the same way didn't I?" Harry starts to object, "It's okay Harry I know I did, believe me if there is anything I've learned over the past few months its people are really good at hurting each other." Shaking his head, "I don't know how to change, but dammit Harry I know I need to..."

Chapter 59

Nothing had been resolved that night over salty tortilla chips and tangy guacamole, but Jake had agreed to take Maria with him to see Larry Johnson and face the man his father had left screaming in the woods outside an old plantation thirty years ago.

The summer was starting to wane, the shadows lengthening in the late afternoon light, and the hint of cool on the evening air were the first signs change was afoot. In the fields the last of the summer hay was being cut and the silky tops of the corn stalks were beginning to brown. The golden glow of late summer lay across the upstate, hiding in the valleys and glens, burnishing the peaches to a deep red and orange all the while holding onto the last vestiges of summer knowing it was just a matter of time before the cooling rains and fall temperatures would usher in autumn with its chilly nights and frantic splashes of color.

It was the last weekend in August and Jake was busy finishing a number of the summer projects he and the Sanders boys had been working on. There was the decking to complete on the Brown place on Main

Street, the bathroom tile at old Mr. Nelsons, and the basement playroom for the Tanger kid's out by Harry's house. It had been a good summer and he was already lining up his fall projects and it looked he would have plenty of work to keep him busy through till winter. Jake didn't want to leave for Pennsylvania without having everything wrapped up. No point in taking a risk of not getting back on time and leaving one of his new customers waiting. This conscientious Jake was unfamiliar to him and when he took the time to think about it was good for a shake of the head and an inner chuckle. There were times he didn't believe this was really happening and he was actually saying the things he heard himself say.

Maria had spent most of the past two weeks with Harry, she was worried about leaving him and if she was honest about it she was a little scared. Not sure what she would find or what may lie ahead for her was creating some real anxiety. She was sitting on the back porch with Harry as the Saturday afternoon sun began its slow descent, they had been sipping ice tea and talking about this and that.

Harry slows his rocker, "Maria, honey all will be well my dear..."

She gives him a quizzical look, "What are you talking about Harry?"

"Dear, you know exactly what I am talking about, you've been skittish all week, a bundle of nerves. It's okay to be nervous about this trip, I would be too, but I think this will finally give you some answers and maybe help you decide what you want to do..."

"What I want to do?"

"Maria we both know there are no answers for you here, and as much as I appreciate you taking care of me this is no life for a young woman and we both know it. I know you don't mind but there is so much more for you in this life."

"But Harry I love it here, and I love taking care of you... you and Jake are like family to me now, I can't explain it, but I don't want to be anywhere else."

Sighing Harry says, "I know, I know, and I am not saying you need to leave, but you have a gift, it may not seem like it sometimes, but it is a gift nonetheless. Only question left is what are you going to do with it? You can stay here forever, Lord knows I enjoy the company, but we both know sooner or later everyone's destiny catches up with them like it or not."

"Harry I don't know anything about destiny or even what that really means, I just know I left the only family I ever knew not knowing what was going to happen and then I found you and Jake. I don't really understand how or why, but I know I don't want to be alone again."

"I understand dear, I just don't want you to have regrets, to wish you had asked more questions, and honestly I am beginning to think gifts like yours aren't lightly set aside. I'm not trying to scare you, I just want you to go with an open mind and not worry about anything just do what's right for you."

Patting his arm, "I will Harry, I promise..."

Harry didn't believe her for a second but he let it go having already learned his powers of persuasion were wasted on this one.

Chapter 60

Larry had turned eighty-four that spring, but continued to maintain his daily routine with the vigor of a much younger man. He slowly rolled his mat, precision and a meditative silence the trademark of his morning yoga session. With a deep exhalation he rises beginning the seventeen-step journey to his room and the hot shower that signals the formal start of his day.

"Sir, sir, sir..."

Larry hadn't heard the young man approach, "Yes...?"

"Your breakfast sir, should I set it on the table for you?"

"Yes, yes of course, thank you..." He hadn't been this distracted in years he was going to have to take some meditation in the garden later. He gently stirs a teaspoon of honey into his ginseng tea, everything he consumes is either grown or cultivated here at the institute, his yogurt is dotted with raspberries and blackberries from the patches on the north side of the property and the warm zucchini bread had probably been in the oven less than fifteen minutes earlier, a small cup of bright yellow hand churned butter next to it. Larry no longer found any of this amazing, he had been here long enough, but he did find his appreciation for these simple delicacies grew with each passing year. The son of Randy Delhomme, he knew instinctively was the source of his distraction, he had long ago dealt with the vagaries of his past and the specter of his heritage no longer plagued him. The truth is he had been isolated from it, but that didn't mean he had forgotten or that the memory was any less sharp. No Larry Johnson would never forget where he had escaped from, it was one of the cornerstones of moving forward, acknowledgement of your true self required you to face the hard realities of our subconscious personality before learning to no longer be enslaved by it. It had taken him years of constant study and work on himself but he had reached levels he had never thought possible or had even knew existed for that matter. Admittedly the visit from the old attorney had caught him off guard even with Janice's forewarning. That was something so not easily accomplished these days, but it hadn't taken long to come to the realization that possibly this was his last task... for it is one thing to achieve a higher level of consciousness yourself, but an altogether different thing to lead another there. He smiled to himself, well, no better test than the seed of the most incorrigible and wayward bastard he had ever personally met, it was poetic he thought to himself.

There was the girl as well, he had decided her special gifts were clearly outside his experience. He was going to have her meet with Janice Springerhausen who had been doing some amazing work with higher energies and people with the "sight". It was definitely the early stage, but there seemed to be a rapid influx of information and people experiencing these types of gifts. Janice and her team were trying to determine if this was a new phenomenon or if they were just starting to tap into a previously unknown or undiscovered set of energies. He had only kept up with the periphery of it, but had met with Janice a few times mostly to satisfy his curiosity, but also he had never forgotten that night they had been waiting for him, they had known he was coming.

Ms. Sally had the gift, he was sure of it. They had never discussed it, once he had agreed to come to the school it really hadn't been relevant, but she always seemed to know things well before other people. Maybe it was just her elevated state of consciousness, he had never met anyone like her and he missed her dearly since her passing a decade ago.

She had personally worked with him and had never, not once, said anything even remotely unkind, and if anyone had earned it he had. He hadn't thought about her like this in a long time, it was turning into a strange day.

Those early years had been difficult, he had agreed to the program, but he had no intention of making it work especially since they had left him little choice but to go. He had reflected on it more than a few times over the years and truth was he probably could have just said no and that would have been the end of it. He had been scared though and everything had seemed so official he hadn't thought to chance it. His cowardice had saved him, in the end he had stayed. Even more than that he had been so overwhelmed he found himself wanting what these people had, wanting something real in his life, a meaning for being here. He had finally reached the point of asking that inevitable question driving all men whether they acknowledge it or not: *why are we here and what's it all about?*

Chapter 61

Larry picked through the salad looking for something, anything that looked halfway appetizing, Jesus, what he wouldn't do for a fucking Big Mac, fries and a couple of cold Budweisers, this healthy food was coming as a bit of an adjustment. It had been six weeks and four days since that fucker Randy had left him in the woods outside the plantation and he was gonna seriously kick his ass if he ever got out of here. He still hadn't figured out how they had known he was coming and no one seemed interested in explaining it either. Looking around again he just couldn't wrap his head around why all these young people would voluntarily come here and live like this. They were mostly in their early twenties and seemed to be from pretty well off, mostly northern families. Hell he was fuckin' ancient compared to these kids, probably as old as their parents and proud to be a redneck on top of that. They couldn't work for shit though that was for sure. He ran circles around them and most acted like they had never seen a hammer before.

Most days started out the same, community

breakfast in the main building, it looked like they had renovated the kitchen and dining area first and that made sense to Larry if you were going to have a bunch of people working you had to be able to feed them. Lots of eggs, oatmeal and bacon, no grits or sausage gravy anywhere to be found, never mind a biscuit, definitely no southern influence in this kitchen. Every breakfast ended the same way, a short "meeting" with Ms. Sally or the "teacher" as these kids called her. He couldn't follow most of it; she would give out the work assignments and then spend another fifteen minutes babbling on about working on one's self and making observations. It was some pretty weird shit he thought.

Dinner was when they took odd to a whole new level though, not that the food wasn't good, truth was whoever was in charge of the kitchen really did know how to cook. Plenty of things he had never tasted or even considered tasting before, but admittedly he hadn't found anything he didn't like. Curries, stews, leg of lamb, and honey wheat bread that was dense and chewy but delicious with slabs of butter spread on it. Two or three times a week they would have what Ms. Sally called ambrosia, he could not get enough of it, a mixture of sour cream, honey, nuts and fruit, it was cool, refreshing, sweet, crunchy and tangy, all rolled together. He had never tasted anything quite like it before. There was always a group of four or five that were assigned cleanup duty, but everyone else would form a semicircle around Ms. Sally and they would have these meetings that would seemingly last hours. The first couple of weeks he had tried to sneak out, but there was always someone appearing at his elbow asking if he needed something, "yeah, I need to get the fuck out of here," was his typical response. His rebellion had only lasted about two weeks before Ms. Sally had sought him out and asked him to make an effort to stay for the meetings, explaining he didn't have to participate but it would be important to for him to stay. She had some weird power over him cause he hadn't been able to say no to anything she asked. He would never admit it but she also scared the shit out of him.

She is gentle and soft spoken, never seeming to raise her voice or get agitated, but there is some kind of unspoken power or strength seeming to emanate from her being that is honestly just unnerving and it's this odd sensation that fills your being and you find yourself saying things you would never tell anyone. It was like somehow she could read your darkest fears and secrets. He had his first experience with this just a week ago at the Thursday evening meeting, he had been drifting off leaning against the back wall as he usually did. Staying but not participating when he noticed the silence. That sensation you get when everyone has stopped talking and is waiting for something, but you have been off somewhere else and are late getting back. It was akin to daydreaming in class, and then being called on by the teacher for an answer, but much more intense and unnerving. He instinctively knew he was on the spot, but had no clue why.

She had saved him of course that night and many more times since, "Larry... Larry tell me about your day today, you were framing out the pottery studio weren't you?"

"Um, yeah, why..." Ms. Sally looked at him and he felt like she was looking right inside him seeing his thoughts... "I uh, uh, mean yes ma'am, I spent most of the day framing out the studio."

Softly she says, "so Larry tell me about your day framing, start at the beginning and tell me everything about it..."

"Well, um, okay, I started after breakfast, I was about five minutes behind the others, but it's because I like to check my tools and supplies over before I get started for the day, always saves me a trip or two back up to the tool shed. Anyway, I wanted to grab that big square you have in there. I figured we would get as far as the windows today so we were going to need it, that and some more nails." Nodding in the group's general direction, "these kids ended up making three trips up and down yesterday, waste of time, get what ya need the first time... umm, no offense but..."

She just smiled at him and said, "it's fine, no one's offended here, go on..."

"Well okay, but I didn't mean nuthin by it... so first thing I always like to do is sharpen up my pencil, you need a good straight line, mark it twice, cut it once I like to say." Hesitating a moment he asks, "Why do you want to know all this anyway?"

Sally doesn't answer him, "John, what did you do today?" she asks a young man in the front row.

John, a twenty three year old philosophy student from upstate New York hasn't been here much longer than Larry. He knows the lingo though and launches right in, "our task for today was to make an effort to be aware of our surroundings, with particular attention to the people we were working with. I was working with Larry there and Mark and I believe Tom was helping for a while as well. We framed out the walls and Larry showed us how to cut the windows in and frame them out."

"So what did you observe?" Sally asks pointedly.

John hangs his head, "I don't know, I worked with Tom and Mark most of the day..."

"So Larry what did you observe today," she asks turning back to him.

Larry hesitates for a moment looking for the trap but not seeing any way not to answer her so figuring what the hell he goes for it. "Honestly I don't understand this whole observe thing you people are talkin' bout, but like I was tellin ya earlier we got as far as framin' out the windows today. Now I don't mean to be talkin out of school on nobody, but John here can't seem to remember from one day to the next how to drive a nail properly. I've showed him half dozen times but it don't seem to be stickin. Mark over there, he can drive the hell out of a nail, but seems to me he is mighty angry about something cause even after that nail is in he pounds it a couple more times just for good measure, just seems to be something angry about it though. So I guess that leaves my boy Tom," he gestures in front of him, "I like ol Tom here, he is always willin' to help out, gives me a hand whenever I need it, but I'm on to him..." With a sly grin, "yeah Tom here thinks nobody notices him slippin' out to catch a smoke three or four times a day, and I can tell ya those aren't Marlboros he's smoking either..." faltering he comes to a stop realizing he has been rambling on comfortable as can be.

"So Larry, tell me did you observe anything about yourself today..." the question hangs in the air as Larry looks around knowing he has probably crossed some line with these people.

"Well now let think on that for a sec... I guess if I had to come up with something I'd say that uh I, and I didn't 'spect this, fact couldn't help myself... but I kinda wanted to teach these young fellas how to properly frame up the building. You know kinda hopin' they would ask questions so I could show em how to do it right. My boy Mark there could be a good carpenter with a little work... So I guess I was wantin' to show that I knew something that was uhhh, valuable..."

"Why do you think that was Larry?"

"Well ummm, these kids are bright, anyone can see that, but they don't know real stuff and well," pausing for a moment Larry hesitates, "I guess the truth is I was feelin' not quite as smart as they are and I just wanted them to see I uh, I knew things that were important too..." He hangs his head tears welling up in his eyes he starts to get up, "fuck this I'm outa here..."

"Larry you saw more today than any of these young students..." her voice touches him inside somewhere and he sits the tears unbidden streaming down his cheeks, he looks up and sees her smile and he wants nothing more than to sit here and learn whatever it is she is willing teach him.

"Larry, I want you to think about the difference in what it meant to observe the three young men you worked with and then to observe something about yourself... that's the real work. What you will come to understand is the difference between your 'essence' and your 'personality'. Simply put your essence is who you are, it's what you are born with, it's our being if you will, you don't have the power to pollute or sully it, however your personality is that which you acquire through observation, experience, teaching and your environment. It is the summation of those influences you experience from early on through your adult life, unfortunately most people never truly examine this for what it is and in that state the 'personality' dominates one's 'essence'. What I want you to learn is to see past that, see who you truly are, who you are capable of being and do the work necessary to shred the prison of personality..."

Larry didn't honestly understand any of this personality or essence talk, but that night was the beginning of a long journey to self-awareness.

Chapter 62

They had stopped just South of Harrisburg at the Enola exit off Interstate 81 pulling into the Quality Inn parking lot. Jake shuts the truck off and stretches, working the kinks out of his neck and back, "hey Maria we're here, wake up kiddo," he says shaking her shoulder. "Alright, sit tight I'll get us a couple of rooms, be right back..."

Jake hops out and heads into the lobby as Maria rubs the sleep out of her eyes and sits up looking around, she can see the late summer moon reflecting off the river across the highway as the lonesome whistle of a locomotive drifts up from the rail yard further down the river banks. It all seems strangely familiar to her, not in the same sense as her dreams, but in the way most of us feel a sense of déjà vu every now and again. She didn't remember falling asleep, but it had been long enough for a bit of crustiness to form around the corners of her mouth, *Oh God*, she thinks, *I was probably snoring my head off.* Maria was wise beyond her years, and had experiences most people never imagine but she was also eighteen and suffering with all the self-imposed societal expectations young people tended to place on themselves.

The Summerdale Diner shared a parking lot with the Quality Inn and was already filling up at 6AM as Jake and Maria take a booth off to the side, Jake preferred to sit at the counter, but the locals weren't making room for anyone new this morning. It was a classic setup: dining rooms on the right and left, counter and kitchen in the center and a dessert case with the requisite meringue topped pies and cheesecakes daring you not to have a piece. Maria stuck with her standard order of French toast while Jake almost gave into the scrapple and eggs, well that was until the waitress explained scrapple to him, turns out Jake wasn't all that adventurous when it came to breakfast meats.

Jake felt right at home here, the steady traffic of Pennsylvania blue collar workers grabbing coffee and a breakfast sandwich before heading back out to their work trucks. Across the river the sun glinted off the dome of the capitol building, most people thought Philadelphia was the capitol, not the small city of Harrisburg on the banks of the Susquehanna River, a fact that escaped Jake this morning as well.

They were headed up Interstate 81 to

Carbondale, a once thriving coal town that had seen its heyday in the '30s. There were only a little over eight thousand folks living there now. They would pick up PA 6 for the quick twenty minute drive into Honesdale, the small Pocono town just minutes from the Institute and Jake's date with both his past and maybe just maybe the possibility of a distinctly different future. The miles spin quickly by, both of them caught up in their thoughts and fears, an anxiousness in the pit of their stomachs, both sharing the feeling but unable to talk about it. As Route 6 dumped them onto Main Street Jake felt himself take a deep breath as if he had been holding it for the past three hours. Sitting there at the light Maria points across the intersection to Days Bakery "let's get one of those donuts Harry was all excited about..."

"Yeah, good idea, I could use a coffee anyway," Jake mumbles ignoring the now cold three quarters full cup sitting in his cup holder. At this point any reason to delay the inevitable was good enough for him. Pulling over to the side of the street. They ease out and enter the bakery; it looks like a converted house more than a bakery, but the glass display cases are filled with every kind of pastry and donut you can imagine and the smell makes you smile without quite knowing why. "I'll take two of them; whatta ya call them, yeah 'nutty donuts' and a small black coffee." Turning to Maria, "you know what you want kiddo?"

"Sure I'll have two also and one of these orange juices," she says reaching into the drink cooler extracting a carton of Florida orange juice.

Eying the young woman behind the counter, "so you know anything 'bout this institute place up the road?" She gives him a look, like this might possibly be the dumbest question anyone has ever bothered to ask. "Geez, never mind, I was just curious," he mumbles as he turns to leave.

"Sir, there isn't anything I can tell you that won't learn for yourself soon enough..."

Back in the truck, "Ok, that freaked me out a bit... how bout you?" Jake says taking another bite of donut and a sip of the steaming hot coffee.

Maria ignores the bait while munching down on her donut, "ummm, these are even better than Harry said, I could eat these till I was sick." This is a common game with Jake by now: ask a question about something he wants to talk about with no real interest in your answer. Marie isn't playing along today though. Nothing really "freaks" her out since she started having the dreams.

Jake drops the truck into drive, "well, nothing left but gettin' it done I guess."

Chapter 63

Man has an overwhelming tendency to believe he controls his environment, controls what happens to him, controls his reactions, his decisions, and at his most delusional that he can control others. Jake would be indulging in all of these today.

Jake and Maria share a look as he parks the truck in the main parking lot, "Geeezus, this place is fuckin' huge," Jake mutters mostly to himself. Turning to the girl Jake asks, "You ready to do this?" Maria just nods, no words escape her half open mouth as she peers out the truck window.

She feels nervous, excited, and a bit scared all at once, Jake's palms are sweating and he is on the verge of hyperventilating. He couldn't tell you why, just an overwhelming feeling that everything is closing in on him. Standing in the parking lot the morning sun is beginning to heat the day, it feels good on their faces, even while a cool breeze passes through the trees caressing them on its way by. Slowly their senses tune in and they can smell the fresh cut grass, there is the soft murmur of voices and gentle laughter somewhere just beyond their sight. Jake turns and watches the sun glint off the traffic winding through the gentle curves across the valley. There is a peacefulness that engulfs them, similar to the feeling of coming home after a long journey, gone is the anxiety, the fear, the tension and Maria turns with a childlike smile and softly says, "let's go Jake, we are finally here."

Jake would have trouble relating with any real precision the specifics of that morning, but he knew unequivocally that he would never be the same again. Much like Harry they were greeted by a well-mannered if somewhat solemn young man who ushered them down a hallway lined with portraits to a sitting or maybe reading room, Jake wasn't really sure. Fresh brewed coffee, baked zucchini bread and butter were laid out on the side table. Jake had just slathered up a piece with the creamy butter when the door opened revealing a fit older man dressed comfortably in linen drawstring pants and a short sleeve matching shirt. He was mostly balding and you could sense more than see the age in him. "Jake, Maria, I am really delighted you accepted my invitation."

"I can't believe it, Larry fuckin' Johnson," Jake murmurs to himself.

"Believe it Jake, I am no longer the man you remember, but I assure you I am the Larry Johnson that was a good friend of your father's." Turning to Maria and taking her hand, "Young lady, I am very happy you agreed to join us, I have some people I am going to introduce you too that I believe may be able to answer some of your questions." Turning back to Jake still holding Maria's hand, "let's take a walk and I will give you some background on the school and answer any general questions you have. Jake, I have set the afternoon aside for you to spend some individual time together, does that sound okay to both of you?"

Jake can't speak, he can barely believe this is the same man his father was such good friends with Maria answers for them both, "thank you Mr. Johnson, that would be wonderful."

"Oh young lady, please call me Larry..." he says taking her hand again and turning to Jake, "Are you ready Jake?"

Jake wasn't really ready for any of this, but all he could do was nod.

It had taken a little more than an hour to cover the grounds completely, Jake was amazed at not only the size of it, but you could really feel the peace and tranquility seemingly infused into the very buildings. Larry showed them the Pottery Studio, telling the story of his first days at the school and how Ms. Sally had initially taught him the basics of self-observation. The fields of vegetables and the small orchard of apple, pear, and plum trees fascinated Maria. Larry pointed out the row of bee hives flanking the fruit trees explaining to Maria how the bees were a vital part of the pollination process for the various crops. The school used each crop for the daily meals or canned the excess for later use. On the far side of the property was the working farm including the horse and dairy barns. The farm produced its own milk, cheese, butter, eggs, and even had a facility for butchering, smoking, and curing meat. Larry explained that they raised their own hogs, sheep, and beef cattle in small quantities sufficient to support the staff and students at the institute. Self-sufficiency had been a lesson learned many years earlier and was an important part of sustaining the "healthy" lifestyle that was an integral goal of the school.

They made their way back to the main building entering through the back doors of the kitchen. Larry explained they were equipped with a full commercial level kitchen capable of producing meals for up to five hundred at a time, although the full time staff and complement of students was substantially less. Back in the main building he points out a series of classrooms, conference rooms and offices, stopping next to one of these he lightly taps on the door, but it opens almost simultaneously.

Janice Springerhausen appears to be in her late thirties strikingly blond, wearing glasses and very pretty, but it's the intensity of her deep blue eyes that really captures one's attention. "Mr. Larry, always good to see you, is this the young lady you told me about," she asks turning toward Maria.

"Yes, this is Maria, I've just finished giving them the ten cent tour but I need some time with Jake here if you are ready for Ms. Maria?"

"Yes of course," with a smile "we have been expecting her."

"Well, I will leave you to it then, shall we Jake?" Larry asks turning towards Jake.

The tour complete and Maria meeting with Janice, Larry leads Jake down the hall and into a small library. The late morning sun filters through the tall windows creating long trails of shimmering light as microscopic particles ride on invisible waves of air the faint smell of furniture polish a blend of wax, lemon and pine mixes with the scent of the endless rows of leather bound books. You can sense the quiet and feel the stillness of the room, as if it has been empty for a long time, but not stale or dormant, just waiting alive but dozing in a quiet slumber waiting to reawaken when needed. On the far wall an ornate oil painting of a regal Arabian black stallion seems to stare down into the room. A tapestry of oriental rugs cover the floor and two comfortably worn leather chairs face the windows bounding a rugged hand carved coffee table between them. A crystal decanter of ice water just starting to condensate and a small plate of shortbread cookies stands at the ready. "Please Jake," Larry motions to the chair on the right, "sit, let's and talk a bit..."

Chapter 64

It had taken five years to accomplish the initial build out of the school and its accompanying buildings, the stables had been added two years later, but by 1990 the work was complete. Those seven plus years had seemed to pass quickly for Larry, that first Thursday night breakthrough had been a true watershed moment for him opening a thirst he hadn't known existed.

Let there be no mistake Larry's evolution was not a miracle healing or anything of the kind, but a dam had been broken inside him that evening and he had opened himself to the possibility of change. Ms. Sally had brought him along slowly knowing trust would need to be established first, it wasn't possible or probable to erase fifty years of conditioning in mere moments. The seeds had been planted and the desire was evident even if not entirely understood. She had added a one on one session twice a week to the evening meetings for Larry and assigned him some very basic reading on the human condition. Larry needed to establish a basic understanding from which to work from, that was his major disadvantage to the young people around him. Ultimately it would turn out to be his major strength and advantage and would have Ms. Sally evaluating the school's overall approach. Sure, these young students came in with an understanding of philosophy, most of them transitioning or matriculating out of university philosophy departments, but in many respects that was part of the challenge of reaching them. They had no real experience, no life lessons learned, no exposure to the human condition beyond their sheltered existence in whatever suburb their parents had settled in, they hadn't tasted enough personal tragedy. So there was an arrogance and sense of self-entitlement permeating their efforts to work on themselves. Larry had no such preconceived notions, no, his issues were born of a life of societal conditioning, lack of education, culture, and example. Certainly not easily overcome but not punctuated by an arrogance preventing him from hearing what the teacher was saying either.

He had continued to share on a limited level during the evening meetings and early on had admitted to Ms. Sally that reading had not always been a strong point for him. She had set him up with one of her assistants who had been a teacher in a previous life, they had worked every evening before dinner on improving Larry's basic reading skills. Over the course of many months he had progressed to the point where he could handle the basic texts Ms. Sally was giving him to read. He had also taken charge of his own building crew with Mark as his assistant, the young man had the makings of a good carpenter and Larry was enjoying teaching him the craft.

During these years the prescribed timeline for Larry's "probationary" period under the authority of the Governor had expired. He clearly remembered the day Ms. Sally had called for him to meet with her after the breakfast tasks had been assigned. It had been late May 1987 and they had been working on the first of the barn foundations, he had made sure Mark was clear on what needed to be accomplished before washing up and heading toward the main building.

Larry nervously reviewed the past few days hoping some mistake had not generated this meeting request. He felt secure his work group was progressing on all their tasks properly, but that feeling of getting called to the principal's office was not easily discarded. He knocked softly on the office door almost hoping there wouldn't be an answer. Larry had made a great deal of progress over the course of six years, but somehow he sensed this meeting was different.

"Come in Larry it's open..."

Suppressing a smile, she always seemed to know when it was him. "Good morning Ms. Sally, you wanted to see me?"

"Yes Larry, have a seat, I need to review some paperwork with you and then we can discuss how you want to proceed."

"Uh umm, what's this about? What kind of paperwork?" Larry asked, trying to suppress a rising sense of panic.

Ms. Sally looks up at him, "Larry, you have completed your prescribed time here, you are free to do whatever you like, even go home if you want to."

"Oh..." the word hangs in the air, "do I have to?" He can feel himself tearing up, "I mean, do I have to leave, I don't want to leave, please, please don't make me leave..."

"Oh Larry I am sorry, of course you don't have to leave, but now you will be here because you have chosen to be here, of your own free will and volition." She smiles at him and pats his hand across the wooden desk. "Do you need some time to think about things?"

"Ms. Sally, I made my choice the first Thursday night you made me speak, I won't leave here unless you make me," and the tears come unbidden, but with a smile this time.

Chapter 65

Maria spent the morning with Janet and her staff. Janet had explained that to start they just wanted Maria to tell them her story in her own words, don't worry about the dreams in particular, we want to know about you, where you come from, what your family is like, how you grew up, tell us the story of Maria she had said. Maria had been a little unnerved wondering why they didn't want to just talk about her dreams.

Janet explained that the "sight" as they were calling it, had a scientific name for the phenomenon, but they had all agreed the sight was just easier than precognitive somnum-oculis. Some brilliant researcher had decided to invoke the Latin terms for "sleep sight" and it had stuck. Anyway, they were looking for markers or common experiences in each person's history that might give them a clue to the sight's origins.

Maria led them through her life story as far back as she could remember. It was more difficult than she imagined and before long she experienced a deep aching sense of missing her family. It had probably been there all along but she had managed to bury it amongst the day-to-day demands of life with Jake and Harry. Recounting her story though, she knew she was going to have to find a way to contact her family, find a way to apologize and try to explain things to them. She had no illusions of that working but she would try anyway. As she recounts the details of leaving that night not so long ago and the dream of Jake she falters and pauses, looking up she mistakes the amazement in Janet's eyes for something else. "What, don't you believe me?"

"No, I believe you Maria, your story is simply amazing for someone so young." Janet sets down her notebook and pen spreading her hands out, "we have heard amazing stories of the sight, clairvoyance, even gypsy fortune tellers, but your life story with or without the dreams is pretty incredible young lady." Shaking her head, "we tend to be so focused on the analytical portion of what we are doing you lose sight of the real courage and tenacity life requires all by itself. Your story is a reminder of that, combined with this incredible gift you seem to have and well, it's a bit overwhelming even for us."

Maria hangs her head sucking her bottom lip in and twisting her fingers together, "but, but can you help me Ms. Janet?" Looking up, "I don't know if I want to have this sight, these dreams, I don't know, it's just that, well sometimes they scare me. I don't want to be responsible for what happens to people..."

Janet nods, "I understand dear, I really do, but no one can take this from you. I can tell you this: you are not responsible for the people in your dreams. In fact let's take a quick lunch break and after we can talk about your dreams and I think you will see that the ability to change events wasn't within your power."

Maria nods her head, "ok if you say so..." not quite believing her. Then, as if remembering something, "can you help me track down my parents, I really need to tell them I am ok."

"Sure we can," turning to one of the young men that had been operating the recording equipment, "Matt, see what we can do to track down Maria's parents." Checking her notes she relates their names and last known address as well phone numbers, turning back to Maria, "Matt is pretty amazing at finding people, even people that don't want to be found, so let's get some lunch and see what he comes up with."

Chapter 66

Jake had settled down considerably by the time he and Larry had made it to the small library and the invitation to talk was hardly necessary, he had questions that needed answering.

"Mr. Johnson, Larry, there are just some things I need to know, stuff I gotta ask you is that okay?"

"Sure Jake, I will try to answer your questions, but sometimes the answers aren't going to give you what you are looking for."

"Sir I don't know what that means in fact," waving his hands around, "I don't get most of this honestly but you are the only one who can answer some of these questions for me."

"That's fine Jake, but when we are finished the questions of the past are going to remain the past and we are going to discuss the future, where we go from here, how you in particular move forward."

"Okay, I get it everyone seems to think I have this big opportunity to change, to travel down some other path as Harry likes to put it, I don't know about that, maybe you can explain it, but right now I want to know two things in particular." Larry nods and motions for him to proceed. "Sir I know this is a long time ago and maybe not a fair question, but when I was six years old I was in that pine grove, I saw that ni... that black man on the rope and I am pretty sure my daddy lynched him, but I can't really ask him now can I? So I just need to know for absolute sure did, did my daddy lynch him..." it hangs in the air the silence taking on a thick quality and the sun seems to darken just a bit... "I have to know sir, I have to know for one hundred percent, am I the son of a murderer?" It's out and the tears follow he just can't help; this secret has haunted him for more than forty-five years.

"Jake, son I..." Larry fumbles for what to say and the tears well up in his chest choking him, "I am so sorry I had no idea you were there, your father never told me..."

"Did my dad kill him?!" Jake explodes all the years of hurt, loathing, and frustration coming out at once.

"Yes... yes, we did, I don't know if we meant to at first, but once we got started I don't think there was any changing that path. Your Dad and Sewie had the rope, but we all knew what was happening and none of us stopped it, I am as guilty as anyone." The words barely a whisper, "Jake, there isn't a day I don't meditate on my guilt, my weakness, the sins of my life, but Jake I am not that man anymore, I haven't been for a long time and I was saved from myself right here." Leaning forward, "Jake, you are not that man either, you don't have to pay for the sins of your father, you are accountable only for yourself."

"I know I really do, but I am the same, I have acted the same way, maybe I didn't lynch nobody but I spoke the hate, I treated 'em like niggers, didn't matter and if that wasn't enough I even treated that sweet girl Maria the same way and I know she didn't deserve it... God what is the matter with me?"

Larry stands up moving over to the window, his hands clasped behind him seemingly lost in thought, "Jake I can answer that for you, I can even show you a path to somewhere else, but first ask your last question, because there is nothing easy about changing oneself, there is no quick fix, and maybe more than anything it requires a degree of honesty most people are not comfortable with. So I'll answer your questions, but you are going to have to decide where to go from here..." Turning around and facing Jake, "so what else do you want to know?"

"I want to know what happened that night, the night you left, my Dad would never talk about it, he was never the same, I mean he was a miserable son of a bitch, but after that he mostly just kept to himself..." So Larry told him, told him about that night, about the deal he made to stay out of jail, how it ultimately probably saved his life, told him about those first days and weeks at the school. The meetings, the meals, the breakthroughs, even learning how to read, and most of all about Miss Sally, her wisdom, kindness, the ability to see through your bullshit, to point out the truth of something with just a few words, and maybe more than anything how she saved him over and over again...

Chapter 67

Maria sat with Janet and her team, but she was lost in her own thoughts only looking up occasionally, *was it really possible they could track her mom and dad down*? She picked at the salad and nibbled on the BLT crisp lettuce and juicy tomatoes stacked with thick bacon on what had to be freshly baked wheat bread, it tasted wonderful but she had no appetite for it. What could she possibly say to her mother that could explain all this, that would make leaving in the middle of the night all right? She hadn't considered before now how selfish it had really been and how distraught her parents would be, sure she left a note, but it had been the rambling platitudes of a teenage girl. She had done a lot of growing up in the months since leaving and there was still the issue of how to explain the dreams.

Janet patted her hand across the table, "Maria it will be okay, give your parents a chance to understand."

With tears in her eyes, "I know, but it was so selfish of me, how could I just leave like that?"

"Honey you did what you thought you had to, no

one can fault you for that, it was incredibly brave even if you think it was selfish. Remember your parents have shown the same bravery, they put everything on the line to bring your family here and make a better life for you, I think they will be much more understanding than you think."

"I hope so, but..." the resilient spirit of youth kicks in and she dries her eyes with her napkin and picks up the glass of hibiscus ice tea, its deep burgundy color punctuated with the bright yellow of a lemon wedge. It reminds her again of home and her mom making hibiscus sun tea on the tailgate of the family's pick up those sunny Saturdays at the fields. She smiles and nods to herself, *Janet was right her mom hadn't been much older than she was when she had made the trip to this country so she would understand.*

Janet breaks the spell, "why don't you finish up and we will go see if Matt has had any luck finding your parents."

"Any luck Matt?" Janet asks as they enter the conference room.

"Actually, yes not too hard at all, from what I can tell they are still living outside of Tampa, same address, same phone, and same jobs as far back as the last two years."

Janet turns to Maria, "do you want to call them now or wait till we finish up and have had a chance to talk about your dreams?"

"Oh, umm well, let's finish first then maybe I'll have a better idea how to explain all this to them, I am not sure they are going to understand..." Now that it was possible to talk to her parents Maria was hesitant, well, scared is probably closer to the truth. She wasn't sure her parents would understand and she was worried they wouldn't respect her decision to leave. There was a great deal more wrapped up in this conversation than a simple "hi mom I'm okay, don't worry about me..." No there was still a cultural expectation that as a young Mexican woman she would defer to her father's leadership of the family and do what she was told. That had never really been how she viewed things, having grown up torn between two cultures she had forged her own identity and although she tried to keep the peace with her dad more often than not he would end their conversations with some variation of "ni~a dificil" or "cabeza dura." She didn't mean to be difficult, but she just didn't see why she needed to conform to the rules of some country she had never even seen. Of course it hadn't occurred to her that basic respect for her father should have been enough, typical teenager.

With the digital recorder back on Janet walked Maria through each of her dreams concentrating on the specifics of each dream's composition, the timing in relation to the actual events, and whether there had been any deviation from the dream even if just something small. Maria mentioned that she had five dreams: the very first one with Jake, the second with the Pickering boy, the third with Harry coming by the house, the fourth their trip here, and her most recent one that she had not shared with anyone. This dream had just come in the past week and she wasn't exactly sure if it fit, it had been shorter than the others and she had been unsure whether this was really the same type. She held back her dream about Harry's accident, not quite sure if she was ready to talk about that one since it was more of "message" from Harry than a dream and it scared her more than the others.

Janet looks up from her notebook, "tell me about this last dream, you say you have not shared it with Jake or anyone else?"

"No, I wasn't sure about it, seemed more broken up than the others and well Jake's been a bit worked up about this trip so I didn't want to take a chance on making things worse." Maria paused, "do you think we have, um, well, like an obligation to tell people about our dreams when they are in them?"

Janet sets her pen down and motions to Matt to turn off the recorder, "I am honestly not sure how to answer that, Maria your dreams are a bit different than those we have been studying, they are more personal and in the present if you will, does that makes any sense to you? Tell me about this last one and I will see if I can help you decide," motioning for Matt to turn the recorder on she picks up her pen and waits.

"Well, in my dream Jake is in Florida, I can tell its Florida from the palm trees and it just seems like it, but I don't recognize the area at all. I saw him driving and then sitting in his truck like he was waiting for someone. I couldn't see if there was anyone else there, but it didn't seem like it, just him by himself if that makes any sense. Then it flashed over to him in a room like this morning. It seemed like he was alone but I could only see him so it's hard to say. The dream ended with him playing with a little boy in the back yard of his house in South Carolina, I didn't recognize the little boy either so not sure if it's someone he knows or what. I didn't mention any of this to him cause it was so much more broken up than my other ones, but it feels the same if you know what I mean and I remember it very clearly just like my other ones. What do you think Ms. Janet, is this a real one?"

"I think so Maria, this is actually more in line with most of the people we have been working with, they have glimpses of events, your other dreams are actually fairly unusual since they are a complete sequence of events. Now whether you elect to tell Jake about it is up to you, normally we don't get involved in that decision, however I will tell you our default position is that it is usually better not to share. It's complicated but the simple explanation is how do you decide what should be and what should not be, it's impossible to know what impact foreknowledge of an event will have on someone." Janet twirls her pen thinking, "Our dilemma though is if we can prevent some type of catastrophe or criminal event is there an obligation to intercede? Our people spend a lot of time debating the pros and cons of these types of situations and there is no clear answer, in fact we don't even know if we would be able to affect an outcome or not. I'm sorry Maria, I just don't have a clear answer for you."

"I think I understand, I'll have to think about how or even whether to tell him..." biting her lip. "Miss Janet there's something else I need to tell you too..."

Chapter 68

Larry and Jake had taken lunch in the small
library opting to continue their conversation rather
than join the others in the dining room. Chunky
chicken salad sandwiches on the rich fresh baked
bread with a fresh fruit salad and the tangy hibiscus
tea had left Jake satisfied and raving to Larry about
how good everything was. He couldn't really describe
it, but everything just seemed so rich and vibrant,
exactly how you would imagine things were supposed to
taste. Larry smiled at him, he knew the feeling, the
food had always been excellent even in the early days
when they were just getting the farm up and running.

It was deep in the afternoon before Larry had
finished recounting the tale of his days here and the
journey of self-discovery he had undertaken. Jake
struggled to understand the concept of "work on
oneself" this journey of discovery Larry kept
referring to where a man stripped his conditioning
away examining every level and cause along the way
till he found his true essence, and what was essence
anyway? Larry had described it as your being, the
"you" that existed before the influences,

experiences, parental examples and education or lack of, created the personality that we filter everything through. Miss Sally had taught him that personality was the lens through which we interpreted our daily lives allowing that part of us to control our reactions, perceptions, and even decision making. Larry explained that once you began to recognize this for what it was you could step outside your personality and begin to make efforts and have experiences that were not polluted by this filter. Difficult concepts for Jake to grasp having no real background or time to digest any of this.

"It's getting late in the day Jake, I know this has been a great deal to try to absorb and honestly it took me many months to just grasp the very basics of some of these concepts. Let's call it a day and regroup in the morning, I think I can maybe provide some real life examples that will make this easier."

Jake gets up, stretching, "That would be great sir, I can't say I really understand any of this, but I'm already here so I'm game if you are."

"Thank you Jake, now let's go find Maria and see about making sure you are all set for dinner, there are some great little places to eat in town." Smiling, "sometimes a good greasy burger and fries with a cold one is still required!"

"Well I understand that anyway," laughs Jake, "although honestly I haven't had a drink in months and feel better than I have in a long time..."

"Good for you Jake, are you guys staying at the Hotel Wayne right on Main Street?"

"Actually we didn't make any arrangements, we drove up from Harrisburg this morning, stopped in at that bakery downtown for a coffee and came right up." Sheepishly, "I wasn't sure how this was going to go so I didn't bother settin' something up for the night."

Larry smiling, "skeptical were you, that's okay we have an arrangement with Hotel Wayne, its right on the corner across from Days Bakery, they have the best nutty donuts by the way."

Jake laughs, "Old man Harry warned us about them, but we picked a few up this morning just to make sure he was telling the truth!"

Larry smiles, "I enjoyed Harry, smart fella. Well, I'll have the rooms set up for you two. Grab some dinner first, I recommend O'Malley's right on Main Street, great burgers and Rueben sandwiches and the man knows how to make fries..." Larry didn't say so, but James O'Malley was a friend of the institute and didn't allow trouble of any kind in his place.

"Thank you sir, that sounds great, what time do

you want us to come back tomorrow?"

Larry pausing with his hand on the door, "Let's
check in with Janet and see how Miss Maria is doing
and then we can decide."

Chapter 69

As Larry and Jake walked down the hall they found Janet outside the conference room talking animatedly on her cell phone, holding up a finger she bids them wait just a moment.

"...I am telling you this is not the same thing," she pauses, "no, no, no, this girl is different, we are talking about a completely different set of skills..." holding up her finger again pursing her lips together... "Listen I'll email you the recordings and you can decide for yourself... ok... thanks, bye."

Before Larry can say anything Jake breaks in, "Is Maria okay, did something happen to her?"

"What? No, no, she is fine..." Janet looking at Jake a bit puzzled, "What would be wrong with her?"

"I don't know, it just sounded like something had happened..."

"No she is fine, in fact she is inside talking to her parents, I just haven't seen anyone with a well developed sense of precognition as her before..."

Jake a bit nervously asks, "Is that good?"

Janet smiles, "it's not good or bad Jake, it just is..." Looking at Larry, "Jake if you have time tomorrow after you and Larry finish up I would be happy to give you an overview of our work here, if you're interested?"

Smiling sheepishly, "Sure, I probably won't understand half of it, but that sounds great..."

While they are talking Maria steps out of the conference room, it's clear she has been crying, but is trying to pull herself together.

Jake turns to her, "are you okay?"

"Yeah I'm fine, I just hung up with my mom, that was way harder than I thought it would be..."

"Didn't go well..." he asks.

"Uhh no, it went fine, she was pretty calm actually," Maria smiles. "I kinda expected her to be a lot more upset, I mean she wants me to come home, but I'm not ready and she wasn't too happy about it..." Her smile fades, "my dad is pretty upset though, didn't want to talk to me yet..." and Jake can see the tears well up in her eyes again.

Jake puts his arm around her shoulder. "Well, what say we go get a burger or something and you can fill me in?"

They shake hands all around in the foyer, Jake and Maria head out to the parking lot while Larry and

Janet watch from the steps. It's obvious Maria is leading the conversation her hands moving the whole time while she talks. With a smile Janet turns to Larry, "that young lady is something special..."

Turning back inside Larry says, "let's grab a tea and you can bring me up to speed on your day."

"Sure let me stop by the conference room. I need to email those recordings to the folks in DC as they are skeptical to say the least, meet you in the study, say, ten minutes?"

"Sure, that works, this old man needs to make a pit stop anyway, I'll have the tea brought up, mint?"

"Perfect..."

When Janet entered the study the tea was steeping on the side bar and Larry was leafing through a half dozen books scattered in front of him on the coffee table.

"Planning some light reading?" Janet teased.

"No, I want to give Jake some basic reading, try to help him understand a little bit better..."

Janet sits down looking through the books, "good choices, these are all pretty straightforward texts..."

"I know I actually started on a couple of these myself," Larry smiles. Somewhat to himself, "I wonder if I was this difficult to get through to..." knowing he was and maybe even more so.

"So, challenging case?" Janet asks.

"I don't know actually, he is about the same age and from the same background as I was when I first got here, real difference is he is looking for something different in his life and I wasn't." Looking up, "so I am not really sure if it's difficult or just a question of finding the right way and person to feed him..." Setting the books down, "tell me how it went with the girl today..."

Janet gives him a brief background on Maria's history including the story of how her parents brought her to the United States as a baby. It's no less amazing the second time around. Janet explains their first impression had been that Maria had a very developed "sight" undisciplined in that she had not tried to use it consciously, but when the dreams came to her they were very specific and much more complete than most of the people already in the program.

"But Larry, that's not the half of it, this girl has another level altogether, I am not sure what to even call it..." Shaking her head Janet explains, "she has the ability see things in real time almost as if someone was sending her a video message. I've heard of this type of phenomenon before, but I haven't actually talked to anyone who has experienced it. Most of the folks in our field doubt the viability of the 'sight' never mind advanced psychic messaging. Although if you think about it, it almost makes more sense since it's a real time type of communication if you will, not some foretelling of something that hasn't happened yet."

Larry purses his lips thinking, "you think it's real or does she just have a good imagination? Sometimes the timing on these dreams is a little tricky, we know folks sometimes have subconsciously picked up news items, or conversations then infused them into their dreams not realizing those ideas were basically planted there. Any possibility that's what we are dealing with?"

Janet bites her lip for a moment, "no, and here is why not, you met with the old man Harry right?"

Larry nods, "I sure did, knew him from before, *a very intelligent person and as straight a shooter* as there ever was."

"Well you know after he left here he stopped late the next evening on his way back home, had a few drinks and just about died in a really horrific car accident. What you may not know is he hadn't told Jake or Maria what he found or that he was even headed home. She swears she woke up from a dead sleep with a clear picture of the old man drinking at the bar and then getting into the accident, even saw him slumped over the wheel. They went and found him, he would have died if they hadn't shown up, in fact he's still recuperating." She shakes her head, "I don't know Larry, I would need to talk to Mr. White and maybe Jake as well, but if she can really tune in things like this we are talking about something way beyond what we are doing here."

"Hmmm, that is something else, well, we can talk to Jake about it tomorrow, I am sure he would be willing to meet with you. I don't think Harry, you know, Mr. White can make a trip back up here, but we can put him on the phone in the conference room with the two of them and walk through that evening."

"Ok, that's perfect I really want to tie this down a little tighter, what do you think about Maria overall though?"

"Well, what do you mean what do I think, seems like a nice young lady, probably needs to go back to school, may even need to go back home... but you know that isn't up to us... I can see you're spinning something up what is it?"

Janet smiles, "am I that easy... I want to ask her to stay here and work with us, we have enough resources and teachers we could help her finish up school and maybe even do some virtual college course work if she wants. In return she can help us document and test what she is able to do."

Larry frowns, "look we are not going to make a guinea pig out of her, that's not what we do here..." he smiles though recognizing immediately the irony in that statement.

Drumming her fingers on the table Janet takes a sip of tea, "you think I don't know that." A bit too sharply perhaps, "I'm sorry Larry, I know I just don't want to miss an opportunity to work with someone so advanced."

"It's okay Janet, but keep in mind her sight might be advanced, but she is still just a young girl and not as advanced as she probably seems, I just want to make sure we remember our first priority has be what's best for her..."

Chapter 70

O'Malley's was all Larry had advertised, a clean and bright pub with a bustling James O'Malley directing traffic and the two waitresses from behind the bar. A big fella, James must have been at least six foot five, two hundred seventy five pounds, with a great red beard and an unquenchable smile. They had entered the "kingdom of O'Malley" where good cheer, good beer, great food, and real football reigned. Finding a booth against the back wall Jake and Maria took it all in before bending to their menus.

"So folks what can I get you tonight?" Karen shared the freckles and red hair leaving no doubt she was James' daughter. "We have a couple of specials not on the menu... but let's get you some drinks started first."

Maria orders her standard Diet Coke and Jake sticks with water.

"Any recommendations," Jake asks when Karen returns with the drinks.

"Sure, my Aunt Pat is the cook so everything is great, but we make our own corned beef so anything with that is terrific, the shepherd's pie is my Dad's favorite and we also have a great burger made with local beef on a fresh baked bun..." Flipping up her pad, "Let's see specials tonight are corned beef with cabbage and boiled potatoes and lamb stew with fresh baked soda bread. I'll give you a few minutes, anyone need a refill?" They both shake their heads, "ok back in a bit then..."

Jake studies the menu intently not making eye contact with Maria, not quite ready to talk about his meeting with Larry. "So what ya gettin' kiddo?"

"I'm going to have the stew special, my mom used to make lamb on the holidays sometimes, what's soda bread?"

"Hell if I know..." Jake says shaking his head, "I'm going to have the shepherd's pie that looks like it's got all good stuff in it." Karen approaches pad out but before she can say anything, "So what's soda bread anyway, you put cola in it?" Jake asks.

Karen smiles, "not quite, my grandmother makes ours. It's just baking soda, salt, flour and buttermilk, it's a traditional Irish bread. She makes it in this old cast iron pot, been in our family forever, everyone loves it, but when we run out that's it." Clicking her pen, "So what are you two having tonight?"

Maria answer first, "I am going to have the

lamb stew, my mom used to make lamb for us sometimes," it comes out more wistfully than she had planned.

Karen nods, "you'll love it, old family recipe, we get the lamb from the Institute when they have it available, it's slow cooked with vegetables and a Guinness base, let me know what you think." Turning to Jake, "and for you sir?"

"Well I was going to have the shepherd's pie, it sounds like it's full of the stuff I like, but what do you recommend?" he asks setting the menu down.

"Can't go wrong with shepherd's pie, we make it from scratch for each order but our corned beef special is really excellent too, up to you, like I said, can't go wrong either way."

"Oh man I hate choices like this, alright, alright... hmm, I'll do the corned beef, never really had that so I guess I'll give it a go."

Maria just shakes her head and gives Karen a look like, see what I have to deal with, Karen laughing "Ok, you won't be disappointed, I also have an order of homemade chips with Guinness gravy on the house coming for you..."

The chips are long gone and Jake has demolished a second helping of the soda bread with his dinner, there is only a small trace of the melted ice cream that had set astride the warm bread pudding left as any evidence it had been there at all. They have been heads down in conversation since placing their orders and Karen has left them to it interrupting only to refill their glasses.

They have been through it a dozen times. Maria is torn between staying at the institute, going back to Peakeville to take care of Harry or maybe most of all heading home to her family. Unfortunately Jake has little or no experience providing sage advice, his focus has always been himself and what he needs or wants in the moment. But he sees the combination of fear and confusion in Maria face and finds himself caring more than he thought possible.

"Maria why does it have to be one or the other? Why can't you go home patch it up with your parents, finish school if you want and then come back?" Jake finally asks trying to find some middle ground. "Look, you know I'll make sure Harry is okay and he has all them folks taking care of him, hell I'll hire someone to come take care of stuff during the day, not like he can't afford it..."

"Oh Jake I know you would take care of Harry, I don't know I guess I am scared if I go back that will be it, I'll be stuck there I am not sure I could leave again..." elbows on the table and chin in her hands she looks at him. "I mean what if my parents try to stop me, I can't run away again, that probably wasn't the right thing to do in the first place..." Jake starts to protest and she can see the hurt in his eyes. "Jake, look I have no regrets, that's not what I mean I wouldn't trade these last months for anything, you and Harry are like family, a weird family but still..." and she laughs a little.

"Alright, alright I get it, but listen if you want to come back here or Peakeville all you have to do is call and I will come get you, it's the least I can do and Harry would have my ass if I didn't anyway," he says smiling sheepishly. "What about these folks up here? They seemed pretty excited about you..."

"I don't know Jake, I mean they are real nice and all... but I gotta go home first then I can figure it out. I guess I didn't really know that till now." Maria purses her lips "you know they seemed really surprised when I told them about that night with Harry and the accident..." Leaning forward and lowering her voice, "Jake, it's just not as important to me as it is to them, I mean I thought it was, but when I heard my mom's voice well I knew I had to go home... does that make any sense?"

Jake tries to sound convincing, "I'm sure there is an explanation for all this, I wouldn't worry about it, you gotta do what's right for you..." Jake knows that's not quite true, nothing he can think of will ever explain that first day on the road, or the young kid in the BMW, but he cares enough at this point not to make things any harder for her.

Most of the folks have drifted out of the pub by this time except for a few old timers on their favorite stools trading laughs with James as he polishes the bar and places the clean glasses back in their perfect lines on the shelves behind him. Karen stops by one last time to check on them as they prepare to leave. She wonders briefly what their story is, *an odd couple to say the least* she muses, but Pat calls her from the back and she turns before the thought goes any further. Funny, you know the strange, funny, how people pass in and out of each other's lives for brief moments of time with a warmth and shared intimacy that is as genuine as it is temporary and so easily forgotten.

Chapter 71

Jake had managed to avoid having an extended conversation about his time with Larry. Maria was sharp enough to see he didn't want to talk about it and she hadn't pressed the issue, being caught up in her own thoughts and worries about what was to come.

Although more nutty donuts were on the schedule, they walk the few blocks down Main Street to the Honesdale Diner for some breakfast and coffee first. Both were up early not having been able to more than toss and turn the night through. The diner was a gleaming chrome classic diner with an added dining room to expand capacity. The menu reminded Jake of McElroy's with its hearty omelets, real home fries, and eggs any way you could imagine them... well minus the biscuits anyway.

Over a perfectly prepared western omelet with rye toast and home fries Jake starts to update Maria on his conversation with Larry. He didn't want to get into any of the real details, especially Larry's confirmation that his father had lynched a man those many years ago. In fact Jake realized it probably hadn't been just that one occasion, he had opted not to press Larry, more because he just didn't want to know than any concern for the old man. The story of Larry's transformation however was pretty amazing and Jake had a hard time believing that he had: one, decided to stay up here and two, how different he seemed. Sure, some of the southern accent or phrases would creep in here and there and his laugh was the same as Jake remembered, but there was a peaceful, kind, and caring spirit where none had existed before. Jake remembered a hard drinking, womanizing, rattlesnake mean son of a bitch and clearly that person was no more.

He tried to explain it to Maria but the words tumbled out on top of each other not really capturing what he wanted to say. You really couldn't grasp it if you didn't have an understanding of where the man had come from, Harry would know what he meant having seen it himself and having known Larry all those years ago. More than anything though he was struggling with the underlying thread of what did all this mean to him, why did it feel so important but seem so unclear? He just wasn't able to picture himself walking away from his life and spending the rest of his days in a place like this and he was pretty sure if Larry Johnson hadn't been forced to he wouldn't have either. He wasn't even sure what the old fella expected out of this visit. They hadn't really talked about that, about the future, or even about Jake for that matter.

The resentment, anger, and stubbornness that had plagued Jake his whole life hadn't gone away, it wasn't repaired or dealt with, but he was seeing glimpses of another life, another pathway, an improved version of himself if you will. It was this glimmer that held him back, that had him willing to sit in this diner with Maria. It would lead him back up the hill to Larry Johnson to see what there might be in his own future. It didn't occur to him but he was shedding the victim consciousness he had been bathed in as a child. That belief that everyone was out to get you, that things would never go your way, that more times than not fate was conspiring against you. It was in these shadows the demons of prejudice, hate, mean spiritedness and addiction grew so powerful. Jake had managed to look up somehow in the past few months and see the sun shining on just the other side of that door. It was just a question now if he could make the journey through and take possession of that other existence that seemed just out of his reach. He couldn't articulate any of this it was just a feeling, a tug he could no longer ignore.

With a half dozen nutty donuts still warm in the box between them on the truck seat Jake and Maria head up the road back to the Institute. One of them was thinking wistfully of home while the other was a jumble of emotions unsure of what lay ahead or if he even had the courage to find out. The sun was climbing with a glorious brilliance into the cloudless fall sky and the fire of a few early maples dotted the hillsides, but the cold morning air captured in the cab gave Jake a slight shiver as he pulled into the parking lot.

Chapter 72

The solemn young man led them down the hallway past the rooms they had occupied yesterday and into the dining room, Larry and Janet were sitting at a table on the far side by the French doors leading to an expansive outdoor patio. It was obvious even from the far side of the room they were in the middle of some intense conversation. Jake hesitates a moment wondering if they should let them finish before interrupting. Larry looks up and motions them over answering the question for him.

Larry spies the bakery box and breaks into a big smile, "is that what I hope it is?"

Jake laughs, "well, if you mean nutty donuts than yes it is... these are seriously addictive, almost didn't make it here."

Larry still smiling intones, "bless you my son, you are truly a virtuous man," as Janet starts to laugh.

"Larry has a serious weakness for the nutty donut, you two just made his favorite people list, and I sure hope there's one in there for me," Janet asks still laughing. "You two want some coffee or tea? Everything is on the counter over there, help yourself," she says pointing to the left.

Maria heads over, "Jake, you want a coffee?"

Looking her way, "Sure thanks, appreciate it..." Turning back to Larry, "so what's the plan today? You mentioned something last night about next steps and wanting me to meet with Ms. Janet here?"

Maria returns, handing Jake his coffee and setting a small stack of napkins on the table, "what are we talking about?"

Larry answers first, "if you and Jake wouldn't mind, Janet would like to run through the night of Harry White's accident again, see if Jake can add any further details."

"Oh man that was one messed up night, I thought Harry was going to die on us, he looked so bad lying there in the car, I sure don't want to see anything like that again." Jake mutters almost to himself. Looking up at Larry and Janet, "I'll walk through it with ya, not sure what good it'll do, honestly Maria was the one tuned him in and knew what was going on. He definitely wouldn't have made it if she hadn't rousted me and got us moving."

Larry stands up, "alright then, I have a couple of meetings I wasn't able to change this morning, so I leave you in good hands with Janet. Jake, lets plan

on getting together around eleven thirty, we can get
an early lunch and finish up our talk, sound good?"

"Sure works for me..." Jake answers looking
over at Maria, she just nods.

Chapter 73

Janet leads them to the conference room she and Maria had been using the day before and introduces Jake to her team. They spend the next two hours going through the events of that evening in exhaustive detail. The team has reviewed the tapes of yesterday's sessions and has a series of questions or really clarifications for Maria, she remains steadfast in her telling of the events though. Then it's Jake's turn and to say he was flustered did not quite cover it. He chooses to relate an abbreviated version leaving out almost all of the interaction with officer O'Neill. Jake may have been open to thinking about some things differently, but that didn't necessarily extend to trusting people he didn't know and it certainly hadn't changed his reticence about law enforcement. Of course Janet and her team have a great deal more information about that evening then they have initially disclosed so there are some awkward moments as they lead him back through the story adding details he hadn't chosen to disclose in the first place.

Just when it seems they have asked him the same

questions a dozen different ways, Janet turns to him leafing through her notes, "Jake tell me what you meant when you said 'Maria was the one tuned him in'."

"When did I say that?" Jake asks looking lost.

"Just this morning when we were having coffee in the dining hall..." Janet says giving him a look over her glasses.

"Oh yeah, well it just seemed that night like Harry was sending her a message or something. I don't know, the timing was just weird, I mean some of what she was telling me had to be happening right then or had just happened. I mean he hadn't been in the car but maybe a few minutes when we pulled into the bar parking lot. Umm, if I remember right she said it was like getting a message so I just figured she must have tuned into what was going on so to speak, why, does that mean something?" Jake asked looking hopefully around. He didn't really think he had anything to add that would help these people, it wasn't like he was the one having the dreams after all. Hell more often than not he felt out of the loop even at home and truth be told he was getting tired of having to answer the same question just cause they asked it a bunch of different ways. *Didn't they believe him?*

Janet looks back at her notes, "Okay Jake, so as far as you can remember you and Maria had not been talking about Harry that evening in the living room before she 'tuned him in', right?"

"Jesus fucking Christ! How many times are you people going to ask the same Goddamn question? I already told you, no we didn't talk about it," losing his temper and raising his voice Jake's frustration starts to boil over. He has been here before and interrogations are not on his list of favorite things to do.

"Jake, Jake, okay I understand this can be a little frustrating sometimes, we use some techniques developed by the FBI, it's just a way to make sure that people don't add details after the fact that didn't really happen. Certainly we don't mean to frustrate you, and really I appreciate your patience and help with this," Janet says hoping to calm him down and keep things moving forward.

"Yeah well, except for the two way mirror you people might as well be cops, Jesus!" Jake says pushing back from the table. "Listen, I need a break, sorry to blow up, but I'm not a big fan of cops or how they like to do you."

"Alright people let's take ten, back here at eleven sharp okay?" Janet announces taking off her glasses. Turning to Maria, "are you okay, need a drink or anything, I know this can't have been easy for you."

"I'm fine, I'm going to catch up with Jake and make sure he is okay, you don't understand but this whole thing has been really hard on him, especially almost losing Mr. Harry" she says, surprising Janet again that this young woman is only eighteen but mature well beyond her years.

Maria finds Jake in the cafeteria fixing a coffee, "you want one?" he asks, turning as she starts across the room.

"No, I'm fine, you okay?"

"Yeah, that just pissed me off, same damn thing cops do to you, like you're guilty no matter what so they just keep asking you shit hoping you'll slip up or something, its total bullshit."

"Umm, okay so how do you really feel?" she asks laughing. That breaks the tension and Jake smiles.

"Ok, Ok, so I may have overreacted a bit, I'm just not used to this stuff."

"Well, I'm not either Jake, but I think they mean well and they have been really helpful with finding my parents you know and I appreciate that anyway."

"I guess my shit seems pretty stupid compared

to what you're dealin' with," he says looking out the window.

She doesn't answer, just takes his arm, "Let's head back and get this done, Mr. Larry wanted to meet with you too."

"Yeah Larry, I am not sure about the whole Larry thing, I know he is going to want me to do something, I just can't figure what his game is, but yeah let's go get this over with."

"Jake I really think he just wants to help you, he seems like he really cares about you..."

"Yeah I know, it's just so weird, cause he and my Dad were like brothers and my Dad didn't give a damn about me so you know... I guess that really doesn't have anything to do with him does it?"

"Nope, probably not," she says leading the way back to the conference room.

"Hey, I'm sorry about that blow up," Jake apologizes as he takes his seat, "Let's finish this up Mr. Larry wants to meet with me in about half an hour."

Janet smiles at him, "Sure Jake, no problem, we are just about done anyway."

The break seems to have done everyone good, and they finish up with Jake walking back through the time frame as one of Janet's assistants plots it out on the whiteboard. Underneath is a separate graphic representing Harry's timeline, it's obvious they are looking for intersections to determine if Maria had "tuned in", they were all using the term now, or if it was more in line with the traditional "sight" they had been assuming.

Janet suggests a lunch break and points Jake in the direction of Larry's office, "his name is on the door, just knock if it's closed," she tells him.

Chapter 74

Jake hesitates before gently tapping on the door toying for just a moment with the idea of escaping to the truck and hanging out while Maria finishes up. Larry opens the door before he has a chance to change his mind, "come on in Jake, I was just going to order up some lunch, how about you, ... hungry?"

"Sure, I could eat, what you havin'?" Jake answers while surveying the office. There is a large wooden desk facing the door with floor to ceiling bookshelves behind it and two wing back chairs facing it. To the right is a round table with four chairs nestled up against the large windows giving a great view of the gardens and orchard. Larry's desk is neat and ordered, with a stack of books on the corner.

"How about a couple of BLTs on wheat with potato salad and some homemade pickles?"
"Well now I am definitely hungry..." Jake grins.

Larry laughs, "the food's good isn't it, took me a little while to get used to it, but now I miss it any time I'm traveling and have to eat out. You do O'Malley's last night? That's one of the few places I go, Pat is one helluva cook."

Nodding, "yeah, we sure did, food was great, had the corned beef and man I ate way too much of that soda bread!"

There is a short knock on the door and the solemn young man from earlier brings in a tray stacked with sandwiches, pickles and a bowl of potato salad. He is followed by another young woman carrying a pitcher of iced tea and two glasses, without a word they setup lunch at the round table facing the window.

Jake can't help but ask, "What's the story on the young fella, he seems, I don't know, kinda bummed out all the time?"

Larry nods, "seems that way doesn't it, well he isn't that young for starters, but came to us when he was just seventeen from India, his father was a good friend of Ms. Sally's, he was going to study directly under her before returning home to his family. Well long story short she passed away less than a year later. The boy was devastated and asked to stay, said he didn't want to go back, brilliant and unbelievably polite but he never was able to shake off that sadness you picked up on."

"Hmmm, that sucks, how long ago was that? Did something happen to her?"

"Well Jake, it was about ten years ago last month, I wouldn't say anything happened to her, she had cancer, never let on to anyone about it either, I guess didn't want it to be a distraction to anyone here. She was an amazing human being and there isn't a day goes by I don't miss her."

Jake isn't entirely comfortable with the conversation, especially since he hasn't ever really felt that way about someone, well maybe Harry, but still...

"Jake, Jake..."

"What? Oh sorry, guess I got a little sidetracked there..."

"Happen a lot," Larry asks.

"Well, seems like more lately, I'll get to thinking about something and before you know it... well you know. I was just thinking, I've never really felt like that about anybody, maybe old man Harry, I was going out of my mind when he was in the accident. Hell, I didn't even feel anything similar when my mom or dad died. You know how my old man was, I sat in the nursing home and watched him die seemed like weeks and ya know during the whole time the old bastard didn't have a word to say to me, no explanations, no apologies, no nothing..." Jake shakes his head like he is trying to get rid of the memories, "You know I left town for three years after that, lookin' for something I guess, never did find it though..."

"Well son, maybe you have now... maybe this is what you were looking for, maybe not, but if you're tired of the hate, the anger, feeling like everyone is against you, if you are ready to be free of those things keeping you from being a person in control of his own life. If you are looking for clarity for a chance to escape the path you're on well maybe I can help, but Jake, what you have to understand is if you want to change and grow as a person, a real person, not some carbon copy of your father, well you are going to have to make the investment in yourself, you are going to have to do the hard work."

"Sir, I heard pretty much the same thing from Harry, but I have to be honest, I just don't understand what y'all are talking about, what work?" Jake picks up a pickle crunching down on it before continuing, "hard work isn't a problem for me, I know how to work, really I do, but can you explain to me what you are talking about 'cause I just don't get it."

Larry nods to himself, "you're right of course Jake, I had forgotten what it was like for me when I first got here, didn't understand a word they were saying honestly." Picking up his sandwich, "let's do this, tell me a little bit about Peakeville while we eat and then I'll see if I can simplify things for you deal?"

"Sure sir, I'm sorry, I just don't get it..."

Chapter 75

With lunch finished Larry sips his tea and works on finding a simpler way to explain things to Jake, who desperately wants to understand but just has no frame of reference for a conversation like this. So Larry starts over, "okay Jake this may be a little uncomfortable, but it was one of the first things I had to deal with head on. Now you and I both know your old man was a mean spirited racist until the day he died is my guess... and if we are being honest you spent many years thinking the same way. Well, let me ask you, do you think that is something he taught you or something you were just born knowing?"

Jake bristles a bit, "hey, now I am trying not to be like that..." he doesn't get a chance to finish.

"Jake drop the defensiveness, I am not attacking you so set that aside, just answer the question honestly..."

"Ok, Ok, I guess he taught me to think that way, at least he was always preaching it at home... but that doesn't make it okay."

Wearily, "Son, you are missing my point... the fact is we are not born hating people, that isn't who we are, you remember me explaining the difference between your essence and all of the things we pollute it with?"

"Sure I do, my mom would have called it our soul I guess... right?"

"That's a fine comparison for now, so listen to what I am saying, all the things you learned, all the things you saw, everything we make part of who we are and how we act those things are not who we are, they are who we have allowed ourselves to become, does that make sense?"

And it finally started to click with Jake... "Wait a minute Sir, if that's all outside stuff then who are we really, or maybe I guess what are we, well whichever, you know what I mean."

Larry smiles at him, "well now Jake, that's the real question isn't it? Who are you Jake, who are you when you strip all the negativity away, all the learned behavior, all the hate, hurt and most importantly all the things you are secretly ashamed of but can't seem to stop doing..." grabbing Jake by the shoulder... "Who are you, that's the question you need to answer!" Sitting back down, "you know the wonderful thing Jake is when you figure that out you can begin taking control of your life, you can achieve a sense of awareness and begin becoming the man you were meant to be."

Jake sighs, "that's all well and good Sir, but how the hell am I supposed to do that?" I mean you saw how long it took just to explain this in a way I could understand..."

Smiling again, "Well Jake I am going to help you... first thing I want you to do is read the books I am going to send you home with... they will probably seem difficult at first, in fact I had to reread some of the chapters three and four times before they started making sense... and the second thing is you have to start recognizing the positive changes you are already making in your life, I want you to start keeping a journal. Write down whatever strikes you, when you question a decision, when you see something and it just seems wrong to you, when you do something then feel bad or good about it, whatever is going on in your day I want you to write it down.... and this last thing is not negotiable, I want you to commit to spending one weekend a month here with me."

"Sir, this is a long way from Peakeville..."

"Jake, this is your choice, your journey, if you're serious about changing your life you will be here, it's really that simple."

"Okay, I get it, how long will this take anyway?"

Larry grins at him, "well, the rest of your life of course..."

Jake smiles, "I knew you were going to say that... I just knew it, alright I am in, I really need this sir, I'm tired, just really tired of how my life has been going." Jake sips his tea and bites his lip, "Sir, can I ask you a question... I need a little advice."

"Sure son, what is it..."

"Well, before I came home this time I was working down in Miami," Jake pauses, "truth is I was drinking pretty heavily and couldn't hold down a spot on a crew, just couldn't get it together, but I met this great woman down there and one thing led to another and we were living together..."

"You didn't get her pregnant did you?.." Larry interjects.

"What??? Uh, no, nothin' like that, but I just couldn't hold it together and I up and left one morning early, didn't say nothin', didn't even wake her up, Sir, I just left like she didn't mean nothin'." Jake hangs his head running his hands through his hair, "you know it's bothered me more and more lately, how could I do that to her?" Looking up at Larry, "I think leavin' without saying anything is one of the reasons I started thinkin' bout stuff this summer and well I just don't want to be that asshole anymore... but what should I do Sir, I can't stop thinkin' bout her all the time."

Larry leans forward, "Jake you probably aren't going to like this cause I think you are wanting me to tell you to go make it up to her and the bottom line is you got to get yourself straight and moving forward before you think about dragging someone else into your mess." Pausing for a moment, "look its simple don't you want to see what kind of man you are capable of being before you go pursuing a relationship, don't you think a woman deserves the best 'you' possible?"

"Yeah I guess you're right, but I really feel like I need to go down there and see if I can at least patch it up or say I'm sorry or something..."

"Jake, you do what you think you have to do, then go home, start in on those books and be back here in a month... can you do that?"

"Yeah, I guess I can do that..."

"Alright let's go find Ms. Maria. I think you two should get on the road before it gets too late, and Jake you make sure you do right by her as well.

She really looks up to you and Mr. Harry, I got a
feeling she is going to need you two to be there for
her."

"No problem sir, I probably should tell her,
but I would do anything for that kid..."

Larry hands him a box with half dozen books in
it as they head out the door, "your homework!"

Chapter 76

Maria and Janet had spent the second half of the day together. Janet had dismissed the team so she could spend some one-on-one time with Maria. In particular she wanted to pitch her on the idea of staying at the institute for at least the foreseeable future. Maria had listened politely enough, but Janet could tell her heart wasn't in it. Maria had already made her mind up.

"So Maria, what do you want to do, you have been politely listening to me for the last hour, but I can tell you're not seriously considering this," an exasperated Janet asks pointedly.

"I'm really sorry Ms. Janet I, have been listening, really I have, but I have to go home to my parents. I didn't really figure it out until last night, but I should never have left the way I did. I need to explain things to my mom and dad face to face, please, please, please tell me you understand?"

Janet slowly closes her note pad and sets her pen down, "Maria honey, of course I understand, I would never want you to do anything you weren't entirely comfortable with. Let's do this, I want you

to promise to keep in touch with me either by phone
or email, and I also want you to begin keeping a
journal of any dreams you have, can you do that for
me?"

Maria smiles, "of course, I already keep a
journal and honestly it will be nice to have someone
to talk to if there are more dreams, I mean Harry and
Jake are fine, but you really get it if you know what
I mean." Realizing what this means she covers her
mouth with her hand, "Oh man, how am I going to tell
them I am leaving?"

Janet takes a card out of her pocket and hands
it to Maria, "all of my information is on there so
anytime you need to reach me don't hesitate, doesn't
matter what time it is I'll pick up. I wouldn't worry
about Jake and Harry, if I am right they will
definitely understand. And listen if you want to come
back at any time even for just a visit let me know,
we can take care of flights and getting you up here."

"Thanks Ms. Janet, that means a lot, you really
think they will be okay? And I really do want to come
back, I just have to do this first. Actually I need
to figure out how I am going to get home. I want to
go back with Jake and tell Mr. Harry everything and I
couldn't leave without telling him goodbye, but...
well, I hadn't really thought past that point."

Janet pats her hand, "if you can't figure it out, just call me and I'll help you take care of it..."

Maria tears up, "can I call my mom and tell her?"

"Of course dear, use my phone, I'm going to go check on Larry and Jake, take as much time as you need... just hit that green button, dial a nine then the number."

Janet lets herself out quietly, she smiles as she hears Maria start speaking rapidly in Spanish, *well* she thinks to herself, *it was worth a shot, but Larry had called it right last night, the girl was going home.*

Chapter 77

Janet ran into Larry and Jake in the hall,
headed her way, she told them Maria was on the phone
with her mother and the three of them headed back
towards Janet's office. Maria had just finished up
and with tears in her eyes, but an unrestrained
smile, she told them her mom and dad couldn't wait
for her to come home. It was then she noticed the
look on Jake's face and wrapped him up in as big a
hug as her diminutive frame could muster, apologizing
she wouldn't let go.

Jake, a bit awkwardly, hugged her back, "hey
now it's okay, no need to cry, I get it, really!"

She is still sniffling, "are you sure, you and
Harry have been so good to me I hate to leave, but I
have to go home..."

Jake smiles at her, "are you kidding? You
probably saved my life girl... and I am going to take
a quick trip to Miami so what ya say I give you a
ride home, it's on the way, besides seems kinda right
doesn't it?"

Larry pats his shoulder and gives him thumbs
up. "Are you sure Jake?" Maria asks.

"Yep, no problem at all, won't even charge you gas money," he laughs. "Just need to check on a couple of projects when we get back then we'll hit the road, deal?"

As they head out to the foyer and the front parking lot one of the kitchen crew comes up with a bag and jug of tea.

"Parting gifts," Larry grins, "couple of sandwiches, jar of those pickles you demolished today, and a fresh zucchini bread, be better than some fast food joint. How far are you planning on going tonight?"

"I am thinking if we can make it to Enola, right past Harrisburg we can stay at the same hotel we did on the way up, catch breakfast at the diner again and make the rest of the trip tomorrow," Jake tells him.

After hugs all around, Maria and Jake head out of the parking lot, Jake lays on the horn a couple of times for good measure.

Maria talks a hundred miles a minute about the call with her mom, she is clearly excited and maybe a bit nervous about going home, and she can't stop thanking Jake for taking her home. Of course he tells her it's nothing, but he is going to miss having her around and he knows Harry will put a good face on it but...

They had stopped at an overlook on Interstate
Eight-One killing the sandwiches, pickles and a
couple of McIntosh apples, perfectly crisp and tart,
that had been at the bottom of the bag. Maria drifted
off as the twilight settled in leaving Jake alone
with his thoughts. He kept coming back to Molly, *what
could he possibly say to her that would mean anything
at this point?* He didn't have any answers tonight,
but he knew he had to see her, had to try, he
wouldn't forgive himself if he left it the way it
was. In Jake's mind he needed to make amends before
starting on this new journey, and maybe just maybe
Molly would agree to come with him.

He shook Maria gently as they entered the hotel
parking lot, Jake went in to get a couple of rooms,
while Maria sat listening to the pings and ticks of
the cooling engine, *man wasn't life interesting* she
thought to herself?

After filling the truck up and a quick
breakfast at the diner Jake and Maria are back on the
road. The trip takes them through the mountains of
West Virginia where the leaves are rapidly changing
creating a kaleidoscope of colors. They stop at a
roadside BBQ joint for pulled pork sandwiches and icy
cold colas before getting back on the road. It's

after dark when they pull into Harry's drive, but the lights are burning bright and they know it's going to be a long night bringing the old man up to date on all that has happened. With a pot of fresh coffee brewed they sit at the kitchen table stumbling over each other trying to tell him everything at once. Harry gives Maria a big hug and there are tears all around as they talk about her going home, it hadn't really hit her till now that she would be leaving these two, maybe never to see them again. Jake shows them the books Larry gave him to read. Harry good-naturedly, wishes him luck. None of them really wants the evening to end, but the clock passes three and the zucchini bread is long gone... I'm just going to crash on the couch Jake says walking into the living room as Maria helps Harry to his room before heading down the hall to the guest room that she has been using.

It's an unlikely trio of souls that fate or the universe has brought together in a moment of need, coincidence maybe if you believe in such things. But tonight the trajectories of their lives are already beginning to separate again spinning in the specific direction each of them needs or maybe finally in the direction each of them has chosen. Time will be the final arbiter of their success.

Chapter 78

Molly hadn't been this nervous about a date since high school, this is ridiculous she thought to herself as she worked hard in the mirror putting on her lipstick and eye shadow, the fact she had fixed hair three times already was not lost on her. It had taken Robert almost a month to work up the nerve to ask her out and to her credit she hadn't said yes right away. In fact he had asked almost two weeks earlier and Molly had thought long and hard about it. To his credit Robert had been a perfect gentlemen telling her no rush, he was happy to wait till she was ready.

She was finally happy and feeling a sense of independence and wasn't really sure she wanted a man in her life right now, school was going great, she had her job with Pete and well, she felt good about herself for a change. But some company would be welcome and Robert seemed like a nice enough guy and it was true this was the first fella she hadn't met in a bar in what, ten plus years? That had to mean something didn't it? She had mentioned it to Pete that night at the bar as they were closing up, he had just smiled at her and said, "You go girl!" She had snapped at him with the bar rag laughing along with him, but she really did want his opinion she didn't have anyone else she trusted and her own track record wasn't really stellar. Pete had told her go, Robert sounded like the type of man she deserved and if he turned out to be a jerk, well he would deal with him.

She had first run into Robert at the Subway across the street from school, he was wiping down tables and had held the door for her, turned out he was an area director responsible for four local stores and liked to spend at least one day a week in each one seeing firsthand how things were working. Of course he seemed to be visiting the Third Avenue store a little more frequently since meeting Molly. She had been worried he would look down on her when he found out she had just started back at school and worked in a bar. They had learned more about each other, leading her to let her guard down and he had seemed genuinely interested in her story. He even said he really respected the courage it took to start a new career at this point in her life, which had immediately turned into embarrassment when he realized he had brought age into a conversation with a woman. She had laughed, never having been self-conscious about her age. They had seen each other in the store four or five more times before he had stumbled through his invitation to dinner.

So here she was two weeks later with flutters in her chest, nervous like a young girl on her first date and well, maybe this was the first date for the new and improved Molly. The knock on the door breaks through memory lane, she takes one more look in the mirror, checks her watch and gives herself a small smile, he was early. Life was funny wasn't it, but she didn't take time to explore that thought, turning toward the entryway she says, "coming, just a moment."

Chapter 79

Jake had dropped Maria off around two that afternoon at her parents' house just outside of Tampa, they had made an early start of it that morning hoping to beat the traffic in Columbia and Savannah and they had done pretty well. The hardest part had been watching Maria say goodbye to Harry, the old man had been a trooper, but hadn't been able to hide the tears in his eyes. She had left with a large sealed envelope that Harry had made her swear not to open until she was safely home. He and Jake had pooled together twenty-five hundred dollars and each had included a personal note for her as well. No real way to explain it other than a token of how much she meant to the both of them.

He had just filled up in Ft. Myers and with a couple of hours left to go the anxiety was starting to set in, maybe this hadn't been such a good idea after all he thought. Jake smiles to himself as he starts across Alligator Alley, things certainly were different this time and still not a gator in sight. The miles pass quickly and soon the outskirts of Miami begin to flash by, Jake is almost in full panic mode by this time, but he keeps telling himself this is the right thing to do. He has reviewed a dozen scenarios in his head, most of them ending with Molly welcoming him back and agreeing to head North with him, Jake knows this is probably just a fantasy, but a small part of him keeps coming back to it.

Jake merges off I75 onto I95 North in the heart of Miami, the memories come flooding back as familiar land marks speed past, he takes the NW 36th street exit toward the beach and Pete's, the neon clock on the Citrus Bank flashes 6:47PM as he passes by. He approaches the light for NE 1st and has to make a decision on whether to go to Pete's first or see if Molly is at home. It's a Friday night, but Molly had alternating weekends when he was last here so she could be either place. He knew it wasn't going to a good scene if he showed up at Pete's, it would definitely be busy and for sure Pete would probably want to kick his ass... and for good reason he acknowledges to himself. All right then, Molly's first, shit he thinks to himself, hopefully she hadn't moved. He hadn't considered that possibility when he had started this trip proving that true to form even with the progress he had made, planning wasn't necessarily a strong suite for Jake.

Jake pulls in the small dirt lot behind Molly's

apartment and sits for a moment collecting himself while the truck plays its lonesome serenade. *Okay, well nothing to do but get to it,* he tells himself shutting the truck door and starting toward the steps. Jake can feel his hands sweating and wipes them on his jeans before rapping gently on the door half hoping she isn't there. No luck, he hears her, "coming, just a moment..."

Chapter 80

As the door opens Jake catches his breath, she is stunning, he had never thought of Molly as beautiful but tonight she is practically glowing and for a moment it takes his breath away. She stares at him as if she doesn't know him...

"Jake, what the hell are you doing here?" she asks glancing nervously past him obviously expecting someone else.

"Molly, I, umm," he is at a complete loss for words now that he is here, "can we talk, I'm really sorry and if we could just talk a little..."

"Uhh, what?" returning her attention to him she is holding the door in her left hand, "no Jake we can't talk, there's nothing to talk about, I have plans and I am not about to spend the night listening to you make excuses why you couldn't have at least told me you were leaving... Honestly Jake you need to just leave, you don't get to fuck with people's lives and then just show back up have it be alright."

"I know, I know," he starts to protest, "but if we could just sit down and I'll try to explain things..."

"You don't get it do you Jake? I am not interested in your excuses, I am no longer available for it honestly, you didn't seriously think you could just waltz back in here months later without a word and just have it be okay, what is wrong with you?" She is obviously angry and Jake isn't sure what to say.

It's in that moment that Jake remembers what Larry had told him and he realizes that this trip hasn't really been about making amends with Molly or even apologizing to her, it's been about self-indulgence, making himself feel better about leaving her in the first place and maybe for the first time Jake has a moment of awareness and understanding of the consequences of his actions and what it really means to be accountable for yourself as a man. Nodding his head he begins to back away from the door, "Molly, I am sorry you're right, I'm sorry, really I am, for hurting you, I get it, really I do," Jake turns and heads down the stairs, looking back "goodbye Molly."

She is still standing at the door framed by the entryway light and he can't help but think about what a mistake he had made, "goodbye Jake," she says as she slowly closes the door. He turns and continues down the steps. A convertible Mercedes pulls up as he is getting in the truck, he watches as the tall fella takes the steps two at a time, flowers in his right hand he knocks on the door. Jake starts the truck up and swings out of the lot heading West back toward the interstate. He stops at the Starbucks on Biscayne and orders a Venti Caramel Macchiato extra hot, sipping the sweet coffee he starts the long drive home knowing he has some reading to do...

Acknowledgments

This book is dedicated to my wife and kids for their unfailing support and belief that this labor of love would one day be a "real" book. Many thanks to the family and friends that have provided encouragement, feedback, suggestions, and have been steadfast supporters through this process. A special thanks to James Coyle for his editing support and taking the time to help a new author navigate this process.

Afterword

This story was never intended to be autobiographical, but I believe it is human nature to infuse our experiences, memories, and personality into the things we create. My own story began on a cold winter night in New York City and I was born on a crisp fall evening later that year. It was 1965 and my parents were deeply involved in the New York art scene and studying the Gurdjieff Work an eastern philosophy of self-awareness and achieving a heightened state of consciousness. I don't have a memory of those early years in New York City; I have the pictures, the art gallery posters and the stories, but my memories start later after my parents left the city for the farmland and foothills of northern New Jersey.

Embracing an entrepreneurial spirit, they started an herb & spice business and a Gurdjieff school in the small northern New Jersey town of Sussex. Clearing the surrounding land and rebuilding an old mountain home located at the Eastern base of the Kittatinny Mountains they created an herb farm and built a school. My earliest childhood memories and experiences inhabit this special place and traverse the spectrum from warm and comforting to disconcerting and unnerving. It seemed my experiences were only limited by my imagination and there were very few boundaries on that. I can't begin to explain most of the strange things that happened in those early days, but I am not so arrogant as to think that makes them untrue. There are things in this world that defy logical explanation or stretch the limits of our adult belief system; however, these are our limitations not theirs.

I don't remember a time in my childhood when there weren't a number of students "studying" with my parents, sometimes as many as thirty to forty people. Young people full of ideas and questions that I absorbed and pondered from a child's perspective. Self-sufficiency and imagination became early survival skills. As is all too often an unfortunate byproduct of success, my parent's marriage did not last, and so began a journey across this great country as my mother sought a place of refuge and new beginnings. Ultimately she landed in rural South Carolina and set up a new school and base of business at an old indigo plantation, it was 1981 and I was fifteen and out of place.

It is the experiences of those years in South

Carolina and later as an adult in central Florida
that form the basis for many of the characters and
the questions that this book and our main character,
Jake, struggles with: generational prejudice, illegal
immigration, and in the end the questions Jake must
answer: Is a man destined to tread the paths of his
forefathers? Is he constrained by the indoctrination
of his youth? Can he overcome his past, his mistakes,
his missed opportunities? And is it ever too late to
forge a new existence that embraces the life that
could one have been living?

Joseph Castagno

Made in the USA
Columbia, SC
27 January 2018